THE HUNDRED MILE VIEW

Thanks for the visit
Great to see you!

C S Decent

January 16, 2022

H THE UNDRED MILE VIEW

C.J. HOWELL

280 STEPS

A 280 Steps Original

Copyright © 2016 by C.J. Howell

ISBN 978 8 293 32684 7

www.280steps.com

For Mon—Aimee is not you!

BOOK I

ONE

The old man's bare feet shuffled over dried out bunch grass and thistles matted into the red earth of the high desert. The frayed edges of his blue jeans left trails in the sand behind him. His feet were calloused and gnarled like little clubs, the skin as hard as shoe leather, but he was not immune to the thorns and pricklers covering the desert floor. Yet the pain in his feet was far from his mind. He had not yet been born at the time of the Long Walk, when the People were marched at gunpoint to Fort Sumner, but his grandmother had been alive then, and he grew up hearing many stories about that time of sorrow and brutality. Now, as he was marched into the wilderness with the barrel of a Smith & Wesson pressed into his back, he knew that sickness had returned. The world was out of harmony. The world had gone insane. Over the years he had come to believe that the youngest generation was lost, and maybe even the generation before that as well, the old ways forgotten, the Holy People disrespected, but he couldn't have imagined how far the Dine had strayed from the path of beauty. The path of harmony. So far, that they might never find their way back.

The old man was handcuffed but he could still grasp the thick necklace of prayer beads around his neck. His knotted fingers ran over the wooden beads worn smooth by time and repetition.

His lips were the same reddish mahogany as the rest of his face, and bore the same deep ruts and valleys from a lifetime of sun and weather. Gasoline ran down the creases in his skin and sprayed off his lips as he recited an ancient prayer in Navajo.

More fuel was poured over his head. He closed his eyes and continued praying, his voice rising. Gasoline ran down his long gray braids and dripped off the ends. All he could smell was gasoline. It was all anyone could smell now.

A semicircle of headlights lit the desert night. The old man was prodded with a stick until he reached the center of a blackened fire pit ringed with stones. The jeers and taunts from the onlookers suddenly stopped. For a moment the old man faltered. He tried to open his eyes but they burned as if already on fire. The sky was black. There were no stars. Through tears and searing pain he forced open an eyelid and saw a man with a shaved head sitting on a rock staring at him thoughtfully. The man lit a match and the flame seemed to jump unnaturally high into the darkness. A cheer rose from the crowd but the man put a finger to his lips and the crowd immediately silenced. The old man began to pray again.

The man with the lit match ran his hand over his shaved skull and smiled. He flicked the match at the old man. For a second or two, long enough for the old man's heart to beat and push his body's volume of blood through his worn veins and arteries one last time, nothing happened. And then the oxygen left the air around him, leaving a momentary stillness, a shimmering darkness, before he exploded in flames. His screams echoed off of distant canyon walls and started the coyotes howling one after another so that the screaming was heard in every direction for a hundred miles.

4

The Shaman stood and walked toward the old man writhing in agony.

"Didn't think such an old man could make such a loud noise."

The people laughed and the Shaman embraced their laughter.

TWO

Special Agent Jake Keller put on his sunglasses for the quarter-mile walk to the mailbox at the end of a dirt drive. The door to his trailer slammed shut behind him and bounced a few times against the thin metal frame before a gust of wind blew it back wide open and pinned it against the aluminum siding. Hearing the banging of aluminum on aluminum he turned around and walked back to the trailer and pressed the flimsy door shut against the wind and braced it closed with a rock.

Jake never got mail. No grocery store circulars or credit card applications or department store catalogues or mass mailed pleas from mortgage brokers. That's how it was on the reservation. He was looking for one thing, and today was the day he anticipated and feared. It was there. A manila envelope from Dickstein & Dickstein, as if one Dickstein wasn't bad enough. The divorce papers drawn up by Aimee's lawyer. He walked back to the trailer and tossed the envelope on the TV tray that served as his dining room table, unopened.

He cracked a beer and paced through the trailer. He turned the stereo on and then turned it off. He opened the sliding glass door in the back of the trailer and sat in a lawn chair overlooking a hundred mile view of open desert. The sky reddened and then faded to orange and purple. As dusk turned to night and the better part of a twelve pack of Busch Light lay in a pile of crumpled cans at his feet, he heard the sudden baying of coyotes, the high pitched yips and cries fighting and circling each other until joining in one long howl. His hair stood on end and his scalp began to tingle. He got goosebumps. He hadn't had that feeling since he was a kid. The howling of the coyotes spread out across the valley floor below until their cries surrounded him, permeating his soul. In the distance he thought he saw a spark like a distant flame. But he knew the eyes play tricks on you in the desert. That night coyotes howled in his sleep.

THREE

Jake woke to the sound of the wind screaming across the canyon lands and the whistle of air moving through poorly caulked seams in the trailer. The screen door banged on its hinges. The wind was a constant out here. Always the wind. Sunlight flooded the trailer illuminating even the dankest of corners. He washed his hair under the weak stream of piss warm water spouting from the near empty water tank feeding his plastic and plexiglass shower box.

He put on jeans and cowboy boots even though neither had broken in after three months in New Mexico. There was only so much you could do to fit in. He took the Ford F-150 into Gallup. He hadn't driven his government issue Crown Vic cruiser since he'd been here. In spite of everything he was in a pretty good mood. Hard to be in a bad mood out here with the blue sky and open space. A feeling you could never have at Quantico or in the grey skies and muggy air of D.C., the cold war era sense of imprisonment the J. Edgar Hoover Building was built to impart.

The inside of the F-150 still smelled new. He loved the smell, the feel of the cool smooth molded carbonite steering wheel, the flawless sound system. Beat the shit out of riding the Metro every day, coughed on, breathed on, the cloying residue of overheated brake pads in the tunnels under the Potomac. The sky was a brilliant blue. Coming off the ridge line with green flashes of trees in the passenger side window, it was cool and crisp, but as Navajo Route 28 merged with US 66 and then became Main Street in Gallup, the earth dried and browned and became hardened and dust blown. Old Route 66 was strewn with the remnants of dogleg motels with names like the Aztec and the Apache Inn, fast food joints, a couple gas stations and drive through liquor stores, and then a few blocks of frontier downtown, old west storefronts and long low adobe.

He parked the truck on Lead Street, a block off Main, in front of a two-story stucco office building. He slammed the door of the F-150 and looked down the street. Empty in both directions for as far as the eye could see. A gust of wind slapped him in the face and he felt his cowboy boots being pelted with sand and gravel.

"This is why you wear the boots," he said to nobody.

The glass in the front entrance door to the building rattled its panes as he opened it against the wind and went inside. He said good morning to Mary, the administrative assistant and the only other federal employee stationed at the FBI Gallup Field Office. She squinted as she worked the mouse tethered to her computer to scroll around the TMZ website.

"How's Aimee?"

"Her lawyer says she's great."

"Well, he would know."

He kept walking toward the stairs to his office on the second floor and then stopped. He never knew about Navajo humor, the vague feeling that everything said was at his expense. His thoughts were interrupted by the crackle of the scanner next to Mary's desk and the late emergence of a hangover.

"Anything this morning?"

"It's one-thirty in the afternoon."

"Really? I'll never get used to this time zone."

"Beer weaker out east?"

"No, I don't think so. Hey, you don't have to be here all the time, you know. You should do one of those flex schedules, work four days a week."

"I am on a flex schedule."

"Oh."

"Four tens."

"You work four tens?"

"Yep."

"Oh."

"You've been certifying my time for three months."

"I know."

"You have been certifying my time, right?"

"Yeah, but I just take your word, I don't really look at it."

"That's good to know." Mary pulled her braids back behind her shoulders, rested her arms on her belly, and went back to TMZ.

"So, anything going on?" Jake asked again.

"Found a body, been burned up."

"Any leads?"

"Skinwalkers."

"It's always skinwalkers."

"Yep."

FOUR

Jake climbed the stairs to his office, ignored the unorganized scattershot of paper on his desk, and stacked in and on top of Redweld folders, and in piles and clumps on the floor, and fired up his computer to check his email and then his fantasy baseball team. He set his team's line-up for the day and then figured he should see about the body. He jogged down the stairs, the wood creaking and groaning under his boots.

"Calling it a day?"

"Going over to Tribal."

"Say hi to Del for me."

"Will do."

The Navajo Tribal Police headquarters was in Window Rock, Arizona, about thirty miles northwest from Gallup, New Mexico. Gallup itself was not actually on the Navajo Reservation. Instead there was a doughnut hole of New Mexico state jurisdiction and the local province of the Gallup Police Department. Everything else for a few hundred miles in any direction was under the jurisdiction of the Navajo Tribal Police, the United States Department of Justice, and the FBI.

Past the red cliffs of Ft. Defiance, Jake got the F-150 up to speed and made Window Rock in twenty minutes. Gray clouds gathered over the giant natural sandstone arch that gave the town its name. Beneath the arch, jammed into the canyon walls, was the Navajo Tribal Police headquarters. It occupied an old brick building that served as the Bureau of Indian Affairs Superintendent's office a hundred years ago, but it was tethered by a concrete sidewalk to the brand new stucco and glass Navajo Tribal Court complex, built with federal stimulus dollars.

Jake parked at the Courthouse and dodged the first heavy rain drops from a high column of towering clouds as he hurried down the sidewalk to the police station. He turned the handle and pushed open the heavy front door, original wood block a century old. A receptionist he didn't recognize smiled at him. The rest of the place looked empty.

"Where is everybody?"

"Out on skinwalker calls."

"Everybody?"

She nodded.

"Even Del?"

"The Chief?" She thought for a moment. Jake eyed the phone on her desk, a red light by Del's name indicated that his line was busy.

"Oh, he's here. Want to see him?"

Jake wrapped his knuckles on her desk and looked around the office. Water stains on the ceiling had black spider veins of mold.

"Next time."

Jake pulled open the thick wood door and was greeted by a blast of horizontal rain from the passing storm.

FIVE

A teenage girl, hands bound, gasoline running down her white ribbed tank top, burning and making her shiver all at the same time. Goosebumps on brown skin. A scream in her throat, choking her. Her legs kick out from under her as she's dragged to the center of a sandstone circle. The dust she kicks up clings to the gasoline and gives her body a reddish hue. She begs for her life.

"I'm real...I'm real!"

"That's what they all say." The shaved head shifts its balance on a well-muscled neck and cocks toward her. She has never seen the man before, but something about him is familiar, deja vu from a sliver of a nightmare. She flails her thin arms but her captors hands are strong, and big, entirely encircling her biceps. Her eyes dart wildly. The night sky whirls overhead. A map of stars jostles and kaleidoscopes in and out of focus. A giant stone monolith towers a thousand feet into the sky, a black rectangle blocking out the spinning stars. She struggles to keep her head up, to face the mob. She tries again to speak to them, this time in Navajo—"t,aa shoodi, t,aa shoodi"—"Please, please," she says, but they don't seem to hear her. She doesn't understand these people. Some are Navajo, some are not. Some are white. They look crazy, like the people who used to visit her uncle, the bad one, the one her grandfather doesn't speak to.

The man with the shaved head stands and spreads his arms, half to the crowd, and half to the night sky and the stark mountain of rock overhead.

"The old man didn't beg like the girl. I guess she has more to live for."

The crowd laughs and their voices rise in a crescendo of ecstasy. She digs her heels into the hardscrabble as two men haul her by her armpits through the ring of onlookers. The skin on the bottom of her feet is peeled off by the scree of little jagged rocks embedded into the desiccated earth, and impaled by cactus needles that dislodge from green flesh and affix to brown. She feels her shins and the bottoms of her legs up to her knees scrape against the large rocks bordering the fire pit as she is dragged to its center. Abruptly, she is dropped on the ground with a thud. The wind is almost knocked out of her and she struggles for breath. A pickup truck's engine revs to redline rattling the hood and brightening the truck's headlights. The girl's eyes widen. They all see the fear. Her fear. The shaved headlights a match, looks around at the circle of revelers, his congregation, and flicks it at the girl.

"They all scream the same though."

The match ignites the gasoline vapors swirling several feet from her body and a burst of flames blisters the length of her right side. She lurches away from the flames even as she is on fire, running reflexively from the brilliant pain engulfing her right arm, hip, and thigh. She pushes hard off her left foot, running from something that has already caught her, fleeing the pain as it consumes her, the fire clinging to her skin and cutting into her. The crowd reacts, the circle flexes, at once adrenalized and brought clear, momentarily aware of actual danger—fire might not kill the Shadow People after all, at least not right away. This one might set a few of them ablaze before it succumbs. The girl on fire runs straight at the watching circle. Her arms stretch out for anyone in reach as the fire covers her back and burns up her neck. The ring buckles, people brake and run. One man juts out his leg at a ninety degrees angle as the girl claws blindly toward him and catches her in the chest with his foot. The girl goes down hard and rolls in the dirt. The fire coming off of her body leaps into the sky and is blown horizontal by the wind. The air smells of burning hair, and then something worse. The circle regathers, links arms, and howls into the night sky. There is a lump of flesh in a raging fire, and a scream.

In the end, the girl's scream is no different than the old man's.

SIX

The storm passed as soon as it started. One of the microbursts that randomly provided a moment of terror and relief from the afternoon heat of the high desert in summer. The desert after a rain smelled like the dawn of time. Desperate life temporarily flourished in primordial puddles. Jake drove with the windows down. The scent of ozone and sage filled the cab of the truck. He was stuck by the beauty of the landscape as he always was out on the reservation, and felt that twinge of melancholy when he hit the outskirts of Gallup, his apartness from it all.

He parked on the street in front of his office, saw that the dashboard clock blinked 4:00, grabbed a paperback novel off the passenger seat, and walked two blocks to the Copper Street Pub for an early supper. He sat at the bar and ordered a cheeseburger, and a locally brewed IPA. A waitress sat at the elbow of the bar hunched over a thick hardcover textbook and sipping a Diet Coke. He began reading his own book but found himself glancing at the girl with unwanted frequency. Blonde hair tied loosely in a ponytail, skinny, pale skin. Unusual in Gallup. Her plastic engraved name tag read, Cally. The bartender brought his burger.

"Whatcha readin'?" The waitress asked, trained her green eyes on him from the crook of the bar. Ketchup coated his three day stubble. He wiped his face with a cocktail napkin, began to speak and then decided it was best to finish chewing before he answered.

"Tony Hillerman novel."

"Looked familiar."

"He writes about here, you know, the reservation."

"My dad read those, but I never have. Guess I should."

"His early stuff is really good. I think he mailed it in after awhile."

"Cool."

She spun away and checked the kitchen window for her orders. She balanced three plates on her left arm and took them to a table with a condiment caddy in her other hand, before returning to the corner of the bar.

"What are you reading?" Jake asked.

"Organic chemistry."

"That sounds fun."

"Well, I can tell you, this guy didn't mail it in."

"He takes his work seriously."

"I think you have to when you're an organic chemist."

"Where do you go to school?"

"Navajo Community College."

"You like it?"

"It's a little weird, but I went to high school here, so I'm used to it."

"Used to what?"

"Used to being a white girl."

"Ah."

Jake didn't know what else to say to that so he turned his attention back to his beer. She crossed her legs on the bar stool, letting a sandaled foot bounce to an unheard rhythm, and turned the page of her textbook by sliding the paper slowly back against itself. He smiled and thought briefly about asking her out, to a movie or dinner, but he noticed that the bartender, at least one cook, and the family at the table she'd been serving, were listening to their conversation, and he became too self-conscious. Embarrassed, really. After all, he was still married, on paper at least, and probably a decade older than the girl.

"Good luck with that book."

"You too."

He walked outside, surprised to see that it was still light out, not even evening. He gained the truck and fired it up, liking the feel of the peddles, the sound of the engine. He eased around the block to Old Route 66, and watched the sun dip below the visor. He pulled into a Conoco station, parked, and went inside the Food Mart. He grabbed a twelve of Busch Light out of the cooler, and got long looks from the woman at the counter. It was illegal to transport alcohol onto the reservation, and outsiders were viewed with suspicion.

"Where you going? You can't take this to the reservation."

"I live here."

"Uh huh."

She put her hands on her hips. A short, round woman, her long black hair flowed past her waist. A turquoise neckless settled over her white Conoco short sleeve collared shirt.

"I mean, I live just outside Gallup."

"How far outside."

"A couple of miles up 28, on the mountain."

"That's on the Nation's land."

"I know, but I'm not going there right now."

They stared at each other for a long minute. Finally, she rang him up. Very slowly and deliberately she fit the beer into a plastic bag, and handed it to him. He thanked her, trying to drain any trace of perceived disrespect from his voice. He felt guilty as he left.

SEVEN

Jake set the beer on the floorboard in front of the passenger seat. As he reached the edge of town and turned onto Navajo Route 28, he cracked one open, and headed up into the hills toward home. The truck geared down for the climb obscuring the country music twanging from the radio, another custom he had yet to adjust to. At the top of the ridge he pulled over at a dirt turnabout where an aging pickup with a camper shell propped up a hand painted sign that read 'Jerky'. Jake parked, finished his beer, and took two cold ones over to the old Indian sitting in a lawn chair by the Jerky sign.

"Evening, Joseph."

"Evening, Fed."

"You're not supposed to know that."

"Everyone knows that."

Jake handed Joseph a beer. "I'll take some jerky."

"Venison or rabbit."

"You make rabbit jerky?"

"I'll jerk anything."

"Heard that about you."

Joseph opened the cooler that he was using to prop up his feet and fished out a vacuum-sealed package of venison jerky. Jake gave him a ten. The wind picked up and Joseph stood, uncreaking his joints one at a time, and folded his lawn chair, and laid it down in the bed of his truck.

"Well, that's it for me." Joseph sighed.

"You packing it in?"

"Good night to stay inside. Bad goings-ons."

"You too Joseph? Didn't know you were superstitious."

"Not superstition. Religion."

"Well, then I'll heed your advice, forgo the many temptations of Gallup, and stay home tonight and enjoy the jerky."

"I know you will."

They shook hands and Jake started back to his truck and then stopped, remembering something.

"Hey Joseph, you see a fire down in the valley the other night, like a flame just come out of nowhere and then disappear?"

Joseph still held the unopened can of beer in his hand. He carefully popped the top and bent back the tab. He gingerly took a sip and looked down the mountainside.

"I did not see it. But I felt it. Second time in the last couple of nights."

"Second time? What did you feel?"

"Like I said, bad goings-on."

Jake nodded, he didn't know what he was expecting to hear, his training had taught him to just ask questions and observe body language. Quantico ingrained it in him.

"Alright then."

Jake got in his truck and started it up. Joseph still stood in the dirt turnoff sipping his beer, looking off into the distance.

"Hey, why do skinwalkers go after people anyway?" Jake called out from the cab of his truck. The old indian turned to face him.

"Sometimes people are cursed. Sometimes witches just create

mischief. Sometimes they hurt people close to the cursed one. They know that can be worse."

Jake nodded and the two men watched each other for a moment over the rumble of the idling V8 engine. Finally, Jake tipped his brow at Joseph and eased the big pickup truck back on the blacktop. He drove a couple of hundred yards up Navajo 28 to the dirt jeep trail that lead to his trailer. He rolled away the rock that kept the screen door shut with the toe of his boot, and went inside. He pulled the chain on a bare light bulb hanging from the ceiling in the front room, and messed with the antenna on an old transistor radio until he got a semblance of the Diamondbacks game retransmitted from a Phoenix station. He looked out over the hundred mile view as dusk fell and the earth dimmed. The baseball game crackled into infinity. He finished the jerky and the beer as the moonless night turned black. He found his bed and closed his eyes, but it was just as black. As he fell asleep, the coyotes began to howl in the distance.

EIGHT

Washington, D.C. — One Year Back

At least once a month, no matter what their finances or their work schedules, Jake and Aimee tried to go out for a nice dinner together. They were both working long hours as new FBI agents so this was no small feat. Recently, Aimee had begun traveling often as the junior agent on a high profile political corruption case, further complicating their sworn ritual evening out. Their favorite restaurant was a wine and cheese place across the Potomac river in Alexandria, Virginia, called Cheesetique. They liked to order a large cheese plate so they could take their time enjoying each other's company, catch up on what there hadn't been time to share during the week, and drink plenty of wine. They had spent many nights sitting on the high bar stools at Cheesetique, a second bottle of wine uncorked, staring deep into each other's eyes, seeing who would blush first, Jake holding Aimee's hand, running his thumb over her fingers, so slender and strong, feeling the sharp bite of the one and a half carat diamond he'd emptied his bank account for, marveling that she was his. That she had said yes.

But this was not one of those nights. The problem with rituals is that they must be done according to schedule, even if no one wants to. Jake knew that Aimee was not in a good mood. She had other things on her mind, and, if Jake were honest, so did he. Aimee had been gone on an assignment for two weeks, and they had been short with each other for the week she'd been back home. But they had reservations, and to cancel would be worse than an admission of defeat. Canceling would be worse than having an awful night. Canceling would mean they'd lost confidence that things could get better. That they weren't even going to try to make things better.

Aimee had her hair blown out earlier in the day and it was parted sharply and cascaded in front of a bare shoulder on one side, beautifully framing her face. She wore a tight black dress that ended midthigh and four inch heels, showing off sculpted arms, toned calves, and lovely brown skin. Looking at her hit him with a kick of anticipation, but also a healthy dose of apprehension. Her mouth was a line drawn tight. Colorless lip gloss. Her high cheekbones seemed to look down at him. She looked too good. She looked like someone with more important things to do.

But what scared him most was the lack of expression in her face. He'd always had trouble reading her, but tonight it was clear that she didn't want him reading her at all. She had a ritual she had to attend. She was keeping an appointment. Nothing more. Or worse, she just had low expectations for the night. Or even worse than that, she was already disappointed before the night began, perhaps disappointed for a long time now.

They decided to take the Metro from Adams Morgan to Alexandria since it was in that rare time of year when the city was walkable without freezing or boiling. It was during the two week window in spring when the weather in the District could actually be called nice. Soon, the heat and humidity would cover everything and everyone in a film of sweat and swamp stench.

But for now, the evening air was soft and pleasant, with a late bite of crispness when the breeze picked up.

They descended the long escalator to the underground platform. Jake stood on the step behind her, his hand just barely touching her waist. He couldn't help but notice the looks she got from those traveling up the escalator, exiting the Metro Station. They were a good looking couple. The attention they received from men and women alike usually felt like an affirmation of their marriage. But now, it felt like an affirmation of something else. The men staring at her a little too hard, as if she could be available.

They had to wait fifteen minutes for the Yellow Line train to Alexandria. Aimee didn't say anything, but he could feel her shifting from foot to foot, getting impatient. His irritation was growing as well. Maybe there were worse things than keeping the ritual.

"Hurt your feet standing in heels like that?"

She looked at him, eyes the color of obsidian, and just as hard.

"You boys have no idea what we go through."

When the train arrived they got on but stayed standing, Aimee holding on to the railing rather than risk getting something on her dress from sitting on one of the seats. The train was over-bright, an unsettling effect. It lurched loudly through tunnels smelling of burning brake pads, but it quieted and the ride smoothed out as the train crossed the bridge over the Potomac. The view was pretty looking back at the District with the city lights and the Monuments lit up. But, the view was short-lived as the train soon dived back into the tunnels underneath the Pentagon and Crystal City. Finally the train arrived at the Braddock Road Station. It was a relief to be let back out into the pleasant spring air.

"Let's cab it back tonight."

She reluctantly smiled at him

"You got a deal."

They walked through a quiet neighborhood to Del Rey, a quaint section of Alexandria that banned chain stores, the business district lined with local artisans' shops, antique stores, and pricey ethnic-themed restaurants. The sidewalks were uneven, bent from tree roots and crumbling from age. Jake held out his elbow so Aimee could steady herself, the heels making walking treacherous, and she took it.

The front room of Cheesetique was a specialty food store with a cheese counter and floor to ceiling wine racks. It was full of people waiting for their tables in the restaurant to open up, milling about holding wine glasses, perusing rare cheeses, artisanal crackers and hand crafted chocolates imbued with chili or crusted with salt. The crowd parted when Aimee and Jake walked in. People instinctively avoided crowding Aimee or standing too close to her. She was often spared the type of shoulder rubbing that everyone endured in the cramped, revolutionary war-era buildings in that part of the world, and not because Jake would have killed anyone who he suspected was crowding her on purpose. People shuffled out of their way, wine sloshing in their glasses, to grant them a clear path to the restaurant. Jake felt every eye on them, and not, he suspected, only because of Aimee's striking presence, but rather because they were an interracial couple, and Virginia was still, after all, the South.

They decided to sit at the bar when two seats opened up, preferring that to formal dining. They ordered a cheese and charcuterie plate with Castelvetrano olives, salted almonds, and an assortment of mustards and membrillos. They started with Prosecco, and even clinked glasses, but the pink bubbly didn't improve the mood any, and to the contrary, seemed to highlight the dim prospects for any true cause for celebration in the near future. Jake finished his glass as fast as he could and ordered a bottle of Willamette Valley Pinot Noir.

Conversation started and stopped. Conversation takes effort, and effort was lacking. For Aimee, to put in effort just for appearances was disingenuous. It cheapened whatever they had left. There were long silences in which they checked their phones or looked around the restaurant at the other couples— white, conservative, letting their hair down with a glass of wine, many still in the clothes they went to work in only with their ties loosened, jackets off, and shirt sleeves rolled up. The silences, more meaningful because in the past they had been so rare. Jake and Aimee loved to talk, spent the first three years of marriage doing nothing but talk. As recruits, their lives were new and every detail of their training could inspire endless analysis. The physical and mental challenges of Quantico gave their marriage sustenance because they each understood what the other was going through. Jake wondered if they'd run out of things to say. As they learned their jobs there was less to say rather than more. Deep down Jake knew that they had never really gotten to know each other. He liked that about their relationship. There were things he didn't want Aimee to know about him. And she didn't ask. One thing they did have in common was a belief that self-analysis was overrated. Talking about feelings didn't change them. Things were what they were.

The cheese board arrived, providing a momentary distraction. The triple creme brie was perfectly runny and the Port Salut was pungent. Jake refilled Aimee's wine glass. Her scowl had hardened to a mask. Jake made another run at conversation, in an attempt to turn around what was fast becoming one of the worst nights of his life, to the one place they had in common— work.

"How's the case against our favorite Congressman coming along?"

Aimee put her phone down and slathered a slice of baguette with brie and quince paste.

"You wouldn't believe this guy. You think when you know you're being investigated you take some precautions. What is it about politicians that makes them think they're invincible."

"Ego."

"Sociopaths."

"That too. How's the C.I.?"

"So bad I can't believe it's working. The wires are hysterical. The guy couldn't be more direct. He sounds like my grandpa—so... Congressman...if I give you this money...which is...fifty thousand dollars...my business will get the government contract...mmm... yes...it is so—and the Honorable Mr. Blakely from the great state of Alaska says "yes", from his Dirksen office no less."

"Idiot."

"Totally."

"I'll never get used to these people out here."

"I like D.C. people, just not corrupt politicians."

"Really? Look at these fucking people." Jake said it a little too loud and a few people turned their heads.

"What? They're interesting. They have jobs."

"They're arrogant and pretentious."

"Isn't it arrogant and pretentious to call a whole city of people arrogant and pretentious?"

"They're weak. They wouldn't last two hours in the wilderness."

"You didn't grow up on a reservation, Jake. I like being around people who have interesting jobs. I'm not squandering this opportunity."

"I know. I just assumed we'd be moving out west at some point."

"Well, you shouldn't have."

"Don't you want to go back and help your people? You know... change things?"

Aimee took a slug of wine, dotted the corner of her mouth with a napkin, and checked her nails. She swiveled on the barstool and looked Jake directly in the eye.

"I am changing things. I'm showing them what I can do. What we can do. That there's more to aspire to than to be some clerk at the BIA."

"You can be an agent from anywhere, you know. You don't have to do it in D.C."

"No, that's where you're wrong. I could, but I won't. This is where the connections are. This is where the power is. It's totally different than being in the field. The freaking Attorney General knows my name. Knows who *I am*. You get that right? Besides, I like it here."

"Don't you miss the desert? The mountains?"

"I can visit. Besides, you had your time adventuring. It's time to grow up."

"That wasn't adventuring. That was war."

"Well, when we got married I assumed you were ready to settle down."

"Well, you shouldn't have."

"Oh no? How unreasonable of me."

"I mean, I just didn't think we'd be stuck here. In D.C."

"I'll go back some day, run for Tribal Council. Maybe after I've got my twenty-pin."

"Twenty years? We'll be like fifty. I want to enjoy life with you while we're young."

"This is life, and I'm enjoying it...for the most part."

Jake broke away from her intense stare. He knew what she was getting at. He was the "most part". They had talked about these things before, where to live, how to live, whether to put down roots. Questions best answered before marriage. But it had always been a discussion. These days it was an argument. One with an air of finality.

The waitress looked apologetic when she brought over the bill, and not because of the amount. The tab was one hundred and ninety dollars. Jake would have rather paid one hundred and ninety dollars to get kicked in the nuts. It had somehow gone from a bad night to a bad marriage. They took a cab back into D.C. in silence. He helped her out of the backseat and held her hand as they walked up the stairs to their apartment. When they got inside the door, he hugged her until she let all the air out of her lungs, sighed deeply, and put her head in the crook of his neck. They undressed quietly, got into bed, and made love for the last time.

NINE

The Navajo Nation — The Present

Jake opened his eyes to daylight and a brilliant blue sky behind the sliding plexiglass door. Bent and twisted blinds rattled by drafts from the wind. He'd patched the holes and the rusty seams in the trailer's aluminum siding with duct tape, but the sun had quickly dried out the glue on the sticky side of the tape, and now dozens of half stuck swatches of duct tape flapped off the walls with the wind like so many tattered prayer flags left to age and decay on some desolate Himalayan mountaintop. It made an eerie sound. A sound that belonged to a ghost town.

He blinked hard, yawned, stretched, scratched, and shuffled to the kitchen to make a pot of coffee. After two cups, and a morning constitutional, he suffered the low water pressure of the singlewide's shower box and put on yesterday's jeans and a passable flannel shirt. He couldn't quite get himself to try the silver and turquoise bola tie he'd bought at one of the roadside curio shops on the way to Zuni. Someday, he thought.

He made good time to the office but Mary was already there, and had been for hours. Mary was always there. He knew that wasn't true because he'd learned yesterday the she worked four tens. But she could also just be fucking with him. It was hard to tell with Mary, and the rest of the town for that matter.

Mary looked up from her computer. "How's Aimee's lawyer

doing?"

"Haven't heard."

"You two on the rocks also?"

"I've never met the lawyer, some ballbuster from D.C."

"Long distance relationships don't work out well. You should know."

"Not my choice."

"Well, you can't expect a D.C. lawyer to move out here for you."

"I'm not...wait...who are you even talking about?"

"Who *am* I talking about."

"Deep, that's deep, Mary. Anything this morning? It's morning, right?"

"Another murder last night, or the night before, they aren't sure. Tribal police found a girl all burnt up."

"Murder...are they saying that?"

"Hard to light yourself on fire with your hands cuffed behind your back."

A vision assaulted Jake's mind. Flames igniting, wrists contorting in handcuffs, skin bubbling, pain everywhere at once, in every nerve ending, desperation, helplessness, horror, an orange blur of fire consuming the world. That was her last sight before her retinas burned away, and her eyeballs boiled, leaving only darkness and stench. Her soul, her consciousness, her essence, fighting to burst free from her skin, to get out of her body, that body. Anything to escape the pain. To end the torture.

Jake shook off the image. He knew not to dwell on such things. Mary stared at him. He shook her off too. He took the stairs up to his office two at a time and started up his computer. He entered his passwords, and as the computer went through its machinations granting him access, he swiveled in his chair and looked out at the empty street and the mountains beyond. When he was logged on he checked his fantasy team. Tulowitzki homered for the second straight game and went three for four, his team was still in first place. He made a cursory check of his email, saw over a hundred new messages, most from Admin that had no relevance in Gallup, and decided his time was better spent investigating the new case.

He made the tribal police headquarters in Window Rock in under half an hour. This time the police station was bustling. He found Yazzie, the only tribal officer he'd formed any kind of rapport with in his three months at the Gallup duty station. Yazzie sighed and rubbed his eyes and extricated himself from a mound of paperwork and carbon copies to shake Jake's hand, his face reading what Jake suspected, that somehow the FBI agent had become Yazzie's burden to deal with by some unspoken arrangement with Del Bradley, the Tribal Police Chief, their friendship, an equally as burdensome byproduct of that arrangement.

"Hey man, busy around here today," Jake said.

Yazzie looked him in the eye, a crooked smile creeping across his lockjaw face.

"Mmm, yes, a lot of activity in the building. The People are worried."

"Another one burnt up, I'm sensing a pattern."

"I can see they taught you well at Quantico. Tax dollars well spent. You have an eye for investigation."

"I do what I can. Seriously, are the murders related?"

Yazzie filled him in on the few details that were known about the latest murder. The crime scene boys were already on location. Jake unfurled his AAA map of Indian Country and

Yazzie used a Sharpie to mark the spots where the two bodies had been found, the old man and the girl.

Jake took Navajo Route 12 out of Window Rock and then Highway 264 East back across the New Mexico line to a little stretch of ground-down black top known as Indian 54. From there he parked and followed a sheep herding trail on foot into a wide plain of desert scrub and ocotillo. He stopped where people and vehicles seemed to have left a circle where the little prickly pears and yellowed thistles were trampled down and a black streak of greasy soot and the burnt fatty clumps of human flesh CSI had missed scarred the desert floor. He found nothing of interest on the ground, but when he rose from his stoop and stretched his back, he was surprised that he was looking at his ridge some miles in the distance. This was part of his hundred mile view. He squinted and made out a reflection of sunlight off of metal siding atop the mountain. His trailer.

The second murder scene was seventy miles away up State Route 491 close to the town of Shiprock. He followed the Sharpie on an unnamed dirt access road that rock climbers used to get close to Shiprock Monument, the iconic giant red obelisk that rose out of the desert like a two thousand foot tall tanker run aground and fossilized. In the shadow of the massive rock, he parked, and walked on the tread marks of emergency vehicles to another circle, this one on loamy reddish sand, and another black stain on the ground. He spent an hour stooped over, fingers running through the withered clumps of grama grass, looking for nothing, when he found something. A metal lighter, not left long in the weather, orange with a rainbow decal. He tried it and a little blue blowtorch flame hissed up.

TEN

Jake drove the hundred miles back to his trailer as the sun reached the horizon. He opened the flimsy aluminum door to the sound of the phone ringing.

"This is Jake."

"Hey, Jake."

"Aimee."

"How are you, Jake."

"Awesome."

"Fantastic. So, glad you're enjoying the rez."

"It's your rez."

"I know. Why are you there?"

"Waiting for you."

"I'm not coming back to the rez, Jake."

There was a long silence while the wind whistled through the gaps in the plexiglass window frames and the loose side boards flapped against their brethren.

"Not even to visit?"

"Visit my family, yes. But not like you want. Did you sign the papers?"

Another silence.

"Do you have the papers?"

Jake sighed.

"From Dickstein? Yeah, I got them."

"Then you've been served."

"When did you become all business, Aimee?"

"I've always been all business. You just didn't notice. What are you doing on my rez, Jake."

"Waiting for you."

"Don't."

"Too late, I'm already here."

He heard her breathing on the other end of the line, probably somewhere in Bethesda, or Chevy Chase.

The line went dead and he held the phone up to his ear for a long time, listening to the wind outside the trailer.

ELEVEN

Jake awoke to a primal scream. It must have come from far away, but it sounded as if it was inside the trailer. He saw the reflection of flames in the windows and thought he was dreaming some long repressed nightmare. But as he rubbed his eyes he realized the color in the windows was from real fire, not from any electric light or remnant dream. He sat bolt upright and leapt out of bed, buck naked as he always slept. He went into the front room of the house and saw that the glow of fire came from the direction of the road running the ridgeline. He ran back to the bedroom and stepped into his sweatpants and ran outside. The night was black and the stars above were disorienting as he ran shirtless and barefoot up the jeep trail to Navajo 28, where he could see flames and smell burning plastic and something else. He gained the highway and ran down the road a couple of hundred yards to a pickup truck on fire. Inside was Joseph still flopping about and writhing in pain, his whole body on fire, the truck burning, paint bubbling. Jake beat the flames off of Joseph with his hands until the inside of the cab became like a furnace and his own arm hair singed and burnt off. He hadn't brought his cell phone—it didn't get a signal on the ridge—so he ran back to his trailer and used the landline to call 911.

By the time the ambulance arrived, Joseph was long dead.

Jake followed the ambulance to the hospital in Gallup. He fished in the truck's glove box for a cigarette. He found a dried out Winston Light in a crumpled pack underneath the owner's manual. He'd quit three months ago but now seemed like a good time to start again. He smushed out the cigarette in the dashboard's plastic ashtray as the ambulance pulled into the hospital's emergency entrance. He followed the gurney with the smoldering body through the antiseptic hallways until they reached the ICU and he was told to wait in the lobby. He walked out to the vending machines and then back to the ICU, but he couldn't see anything through the little rectangular window inlaid with metal mesh.

He felt a hand on his shoulder. It was Cally, the waitress from the Copper Street Pub. He did a double take.

"Hey."

"Hey, are you okay? My mom's a nurse here, we knew Joseph... everyone knew Joseph," Cally said.

"Um, yeah I'm okay." Jake nodded his head and clasped his hands together.

"You must see stuff like this all the time, huh. I mean, with your job and all."

"No, I don't. This is weird."

She put her hand on his chest. His breathing calmed down a bit and they walked down the hall to the front entrance. They could see the dark night outside. She took his hand and squeezed it, and he looked down at her and put his arm around her back and half-hugged her. The duty nurse watched them, frowned and arched an eyebrow at an orderly who shrugged and shook his head.

Jake waited for an hour with no news, not even sure anyone

would tell him if there was any, and then drove home. He took two Tylenol PM to get to sleep, and waited for the coyotes to howl in his dreams.

TWELVE

Two blocks down the street from the Copper Street Pub in downtown Gallup was a different kind of bar called the American. The outside of the bar was painted red, white, and blue, over the bricks and all the windows so that no sunlight ever made it inside. During the day the American was strictly for the professional drinkers, the occasional pool hustler, degenerate gamblers, drug dealers, undocumented Mexicans, and rough necks that worked the fracking fields. At night it wasn't much different except the customers were more heavily armed and drugged. But on Friday and Saturday nights the American booked country and blues bands, and even the occasional reggae band that passed through town making a living on the road in lesser known venues and wasteland outposts. On those nights, the bar reluctantly welcomed a more eclectic crowd, the two-stepping country and western set, the old sixties burners, college kids, and anyone who liked to dance and was brave enough to pull open the heavy steel door, face the tattooed one-eyed bouncer, and stomach the stale beer and old vomit stench.

A tall man in black jeans, a purple button-down, thin neck tie, and black blazer, stood at the bar with a pint of Guinness watching the stage as a Toby Keith cover band finished up a set. The crowd half jeered and half applauded as the MC took the microphone and an odd procession of local country singers took the stage. Sponsors lined up placards, and the house lights momentarily came on, and the sound was cut off. The bar filled with the ambient sound of glasses brushing together and people talking in hoarse hacked off snippets, and laughter. The MC's mic came back and announced the winner of a weeks long sing-off, and presented a wreath of flowers to a beautiful teenage girl who smiled shyly and deferred to her mother who took the heavy arrangement off stage. The room erupted in thundering applause as the MC introduced the hometown girl as the winner of KDOG 102.5's country sing-off. The MC thanked the sponsors and the girl's family. Friends and new friends stood and whistled as the girl slung her guitar and stood in front of the mic.

"This is a song I wrote," she breathed.

Purple and rose spotlights backlit her blond curly hair. The bar grew quiet. She began to play a slow, sad ballad, finger picking minor chords and holding her notes to a chorus that rose as she picked up the tempo, and her soulful lip quiver subtly crept into a smile, and she ripped bar chords in such a catchy tune that by the middle of the song the crowd had picked up the lyrics and was singing along. The song finished with a high note she belted for what seemed like an hour as the audience roared, high-fived each other, and tucked their longneck beer bottles into the crook of their elbows so they could clap with abandon. When she was finished she took a step back and curtseyed.

"Thank you," she whispered into the mic.

The crowd parted as she made her way off stage and hugged her mama. The tall man in the black blazer sidestepped through her friends and extended family, all waiting to pat her on the back, and jammed a card into her hand. She was a little startled, and when she faced him he bent down and whispered something in her ear. She followed him back to the bar and took the seat next to him.

"So, are you an agent?"

"Not exactly."

"So what is it you do?"

"Agility."

The man in black was about to launch into a practiced speech, when a figure at the end of the bar caught his attention. A man with a white shaved head, except for a thin mohawk, stared at him. Except he wasn't staring directly at him, the man was slowly rotating his head, all the while keeping his eyes trained on him, as if trying to see him only out of the corners of his wide and disturbing eyes. It broke his train of thought. He wondered why the weirdo at the end of the bar was staring at him, of all people.

"Agility, what does that mean?"

He reached over and behind the bar and picked up a pint glass, a rocks glass, and a shot glass. He could still feel the weirdo's eyes on him. He lined the glasses up in descending order of size. He poured some of his beer into the pint glass, and then poured some into the rocks glass, and then the shot glass. The rest of his beer he poured onto the bar.

"That's agility."

He gave the girl a self-satisfied smile.

"The beer that's on the bar, that's agility. The part that's lost. That's what I capture."

Before he could explain further, the bartender came over and wiped up the beer on the bar with a rag, and asked him if he wanted another. He stood, all six foot five of him, and lifted his arms in protest that the bartender had ruined his demonstration. The bartender didn't understand, and cupped her hand to her ear, trying to hear what he was saying over the Toby Keith cover band that had started up again. He looked down at the pretty blonde singer on the barstool next to him, but he avoided looking down at the end of the bar. The man with the mohawk rubbed his sweaty white head and made some guttural noise, eyes crazy.

"I don't get it," the girl said.

THIRTEEN

Jake woke suddenly. The trailer was dark. Moonlight behind the crumpled blinds made grayish silver shadows. The trailer always felt alien at night, like this would never be home.

The phone was ringing. He checked his jeans pocket until he remembered that the cell phone didn't work up here, and stumbled naked to the landline on the kitchen counter.

"Agent Keller?"

"Yeah, who's this?"

"It's Mitch."

"Mitch?"

"Your ASAC, you know at the FBI. The ones who are paying you? You report to me, you know."

Jake was silent. He'd met the Assistant Special Agent In Charge once when he filled out his HR paperwork in Albuquerque, and had caught the first whiff of douche. He knew he should be careful now.

"Surprised that I'm calling you at 3:30 in the morning?"

"Why are you calling me?"

"Because people keep bursting into flames in your neck of the woods."

"I know, I was down at the hospital tonight. I knew the guy. Old Indian sells jerky by the side of the road. Well, sold jerky,

THE HUNDRED MILE VIEW

anyway."

"Don't know why you were at the hospital, the body's lying in an alley in downtown Gallup."

"What are you talking about?"

"It's still smoldering. Gallup police are on it."

"Jesus."

"Yeah, you got an epidemic."

"Serial killer, more like it."

"Is that your expert opinion? Agent Keller, you're going to listen to me now. Shut the fuck up. I'm serious. Don't talk. You're a little baby agent and you don't know what you're doing. So I'm going to help you. Keep your goddamn mouth shut. You haven't even been to the crime scene, but you're ready to scream serial killer."

"Where's the body?"

"Behind some bar called the American. Know it?"

"Yeah, it's a shithole."

"A shithole in Gallup, who would have guessed."

Jake leaned hard against the counter and tapped the phone to his head. He listened to the wind outside.

"Is that it, Mitch?"

"I don't know, Agent Keller, is that it? Do you have any suspects for me? Any clues? Do your job before I send someone up there to do it for you."

"Are you taking this from Gallup PD?"

"I would, but honestly, then I'd really be stuck with you. Right now, I'd rather they have to take the heat."

"Funny, they take the heat...you know...because of the fires..."

The line went dead. Jake slowly put the phone back in its cradle and rubbed his eyes. He was suddenly cold. It was summer and in the upper nineties during the day, but it was always cold in the high desert at night. He dressed slowly, he felt no rush. The killing was already done. He opened the door to the outside, not sure of the world he was walking into.

He took the truck into town. He could see the red and blue reflections from the myriad emergency vehicles as soon as he came off the ridge and hit Old 66. All of downtown was cast in intervals of flashing lights, the old frontier brick buildings on Main lighting up and then darkening like the batting of giant eyelashes. He parked down the street from the American and walked up the alley. He had few contacts in the Gallup PD, and didn't know anyone working the crime scene. His badge provoked only passing interest. Everyone was tired and generally disgusted by the blackened corpse and the stench of burnt flesh. The man had been tall, and with the scorch marks he left a huge smear of ash and gore across the alley. Jake squatted and tried to imagine the crime. The tall man had exited the bar by the back door. Was he already on fire? Probably not. The smoke alarm in the bar hadn't gone off. Where had the attacker come from? He looked up the alley and tried to picture someone running at the man with gasoline or some other accelerant but he just ended up starring dumbly at the melted soles of the man's shoes.

The sky lightened as the blood and guts crew finished their work, and enough photos were taken and distances measured for the charred corpse to finally be scraped into a body bag. Jake watched the Gallup boys mill about for awhile. They weren't sure when they could say they were done.

He walked to his office, opening the door too roughly so that the bell clanked once and got stuck upright and wedged in the framing. Mary was quiet. It threw him off. He looked at her and waited.

"You look like hell," she said, finally.

"Thank you."

She nodded. "Did you sleep?"

"Not much. Coyotes in my dreams."

She looked at him. She folded her arms as if she didn't want to say what she was going to say next.

"Skinwalkers."

"Come on."

"They're close to you. Coyotes in your dreams? Can't miss a sign like that."

"I don't believe in skinwalkers. Whenever someone gets drunk on the rez and does something stupid, it's skinwalkers. Whenever a cow wanders on the road and gets hit by a car, it's skinwalkers. It's a convenient excuse, not a religion. But I do believe in coyotes, they're all over the place."

"Why don't you go home and shower. You stink."

Jake looked at Mary and nodded. He gave her a sideways smile and tipped his finger to his temple and turned back around and left out the door. He squinted at the new day sun, stiff and loose at the same time. He found his truck where he'd left it. It'd been a long night and he didn't remember leaving it there, but he could live with that ambiguity.

He took Old Route 66 through the shady side of town, and turned onto Navajo 28 up the ridgeline. The trees were staring at him. He pulled onto the driveway to his trailer and listened to the sound of gravel crunching under his tires. He got out of the truck and felt the earth spin a little bit. He steadied himself and listened to the wind in the trees. His trailer looked small, dented, and rusted. He opened the front door, stepped inside and then stopped cold in his tracks. It felt like someone had been there, inside. He stood still and listened. He felt a draft that wasn't there before.

The phone rang. He stood frozen. He looked toward the tiny kitchen. Nothing moved. He let the phone ring a good seven or eight more times and then picked up the receiver and slowly put it to his ear. He heard breathing on the other end of the line.

"Yeah?"

"Yeah? Is that how you're answering your phone now?" It was his soon to be ex-wife.

"Aimee."

"Who'd you think it was?"

"I don't know. God, I'm glad it's you."

"Mary told me to call you. She's worried about you."

"Mary? You mean my secretary, Mary?"

"She's my aunt."

"She hardly talks to me, and when she does, it's not that nice."

"I told you, she's my aunt."

"Jesus, is there anyone around here you're not related to?"

"Hey, you moved to my rez."

"Why don't you move back here?"

"Why don't you get over me."

"Don't you think I tried?"

"No, I don't think you tried. You moved to the Navajo Nation, Jake. That's not trying."

Jake was silent for a moment, trying to think of something to say. Something to salvage some pride.

"How are things in D.C.?"

"The same, Jake. Things are the same."

"Are you coming home for the Pow Wow?"

It was Aimee's turn to be silent. He waited. He could hear her thinking to herself. He listened to her inhale and exhale. It stirred something inside of him.

"Stay away from skinwalkers, Jake."

FOURTEEN

He slept through the rest of the day. A weird, exhausted daytime sleep. He awoke at night, and expected the phone to ring, but it didn't. He laid in bed watching the dented slat blinds rustle like wind chimes to some unseen draft.

At first light he showered, threw on a T-shirt and jeans, and drove the truck to Window Rock. The Tribal Police station didn't open for non-emergency business until nine, on a good day, so he drove back out to the drive-through Coffee Hut, a converted silver airstream trailer parked on a dirt turn out on the highway to Shiprock. Jake sipped his coffee in his truck listening to the farm and livestock report on AM radio KOA 960—"beans up a quarter, hogs down three and half, corn up one and an eighth, November winter wheat up five and a quarter the bushel, November hogs down one and a half, November light sweet crude up five cent the barrel..."

The morning chill faded and it grew hot enough to start the truck and put on the air conditioning. The cacti moved imperceptibly as the sun lightened the brown foreground to a gleaming white. He donned his sunglasses and walked into the Navajo Tribal Police Headquarters at nine o'clock sharp.

Yazzie was already there, almost expecting him, although he didn't look up when Jake approached his desk.

"How'd you sleep?" Yazzie said, without looking up from the police report he was studying.

"Beautiful, sweetheart, how about you?"

"Oh, I always sleep well. Thank you for asking."

"So, any leads?"

"Mmm...figured out who stole Sally Big Knife's Dodge pickup."

"Solid police work." Jake rubbed his forehead and then pulled at his hair until it stood straight up.

"It was her son."

"Her son? Is that even theft? Isn't that borrowing the car?"

Yazzie looked up and studied him for a long time before he spoke.

"I hadn't thought of it like that."

"Do you know who lit that guy on fire outside the American?"

"Not our jurisdiction. Gallup PD's got that one."

"Okay, do you know who did the three people who got lit up in your jurisdiction?"

"No. But I think that's really your jurisdiction."

"You might be right." Jake nodded and pulled out his cell phone and unlocked the screen out of habit. It had no signal.

"You should see what Gallup PD knows," Yazzie said.

"Do I have to? They don't like me."

"Oh come on now, have you shown them that fancy badge of yours?"

"Yes."

"And that didn't do it? I know for a fact that they are fond of shiny objects."

"No. Come with me."

"How is bringing an Indian going to help?"

"It couldn't hurt."

"Mmm...you are not a student of history."

"Not true, my friend. I can tell you anything you want to know about the French Revolution."

Yazzie crossed his arms and thought about this for a long minute. "Mmm...there is nothing I want to know about that."

"Come on let's go. I'll buy you some mutton stew."

"You should have led with that."

They each took their own vehicles into Gallup, Jake in his truck and Yazzie in his Navajo Tribal Police Chevy Tahoe. The Gallup Police station was a drab concrete building with a glass and steel artifice. They were shown to Detective Yance, a brick of a man, solid muscle buttressed by fat, his square shape reinforced by a close cropped flattop and a blonde goatee, pink skin showing clearly beneath both. Yance was only momentarily confused by the Fed and the Indian. The man was a professional. He briefly studied the Fed's creds. The Indian's green Tribal Police jacket and holstered sidearm, he took at face value. Yance was disturbed by the homicide and shared what he knew freely with his colleagues in law enforcement.

Yance had accomplished quite a bit in twenty-four hours, in Jake's opinion, more than he himself would have, he thought. The victim was an out-of-towner, which was unusual. Recognizably tall, maybe six foot four, and well-off judging by his clothes, shoes, and watch. He was some kind of agent in the music business. Producer maybe. Hailed from Madison, Wisconsin, which didn't make a lot of sense for a music producer or an agent. Yance had learned all of this from the credit card left at the bar, and from interviewing the patrons at the American, including a teenage country singer whose hopes for a recording contract lay in a greasy carbon smear in the alley behind the bar. All and all it was a senseless crime. It left all three lawmen uneasy.

The task of extracting information from the Gallup PD complete, Jake and Yazzie drove their respective vehicles up to Jake's place to try out Yazzie's new Mossberg tactical shotgun purchased with more of that Homeland Security money. Jake grabbed a couple Busch Lights out of the fridge and they walked down to a clearing in the stunted pine trees where Jake had set up some targets. They kicked around what they knew about the case between shotgun blasts. Four murders, that they knew of. Three on the reservation. One in town. Three Indians. One white guy. No leads.

When they'd wasted enough shells, they drove back to Gallup and had mutton stew at Bill's Diner. The stew was thin, the fry bread thick, and the mutton was tough and chewy, just as it should to be.

"Come with me on patrol tonight," Yazzie said. "It will be thick with skinwalkers."

FIFTEEN

The man with the white head and thin mohawk is sitting in a crowded doublewide trailer smoking glass. The Mohawk rotates the blown glass bowl under a flame and exhales white smoke toward the aluminum ceiling. The huge hit of meth doesn't change his expression. He's already high, always high. He's beyond getting high. Now, he just is.

Loud music fills the trailer, alternating death metal, hip hop, and Navajo chants. A few long-haired Indians drink beers. They mill about, nodding their heads with the beat of the music or staring at nothing.

The Mohawk is sitting next to the Shaman. The Shaman sits cross-legged with a placid smile on his face. He is wearing a white terrycloth robe embroidered with Arabic lettering, the emblem of a hotel that no longer exists. The Mohawk passes the pipe to the Shaman. The Shaman bows his head slightly in acknowledgment. He receives the pipe and passes it to a boy lying on the floor. The pipe continues its journey around the room, hand to mouth, hand to mouth.

The Shaman slowly rises, and then walks to the back of the house. He pulls back a sliding glass door and steps outside where a giant bonfire casts huge shadows against a looming canyon wall. There, the diaspora. Skinny white kids with pockmarks,

Navajo, Hopi, Apache, and a few hispanics, dance around the fire as giant speakers hooked up to car batteries fill the desert night with discordant sounds. Their shadows stretch like dark ghouls towering against the sandstone cliff.

SIXTEEN

Jake slept all afternoon in preparation for the night patrol with Yazzie. The couple of beers he had during target practice with the Mossberg made it easy to sleep. But he awoke at dusk feeling none more rested. The sky was a weird graying blue that quickly turned to an ominous black by the time he was out of the lukewarm shower and dressed. He felt groggy on the drive to Window Rock.

The Tribal Police Headquarters was brightly lit and unusually active. Yazzie strapped on body armor under his green Deputy's jacket, and wore his service revolver on his hip, and a Smith & Wesson .45 in a shoulder holster. Jake wore a T-shirt and jeans with his Glock holstered and his FBI badge clipped to his belt.

They started out on patrol in Yazzie's Tahoe, the radio crackling, dashboard lights and console computer glowing softly. The moon was not up yet and it was dark on the reservation. They drove in silence. It was quiet on the reservation. Too quiet for comfort, as if danger lurked just past the reach of the headlights.

The calls began trickling in around ten and peaked well after midnight. Scared people. Strange noises. They raced fifty miles across scarred blacktop and another twenty miles on jeep track to take a call that turned out to be from the girlfriend of an inebriated man who'd passed out too close to a havalina den, and had his legs mauled by a mother protecting her young. He ranted that the girlfriend was a witch until Yazzie talked him down. Jake's hand was on his Glock through the whole call, the drunk man's eyes flicking back and forth between the Indian cop and the white man with the gun.

The next call was sixty miles away at a hogan off a dirt road where an old woman pointed them to a young doe that was trapped in a barbed wire fence, a suspected skinwalker. The fawn flailed its legs tangling itself deeper into the twisted wire. Four small children held hands and watched as Jake blew its head off with the Mossberg. But it was just a deer, not a shapeshifter. After it stopped twitching and the gush of blood had run out into the dusty ground and sunk into the earth, Yazzie cut the carcass loose from the barbed wire and the family carried it to the sheep shearing shed so it could be skinned and butchered for meat.

When Jake and Yazzie got back to the Tahoe the computer was lit up with a license plate number, a description of a maroon 2009 Dodge Ram pickup, and a rap sheet. The radio was calling for assistance with a pursuit on State Route 491, some twenty miles away. Yazzie hit the sirens and floored it and they tore down the jeep trail at seventy miles per hour, the cat claw acacia and tamarisk bleeding into the track, witchbranches scraping the side windows, and the headlights reflecting off the dust, blinding them for anxious moments before the truck bounced through the clouds of dirt and over the under brush, and barreled onward. Jake buckled his seat belt and held onto the roll bar as he was slammed against the passenger side door as the tires kicked over rocks and ruts in the road. He didn't say anything but he looked cockeyed at Yazzie, as if he didn't know the Navajo lawman had it in him.

The Tahoe hit blacktop and fishtailed, the tires screeching and smoking as the truck righted itself and gunned up to one hundred and ten on an open stretch of SR 491. Within half a mile they caught up to a state trooper in a Crown Vic struggling to keep up with the pursuit, and passed it without breaking stride. As the road curved around the cliffs of Ft. Defiance, Yazzie caught up to another Navajo Tribal Police unit riding the tailgate of a DEA Taskforce Ford Expedition, and blew past them both with the benefit of seeing that the two lane highway ahead was clear with all the oncoming traffic pulled over onto the shoulder, headlights illuminating the yellowed grass and cactus on the side of the road. The lead chase cars were up ahead, two across, lights strobing over the dark desert, red and blue pinging off rocky outcroppings, yucca, and sage brush. Yazzie pushed the big block 350 V8 even harder, redlining the tach, and eased behind the two Tribal Police cruisers in hot pursuit of the maroon Dodge Ram that drove right down the centerline. The passenger in the pickup began throwing garbage and beer cans out the window. A McDonald's happy meal box flattened on the Tahoe's windshield. French fries caught in the wiper blades.

The road arced with the curvature of the landscape and the Dodge Ram drifted onto the shoulder and began sliding at one hundred miles an hour. The lead cruiser drifted along side and almost passed the Dodge as Yazzie slid the Tahoe in behind to replace the cruiser. The Dodge suddenly righted as the highway straightened and sideswiped the cruiser sending it in a cloud of dust into the desert. Yazzie swore and ground his boot through the peddle into the floorboard. The Tahoe's hood rattled and the engine threatened to burst loose from its moorings as the truck surged into the back bumper of the Dodge Ram. The pickup swerved once and then t-boned into a bridge abutment splitting in half, both chunks of truck flying mostly over an arroyo and careening into the far side embankment of the ravine. Jake watched through the posts of the bridge's guardrail like an old stop motion cartoon as a body exited the pickup in at least two pieces.

The Tahoe skidded to a stop a hundred yards later, adroitly avoiding the other cruiser and tailing chase vehicles. The highway was shut down and it took forty-five minutes for the first ambulance to arrive, which wasn't a bad response time for a wreck on the reservation. The air smelled of burnt rubber. Jake sat down on the closed highway and watched as the ambulance and fire crews searched the dry creek bed and surrounding desert for body parts. Charley Whitehorse, the Navajo officer who'd been run off the road, had managed to keep his cruiser from rolling and suffered only minor injuries when the cruiser came to rest high-centered on a splintered young cottonwood tree that had been bisected by the Crown Vic's cattle guard. The top half of the tree had toppled over and crushed the cruiser's roof, destroying the siren, and blowing out the windshield. It took two wreckers to haul away the remnants of the Dodge Ram.

Yazzie diligently faced the matrix of paperwork that he was required to navigate. He learned from the DEA Taskforce agent that the pursuit began after a traffic stop where the officer smelled marijuana. The driver had given the officer his license, and then taken off while the officer was checking the computer database for warrants. The search for marijuana continued amid the smoke, twisted metal, melted plastic, and bodily effluent.

SEVENTEEN

Jake became aware of the sound of birds chirping. He was home. It was bright outside and he could see the blue, washed out sky through the rustling blinds. A woodpecker furiously pecked at the aluminum roof at the far end of his trailer, creating a hollow clanging sound, like someone was beating his house with a metal pipe. He blinked several times and sat up in bed, not sure what about last night was real, and what was a dream.

He saw his clothes in a pile on the floor next to the bed. He didn't remember taking them off, or coming home at all, for that matter. He walked naked to the sink in the corner of the trailer that served as the kitchen and splashed water on his face. There were no blinds covering the plexiglass window in the kitchen. He made coffee with the last dried grounds from a plastic drum of Folger's and brownish tap water from the cistern, and drank two cups while looking out at the hundred mile view.

He picked up his jeans off the floor and put them on along with a clean T-shirt. Underneath the jeans and dirty underwear, he found the Glock, still in the shoulder holster. He carried it outside and tossed it in the passenger seat of his truck, happy his truck had made it home with him last night. He drove to the office listening to the farm report on the radio, and got déjà vu. The lack of sleep was beginning to mess with his head.

Mary was waiting for him. It was hard to tell, because she didn't look up from her computer screen when he said good morning, but he got the sense that she'd been waiting for him.

"Heard you were talking to Miriam's daughter at the hospital," she said.

Jake stopped and shook his head. "Who's Miriam?"

"You know, the girl, Cally."

"What are you talking about?" Jake stood dumbly for a long second, and then he realized she was talking about the night before last, when he'd gone to the hospital after finding Old Joe burnt to death.

"I was there to see Old Joe."

"I know, I'm just saying," Mary shrugged her shoulders.

"Jesus Mary, a man died."

"I know, Old Joe. Alls I said was you were seen talking to a girl, let's not make a federal case out of it...jeez."

"I...you...you're the one making a..." Jake stammered and threw up his hands and started up the stairs to his office before he stopped halfway up.

"Why didn't you tell me Aimee was your niece?"

"You didn't know that?" Mary said without turning around. "I thought everyone knew that."

"No, I didn't know that."

"Especially you, being married to her and all...jeez."

Jake started to speak, and then abruptly stalked up the rest of the stairs and slammed his office door. The coroner's report on Old Joe was on his desk. The body was a burnt, bloody mess, but the coroner had been able to determine that the hands weren't bound like the other murders on the reservation. Those were execution style, bodies nothing but charred bone and flesh melted into the sand like candle wax. This killing seemed more spontaneous. A chill ran up Jake's neck. He opened his desk drawer and took out the butane lighter he'd found at the scene of the second murder, the girl's. The safety had been chipped off, like a little blowtorch.

He was suddenly famished, actually felt weak, and realized he hadn't eaten since yesterday's mutton stew. He put the lighter in his pocket and clomped down the stairs and past Mary before she could say anything. He walked down the street to the Copper Street Pub. Cally was sitting at the bar reading a novel. Hearing the door open, she got up off the bar stool, and then saw who it was and smiled at Jake, and then remembered the seriousness of the occasion the last time they'd seen each other, and the smile turned to a sympathetic frown.

"How are you?" she said, gently touching his arm.

"Alright. You?"

She nodded and sat back down on her barstool. He sat down one barstool away, leaving an empty stool between them. He almost wished she wasn't there, he didn't really feel like having to talk to anyone. He needed to think. But she was so easy to talk to that he felt himself involuntarily relaxing. They talked about her classes at Navajo Community College, and about Mary and how Jake had worked with her for three months without knowing that she was his ex's aunt. Even Cally had known that. They talked in subdued tones, almost intimate, like old friends, but not about anything important, not about the murders. She got up to check on the order for a table of tourists, and when she came back he had taken the lighter out of his pocket and set it on the bar, running his fingers over the rainbow decal on the front.

"Whoa, didn't know you were a tweaker. You should lay off or you'll ruin this rugged, slightly disheveled lawman thing you're working on. It'll cross over into disgusting loser pretty fast."

"What do you mean?"

"That lighter's for smoking glass."

"Meth?"

She raised an eyebrow at him.

"How do you know? You..." He left the question dangling in the space between them.

Her nose wrinkled and her face turned crusty. "Oh God no.... please! I was in high school though...like last year."

"Don't remind me," he said under his breath.

"High school's full of tweakers."

"Don't knock Gallup High, my wife went there and it served her well."

"Aimee? Oh, she's a legend, Principal Yepa still has a picture of her in his office. He says she's going to be the first Indian President. Gives the same speech about her to the Student Council every year. Talks about her more than his own kids."

The thought of Yepa with Aimee's picture in his office to look at anytime he wanted struck Jake, where these things always struck him, somewhere between his balls and his heart, although he didn't know why this time, Principal Yepa weighed over three hundred pounds and smelled like a rendering plant.

"Isn't she your ex now?" she said, and then instantly regretted it.

He looked at her, little features and hazel green eyes under those thin but stern eyebrows that spoke before her mouth did.

"Yeah," he said slowly and smiled, smiling again as her face eased. Jake held up the lighter.

"If I were in high school, where would I get one of these?"

"Conoco maybe. Heck, maybe the Walmart."

"What if I were an Indian headed up to around Shiprock?"

"Potter's Trading Post," she said without hesitation.

EIGHTEEN

Potter's Trading Post was a tan ranch style mobile home with faded white trim in a dirt lot off State Route 491 north of Window Rock, not at all like the more touristy adobe trading posts that used huge frequently spaced billboards to lure in cross-country travelers from two hundred miles away. Jake parked the truck and locked the Glock in the glove box. Outside, a stiff wind blew dirt across the parking lot. Inside the trading post it was cramped and dark, the shelves were close together, barely wide enough for a grown man to walk through. On display were fireworks, lighters, cardboard boxes full of ephedrine tablets, herbal stimulants, nitrous whipits, spice, bath salts—anything underage kids could get high on—along with energy drinks and ammunition. A pimply kid was at the counter buying a pack of Marlboro Reds with nickels and dimes. The sales clerk was a large Navajo. He made no effort to card the kid. Jake stood in line while the kid counted out loud in increments of five and ten, sliding the coins across the counter from one pile to another with his middle finger. The clerk watched impassively, his thick arms folded into two impenetrable fortresses. When it was Jake's turn he showed the clerk the lighter.

"Do you sell these?"

The clerk hefted a giant arm and pointed at a rack of the

same type of lighters with the little blow torch flame. Some had the same rainbow decal on them, along with others that had Hello Kitty and weird Japanese anime figures that Jake didn't recognize.

"Did you recently sell this lighter to a girl, about seventeen or eighteen?"

The clerk looked at him without expression.

"I sell a lot of lighters to a lot of girls," he said in a clear deep voice.

"Do you sell a lot of lighters to girls who end up dead?"

The Indian was quiet for a long time and then set his massive knuckles on the counter.

"Probably."

Jake nodded and looked the Indian in the eye.

"We all gotta die sometime."

The clerk returned the stare.

"You could say that."

"Thanks for the help," Jake said and saluted with two fingers as if he was tipping an invisible hat.

"Have a nice day, officer."

Jake let the door bang shut on his way out. He wasn't wearing a badge and never announced himself as the law but he wasn't surprised the clerk called him officer. Still, it bothered him that he was seen as just a cop. He peeled out of the parking lot leaving a billowing cloud of dust over Potter's Trading Post. Childish, but if felt good. He drove north on SR 491 to Shiprock, toward the site of the second murder, where the girl died. This time he drove slowly and paid attention to the surroundings, the trailers, the hogans, the ramshackle compounds. He tried to find any connection to the crime in these buildings, since at one point or another the girl and been here too, they were all connected to the crime to some degree, but his eyes couldn't help but be drawn to Shiprock itself, the giant monolith rising out of the desert, ominous against the darkening sky. Could the murders have been ritualistic? It didn't make sense for a Navajo—ritualizing death, celebrating it in a way, was antithetical to everything the Navajo believed in, everything they are. The Navajo were terrified of the dead. They believed the dead, without the proper cleansing rituals, followed you around in life. The Navajo did not dwell on the dead. So maybe the killer wasn't Navajo.

He turned off of SR 491 toward Shiprock—the rock, not the town. He saw Del Bradley, Navajo Tribal Police Chief, in his Ford F350 dually driving past him, going the other way on the two-lane dirt road. He waved. The Chief didn't wave back.

He retraced the path he'd taken to the crime scene a few days ago. It felt like years had passed since then. He made the turns on the dirt roads slowly. An uneasy feeling dogged him as the truck crossed under the shadow of the towering monument. He stopped the truck and got out. He had to pry his eyes away from the looming mountain of rock blocking out the sun. He was drawn to it, and he kept looking back as he walked to the spot where the murder occurred, as if the massive stone obelisk would topple over on top of him at any moment if he didn't keep it in check with his eyes.

A lot had been disturbed at the crime scene. Tire tracks criss-crossed the site and there was a new fire circle, like people could have been partying there recently, after the murder. He bent down and sifted through the ashes but didn't find anything distinguishing except blackened beer cans with the paint seared off. On closer inspection of the tire tracks he recognized the tell-tale double rear wheels of a dually pickup over much of the area and he immediately assumed that it was Bradley's—it was sloppy police work, but not unusual for Bradley. Some of the tracks even disturbed his own CSI team's markers, little red and yellow flags battered about by the wind, marking some finer point of forensic evidence. The dually tracks were easy to follow and he kept them in sight as he walked back to his truck. He looked up again at Shiprock, and felt compelled to get out from under its shadow, so he followed the dually tracks down the road and back out into the waning sunlight. He was expecting to follow the tracks back out to the highway but the dually tracks did something different, leaving the gravel access road on a barely discernible dirt trail on the other side of the road. He followed the thinly rutted trail as it wound for almost a mile to a doublewide trailer up against sandstone cliffs. The trailer was fronted by a long covered porch and a wooden fence that wrapped all the way around a backyard and abutted the red cliff face. The fence appeared to be cantilevered to the rock wall. Someone didn't want any gaps. The fence was vertical plank wood, like the kind that kept dogs in. But he didn't hear any dogs. Most folks liked an unobstructed view. Navajos in particular, would want to keep the backyard open to the desert. A barbed wire sheep fence would be expected, or a wooden sawlog corral job, but this fence was out of place. The dually had been here recently. This had to be the closest house to the crime scene, so it made sense to canvas. There were no other structures in sight, and one could almost see the killing zone from here, just around the lee side of Shiprock National Monument.

Jake got out of the truck and knocked on the front door to see if anyone saw anything the night of the murder. Bradley would have already been here for that purpose but there'd been no mention of this place in the Navajo Tribal Police report, and he had suspicions that Bradley was mailing it in these days.

There was no answer at the door, so he walked down the porch yelling hello. The windows were blacked out, probably covered up by sheets or tin foil to keep light out. He walked along the fence. No spaces between the slats. Tall, at least eight foot. He found a knot in one of the wooden boards and looked through. The large enclosed backyard was just bare dirt with a huge fire pit. There were fire marks on the cliffs, stretching up quite a ways. Jake was about to turn away when he heard a screen door bang open. He trained his eye on the back of the house and caught a glimpse of a skinny guy with a shaved head and long goatee, tattered jeans with a silver fob and chain link belt in a dingy white ribbed wife beater. The man spun around at noises echoing off the cliff walls, imagined or real, jumping at shadows. Jake pegged him for a weirdo methhead and suddenly everything about the house made perfect sense.

"You okay?" Jake shouted.

The man practically jumped out his skin, did a three-sixty in mid-air and landed in a crouched defensive position with his fists out, scanning the fire marks on the cliff.

"Hey man, want to talk to you about the girl that was killed the other night," Jake yelled with his hands cupped as he stepped back from the fence.

Jake heard the screen door slam shut again. The weirdo must have gone back inside the house. Jake put his eye back up to the knot in the wood to check. The backyard was empty. Suddenly, the screen door flew open and the man lunged outside with a shotgun and pointed it directly at Jake and pulled the trigger.

Jake saw the muzzle flash and a three foot section of fence disintegrated just above his head, splinters of wood lodging in his scalp and neck.

"Jesus fucking christ!"

Jake rose up and fired three warning shots that sailed over the man's head and spun around in one motion and began sprinting to his truck. He heard the shotgun eject its spent shell and cock to fire again. Jake waved the Glock over his head and fired shots into the air indiscriminately as he ran. He heard the shotgun blast as he flung himself into the truck and hammered the gas and tore down the dirt track back to the gravel road and then the highway. His heart rate didn't return to baseline until he was back at his trailer with three Busch Lights in his belly.

NINETEEN

Anybody can kill anybody. The sun came up the next day and Jake felt lucky to be alive. He opened the sliding plexiglass door to the hundred mile view, and lit a cigarette and watched the blood red clouds turn to pink as the sun rose.

He skipped the office and drove straight to the Navajo Tribal Police in Window Rock. Before he left Gallup, he stopped at the Dunkin Donuts and picked up two dozen assorted donuts and a cardboard box of coffee. He was well received at Tribal Police Headquarters. Yazzie loaded up a napkin with three jelly donuts and they went back to his tiny office.

"You finish the paperwork from that splatter job on the highway the other night?"

"Mmmm...some was done. Some was not done. We do not have the same love of forms that your people do."

Jake told him about going out to the scene of the girl's murder and following the dually tracks to the doublewide, and then nearly getting his head blown off and his tailgate peppered with buckshot. Yazzie told him that Bradley had nothing to do with the investigation. There was no record of the house or anyone being questioned there, but it wasn't unusual to get fired upon.

"Stupid to go poking around like that, putting people's lives in danger starting a gunfight," Yazzie said, taking a large bite of jelly donut.

"People's lives?"

"That guy could have been the next Trayvon Martin."

"But I'm not the neighborhood watch."

"If you were, you would have known better than to snoop around people's fences."

"He shot at me first."

"You started it."

"How did I start it?"

"You went snooping around his fence."

"He was methed out and armed."

"You just described half the reservation. You going to shoot us all?"

Yazzie took an oversized bite of jelly donut and leaned back in his chair. He could have actually been angry. It was hard to tell. They compared notes half-heartedly for a while longer and Jake left wondering for perhaps the first time if he really had no idea what he was doing out here on the reservation.

TWENTY

"Am I a racist?"

"Oh lord, what did you do now?"

Jake and Cally were sitting at the elbow of the long laminated oak bar in the Copper Street Pub at what was becoming their usual spot. He sipped a beer even though it was before noon and he thought he had a rule about that. It was only a Bud Light, not a real beer, he told himself. He told her about his shootout, leaving out that he had followed Bradley's tire tracks and that there was no record of Bradley on the case.

"If you came around my back fence like that I'd shoot at you."

"Keep your backside defense up, do you?"

"Around you, I do."

Jake let that one pass. They both looked away and smiled.

"Yazzie says I'm a racist."

"You're just not from around here."

"Said that guy could have been the next Trayvon Martin, like I was hunting him or something."

"Trayvon was unarmed, if I remember correctly. That guy fired first, and apparently messed up your precious hair, if you're to be believed."

"You don't believe me?" Jake bent his head down to show her the dried blood from little cuts on his scalp and the back of his neck from when the pine wood fence had exploded just above his head.

"Poor baby." She brushed his hair out of the way with her fingertips to examine the wounds. It gave him goosebumps. "He really did mess up your hair."

"Yazzie didn't really call me a racist."

"Just called you stupid."

"Smart girl."

"We are all Trayvon!" she said in a deep voice and pumped her fist. He punched her in the arm, liking the feel of his knuckles on her bare skin.

TWENTY-ONE

The Shaman rubs his bald head. It's sweaty. He feels the scars. He is surrounded by a haze of crystal meth smoke. A half dozen kids are sprawled out on the floor of the doublewide. He rubs his head again. The smooth parts this time. He feels like Colonel Kurtz from that American movie he saw long ago. Perhaps that is who he is now. Some of us have many lives. Kurtz. Going up the river to kill Kurtz. The kids are strewn about the floor even though there are two perfectly good couches. Much abused, but still serviceable. The couches, that is, not the kids.

The Shaman speaks.

"We were...met today...no...visited..."

He speaks slowly, his tongue languid, not like the jittering blather-mouthed teenagers he's holding court over. Kurtz with his audience. That's why they revere me, he muses. They want calm. They want wisdom. They want clarity.

"...by the Shadow People..."

He lets this wash over them. If they're listening. If they care. They like to feel like they care. About something, anything.

"...they were here...today...because we vanquished their brethren...we are in a war now...it is an old war...you are soldiers... all of us...we are soldiers."

He speaks louder and his flock stirs, a few pick up their

heads, and then he lowers his voice and he feels their audible slide back into ecstasy.

"I have traveled far to be with you. Across many deserts. I came here today, to this house, to see the black marks myself... see the burnt shadow stains left behind on the rocks... left behind on the mother cliffs...the remnants of the ones we defeated."

He sees a few of them smile. When they have sufficiently settled in, practically melting into the filthy remnants of carpet, he begins today's lesson. The kids don't mind, he knows, because they are high. He starts as he always does, with Conquest, but breezes over the wars with the Blue Coats, the internment camps, the famines, the bounties and the scalpings, the Sand Creek Massacre, Little Big Horn, Chief Red Cloud and Geronimo, for these are topics he has covered many times before. The children have an endless capacity to hear about war. Instead he goes quickly to the 1887 Dawes Act that created the checkerboard reservation, that took the communal land that tribes owned and allotted it to individuals in order to destroy the tribes and turn the Indians into farmers. To turn the Indians into white people. Kill the Indian, save the man. His voice is silky and deep now, like a river running over time worn stones. Rich, like the color of warm brandy. Never mind that one cannot farm without water and land owned by one will divide and divide and divide with each generation until there are so many owners that no one owns anything at all. Never mind that it was easier to steal land from a person than a tribe. And steal they did. Some kids rouse, suddenly angry. Some are too far gone to care, to notice. He jumps to 1934 and the Indian Reorganization Act. If the Dawes Act was meant to turn Indians into white people then the Indian Reorganization Act was meant to turn Indian tribes into white governments. Constitutions, elections, laws, corruption. No more chiefs, no more elders, just politicians. He sees blank faces. He knows they do not understand, are no longer capable of understanding, but he does not care. He does not do this so they will understand. He switches to Pancho Villa and Emiliano Zapata and their struggle against tyranny—something for his Mexican children—and blends their battle with the oppression of all indigenous people around the world. Dictators and Comandantes, puppets and Shadow People. He always ends with the Shadow People, the ones that live out of the corner of your eye. That live in the walls. That can appear anywhere at anytime. The gray shades that haunt your sleepless daydreams. That can only be vanquished by fire. But this time he ends with a warning about one in particular. His voice gains an edge.

"You are soldiers...the one that came here...to this house... defiled our home. Watch for that one...it will return...and you must be ready. We will be ready..."

TWENTY-TWO

Jake spent the afternoon at the office diligently avoiding his secretary. His fantasy baseball team had fallen back to third place—Tulo was out with some phantom rib injury sustained on a hunting trip, disappointing both his fantasy team and the many Rockies fans in Gallup, New Mexico.

At night he drank three beers and when that couldn't help him sleep he moved on to the whiskey and when that didn't put him down he drove to the office. The forensic reports had come in from the Gallup PD and the FBI crime lab in Albuquerque. Record time, at least for the FBI, which had a long backlog from the ceaseless violence along the southwest border.

Jake kicked his boots up onto his desk and leaned back in his chair and studied the reports until dawn. He couldn't get over the differences in the murders. Two bound and lit on fire on the rez. Those were practically executions. And then Joseph, clumsily lit on fire in his truck. That seemed random, but so close to his own trailer, was it a coincidence? Was he in danger? And now the out-of-towner, it turned out from the forensic reports, was beaten to death when the fire didn't immediately kill him, or at least when he took too long to die. The back half of his head was caved in, his brains cooked outside of his skull, charred rather than boiled. And yet, despite the differences, the crimes had one huge similarity. Fire. If the four murders were not done by the same person, Jake knew they were in trouble, the town, the rez, all of them. He had no idea what he was dealing with.

Mary opened the door to the office at nine a.m. sharp, and shook her head. "What are you doing here before lunch," she squinted at him accusingly.

He looked up from the reports, surprised to see her, his eyes bloodshot and bleary. "Let's grab a bite later, you and me, what do you say?"

"Must be the end times."

"No seriously, I'm taking you to lunch. I'm buying."

"I thought you'd never ask."

Jake struggled to stay awake until lunch time, eventually dozing in his chair, until Mary woke him by lifting his boots off his desk and dropping them on the floor.

"I'm sorry," he muttered.

"Yes, you are."

They walked down to the Copper Street Pub for lunch. They sat at a table close to the window. Jake had never sat in the dining area before, only at the bar. Cally came over to take their order. She made eye contact with Jake, but he didn't say anything. They both ordered the special, which was a smothered green chile burrito. When they were alone, Jake asked Mary what she knew about the old man who'd been murdered.

Mary folded her arms and rested them in her lap. It was a long time before she spoke and they sat in silence for a while.

"He was a good guy. He knew the old ways. He tried to walk in beauty. But he had his problems like everyone else. He had four sons who were hellraisers. One died in a horse accident, one is in jail for a DUI, one disappeared from the rez and we never heard from him again, and one was shot to death last year."

"Why was he shot?"

"I don't know. Something to do with drugs, probably."

"What about the girl who was murdered just after the old man?"

"She was a good girl, I never heard anything bad about her, but she was adopted by her uncle after her parents were both sent to the penitentiary. I don't like the uncle, he was involved with bad people, I hear."

"What kind of bad people?"

"Witches."

"Of course, skinwalkers."

"Of a type. These people are not shapeshifters. They cannot change what they are. That is the problem."

"Do you really believe in shapeshifters?"

"All Navajo believe in shapeshifters."

"Even Aimee?"

"You were married to her. You know she did."

"She said she did. But I was never sure. You know, the way people say they believe in Jesus. Maybe they believe in what Jesus taught, or maybe they believe in Jesus, like that he helps them score touchdowns."

Mary took a sip of water, carefully straining the ice with her teeth before she spoke next.

"When I was a little girl, I saw an owl for four nights in a row outside of my bedroom window. Owls, you know, are messengers, bad ones. Owls mean death. And four is always important, the most important number. The four seasons, the four directions, the four sacred mountains. You know. So when I saw the owl on the forth night I called to my grandfather, Aimee's great, great uncle. He was blind but he was a medicine man. He took his rifle out to the front porch. My grandfather made his own bullets. We were poor then, the People were poor, and it was back when people made their own bullets because it was cheaper. They pressed the lead together into the right shape. The owl was sitting high in a tree. He loaded one of his bullets into the rifle and pointed it at the owl and fired and shot the owl."

"He was blind?"

"Yes, but he was a medicine man. The owl fell from the tree, but we never saw it hit the ground. We went and looked and looked all around the base of the tree and up in the branches. But as it fell it disappeared. Vanished. Two days later they found a woman dead in her house, lying in her bed, two miles from our house. She had been shot with one of my grandfather's bullets. This woman was a witch. Everyone knew she was a witch. And she had been messing with our family for a long time."

Cally came back to the table with two giant plates balanced on a tray in one arm and holding a pot of coffee with the other.

"How's your mother, Cally?" Mary asked.

"Good, she had a big buyer, could use another rug."

"Okay, tell her to call me."

"Will do. How's Jess liking ASU?"

"Oh jeez, partying too much I bet." Mary said, flushing slightly from hearing the sound of her daughter's name.

"Yeah, right."

"She tells me she's studying hard. That's why I don't believe her."

"She kicked our butts in high school, don't know why it would be any different in college."

"When are you getting out of here, Cally?"

"I'm working on it." She tucked a blonde strand of hair behind her ear and inadvertently glanced at Jake.

"Don't look at him. He thinks you should go to college too."

"Oh, you do?" She turned to Jake, crossing her arms and sticking out a bony hip.

Jake cleared his throat. "Well, there's nothing wrong with community college."

Cally turned back to Mary. "See?"

Mary shook her head and glared at Jake. "You're the devil."

Cally nodded and carried her tray back to the kitchen.

Mary smacked Jake in the arm. "What's wrong with you?"

Jake shrugged his shoulders apologetically. Just then his phone started vibrating violently.

"Speak of the devil."

"What is it?" Mary asked.

"Three bodies found on the rez," Jake read aloud from the tiny screen.

"How'd they die?"

"Burned alive."

TWENTY-THREE

Cally shoveled Jake's smothered green chile burrito into a styrofoam to-go box and he stood up to leave when he noticed a strange looking man with a mohawk across the street. The man was standing still and seemed to be looking into the window of the Copper Street Pub. The window was tinted against the strong desert sun but Jake could swear the man was looking right at him. It gave him chills.

"Are you coming?" He said to Mary.

She looked up at him while she shook the Cholula hot sauce bottle over her refried beans, obviously quite content to eat by herself.

"Food will get cold."

Jake left two twenties on the table to cover lunch.

"No worries, see you back at the office."

He looked back out the window but the man was gone. He went out into the blazing sun. The street was quiet. He walked to his office looking over his shoulder. He felt like he was walking stiffly, like he'd just dismounted from horseback after a three day ride. The sky was a clear New Mexico blue, but the day's heat didn't seem to reach him. He thought if someone studied him he might look pale or sickly, disturbed. But no one would study him. He was thirty-one and had been in law enforcement for less than five years, but it was long enough to know that people were far too self-involved to pay much attention to people they didn't know, and when they did, it was through the filter of their own self-absorption. People rarely remembered details unless it was something that directed attention back on themselves, a hair style that reminded them of someone they knew, a car or a shirt that they used to have. Details seen through a prism of ego were unreliable, susceptible to change over time. Susceptible to influence. That was how good prosecutors made the facts fit, made the witnesses make the facts fit. Influence. Suggestion. He learned that at Quantico. The trick was to only do it when you really knew the guy was guilty. Of course, he'd sworn then that he wouldn't be that kind of cop, back when it was easy to be an idealist. Now he wasn't so sure. He felt like talking to Aimee. They'd been idealistic together once. Or at least she'd found his idealism endearing. Until it wasn't anymore. He knew what she'd think of the mohawk man. This was no civilian. This was a man who paid attention to details. This was a hunter.

Back at the office he made a few calls and learned that the new crime scene was not on the Big Reservation but was far to the south, south even of Zuni on what was known as the Little Reservation. The Navajo Nation was made up of two distinct lands. The Big Reservation was an area larger than New England covering parts of New Mexico, Utah, and almost half of Arizona. The Little Reservation was a separate piece of land in Arizona and New Mexico, larger still than any one county in the United States, but separated by a hundred miles from the Big Reservation, its people governed by a separate chapter house and family clans with little love lost for the tribal government in Window Rock.

Because of its proximity to the Mexican border, the crime scene was secured by Homeland Security U.S. Customs and Border Patrol agents along with the Navajo Tribal Police working under a cross-deputization agreement, and Jake couldn't see the point in driving two hundred miles on crappy roads to see first hand what could be beamed to his computer in pictures in real time by satellite technology. Or maybe he was rattled. Maybe he didn't want to see charred bodies with his own eyes anymore, or to smell them. He wanted to talk to Aimee. He wanted a drink.

Of all the calls he made, he didn't call Yazzie, who would have the intel the Navajo Police were gathering. He didn't want to know if Yazzie could hear anything in his voice. Hear any weakness, any doubt. Hear if he was rattled. He couldn't seem to get the acrid smell of burnt hair and rendered fat out of his nostrils these days. Death was all around him, somehow connected to him. A shadow on the wall in the corner of his eye. At five he strapped on his shoulder holster and went home. He felt more unsettled and alone than ever.

TWENTY-FOUR

Jake opened his eyes to a strange glow. It was quiet. He registered that he was in his bed. The fitted under sheet had come off and he felt the diamond shaped seams in the mattress on his bare buttocks. It had taken a lot of whiskey to put him down. Whiskey was the only sleep aid the FBI allowed. After the D-Backs closer had blown another save he'd shut off the radio and gone right to sleep but only for a short time, and then his level of consciousness had vacillated in an unsatisfying booze induced stupor, where he didn't feel rested because it didn't feel like sleep. It just felt like lying down in the dark. But he was used to it. When he dreamt, it didn't feel like dreaming because he could swear his eyes were open. When he didn't dream, there was no way to know if he slept.

He blinked his eyes and looked outside the sliding glass door where flames seemed to be dancing, suspended in air somewhere out over the hundred mile view. The physical sensation of the scratchy mattress on his bare skin and the twisted bed sheet intwined in his legs, together with the certainty that his eyes were, in fact, open, gave him the strong impression that he was indeed awake. Still, he lay there for some time until he actually could swear he felt heat and smelled smoke.

He heard something land on the roof with a thud and leapt

out of bed, scooping up his shoulder holster with the Glock in it that had been buried under his discarded clothes. He faced the sliding glass door and could see that the glow was the reflection of flames in his kitchen. There was no fire floating in space over the valley. It was in his home. The trailer was on fire.

Smoke rippled under the ceiling. He was fully awake now. He spun to the kitchen with his gun outstretched before him in both hands. He saw broken glass where something had been thrown through a window, a molotov cocktail he guessed. He heard another thud on the roof and looked up. The ceiling was sweating, melting before his eyes. The smell of burning asbestos stung his nostrils. He heard a hissing sound and leveled the gun back toward the kitchen. And then he remembered the propane tank that fed the water heater.

He holstered the Glock and dove on top of his mattress, grabbing onto the corners with both hands, and pulling it on top of himself, as the propane tank exploded and blew him through the aluminum wall of the trailer. He landed in dirt, cholla, and thistles, bleeding and naked except for the shoulder holster. The mattress that saved his life was lodged in the trailer wall. He sprang to his feet and sprinted around the side of the house. He saw a figure dash in front of headlights. A truck was parked with its high beams on, halfway up the jeep trail to the main road. Jake ran straight ahead, the Glock flopping on his chest in the shoulder holster and his junk flopping everywhere else, not noticing his bare feet kicking over a prickly pear, or the blood running down his back from where the shredded aluminum trailer walls had sliced him open. A shadow ran to the driver's side door and pulled hard as if it were jammed. Jake was close enough to see that the truck was a Chevy Silverado and that the shadow had a mohawk. The truck's door suddenly flung open. Jake crouched to a knee, drew the Glock, and fired a half dozen times toward the Chevy's undercarriage. The truck's tires exploded and deflated so fast that it sat on the ground like a dog done circling. A moment passed and then the driver's side door opened to ninety degrees and from the window Jake saw muzzle flashes and a split second later heard the gunshots.

"Shit."

Jake rolled to his left, diving off the road into a gully and landing on his back, gravel lodging in his open wounds. Poofs of dust erupted on the road next to him where bullets landed, some skipping off rocks and taking flight again. He rose to his knees with the Glock outstretched in front of him. The outline of a man raced into the woods. Jake holstered his gun and gave chase. The man headed downslope off the ridgeline, weaving in between skinny white pines, his descent taking him back toward the flames. Jake plowed ahead in the darkness, smacking the tree branches out of his way when he could, absorbing the needled blows when unseen tree limbs tore at his skin. Jake's jaw was ground shut. He breathed through his nose like a sprinter. Only one thought replayed over and over again in his mind—you are fucking dead.

Jake ducked under some broad sweeping branches by instinct, hearing them before he saw them, and entered the clearing he used for target practice, where he and Yazzie had tried out the Mossberg, just a couple of days before. The shadow was nowhere to be seen. Jake stopped, his chest heaving. He didn't even feel vulnerable out in the open, and naked to boot. Too much had happened. He just wanted it over. He frantically scanned the tree line, ready to see muzzle flashes, prepared for it. And then something in the trailer exploded and he saw movement toward the edge of the clearing. He gave chase again, straight through the heart of the clearing, sensing the drop off to the valley below, that must loom somewhere in the darkness. He caught sight of the mohawk as it disappeared into the trees. He reached the edge of the clearing and plunged into the foliage after it. He skirted a pile of rocks and danced along a cliff face that came out of nowhere, part of the two thousand foot descent that created the hundred mile view. He knew the man must be close, if he hadn't gone over the edge. He skipped along the cliff's edge and swung the Glock around just as the man came out of the trees, his mohawk was illuminated by the burning trailer. By the light of the flames Jake saw the mohawk turn perpendicular, half toward him, rotating back to face him. Jake leveled the Glock and fired three times.

TWENTY-FIVE

His fellow FBI agents, the Navajo Tribal Police, including Yazzie, the local cops, the newspapers, the State Police, Border Patrol, and the Joint Drug Enforcement Task Force, would all say it was a clean shoot. Clean both in that it had been in self-defense and clean because one shot went clean through the suspect's head and two went into, and out of, his heart. But none of that meant shit. The opinion of the FBI's Office of Professional Responsibility, what used to be known as Internal Affairs, was all that mattered.

Jake didn't emerge from the FBI State Office in Albuquerque until evening the next day. He had been questioned by three different sets of agents and taken a lie detector test. He told them everything. He told them about the shooting at the doublewide near Shiprock; about seeing a man with a mohawk earlier in the day; about receiving divorce papers; about asking for and receiving the transfer to the reservation, his ex's reservation; by the end he even told them about the time he smoked pot in college.

He drove back to Gallup with the windows rolled down, happy to feel the fresh desert air on his face. He ran his hands through his hair and scratched his greasy scalp, imagining what prolonged incarceration would be like, if he was this relieved to be outside after only one day of interrogation. But he knew there was virtually no chance the shoot could be a crime. New Mexico had a stand your ground law, and the man had firebombed his house with him in it. No jury would convict him, so no prosecutor would bring the case. Still, he had underestimated the Bureau's thoroughness. He didn't know why. He should have figured all that bullshit about cops having each other's backs was just that, bullshit. Or maybe it was just the Feds that didn't have each other's backs. Either way he drove home west on I-40 to Gallup with the distinct feeling that he'd just been assfucked.

A hundred miles later he saw the lights of Gallup. It was dark and moving on toward ten o'clock. He drove slowly through Gallup and even slower up the ridgeline to his house. He eased the pickup down the jeep trail. The headlights showed what he feared, a burnt out hull of a trailer, not unlike many he'd seen on the rez and assumed were abandoned meth labs. He left the headlights on and took his heavy police issue flashlight out of the glove box and approached the trailer more than a little spooked. This was a place Yazzie wouldn't have gone near. A place haunted by the dead.

The door had been kicked off its hinges. Inside the carpet and linoleum were still wet from the Gallup Fire Department's efforts. The walls of the trailer stood alone with jagged black silhouette edges against the starry sky. The ceiling over the kitchen and the bedroom was gone. Amazingly, a bottle of Jim Beam he kept under the kitchen sink was still intact. He salvaged some clothes, which smelled awful, and tossed them into the bed of the truck. He turned the ignition to auxiliary and drained the battery listening to the country radio station and drinking Beam out of the bottle while staring at the husk of his home in the headlights until he keeled over and passed out with his head on the steering wheel.

In the morning the engine wouldn't turn over. The battery was dead. He checked his phone. There was an email from Division. He was being placed on administrative leave. He tried to call Yazzie to come jump the battery but he couldn't get a signal. He didn't know how he could receive email without cell service, but in the scheme of things this was a small mystery, one that he accepted would never be answered. He fished through the well plundered ashtray for a cigarette butt and started walking.

The morning sun was bright, and the shafts of light cutting through the treetops stung like jabs to the face. The sky was an unbroken blue. He wore jeans, boots and a T-shirt salvaged from the trailer. The dresser hadn't burned but its contents had done their best to vacuum up the smoke and hold onto it like a sponge would water. He reached the main road and stopped, looking both ways. A car headed to town blew by at sixty miles an hour without slowing. He sighed and started walking again. There was no shoulder so he walked next to the road on dirt and weeds. His head didn't hurt like it should because he was still drunk, but his mouth was dry and he yearned for water. He walked on the heels of his boots.

A pickup truck slowed and stopped, half on the road and half sloping into a drainage ditch. Jake trotted toward the truck. An old Navajo man waved at him. He wore jeans, a plaid shirt, and a cowboy hat, and had the seat slid up so close to the steering wheel that it pushed against his belly and he had to drive with his elbows out from his sides. There was an old woman in the passenger seat, so Jake hopped in the bed of the pickup. This seemed to confuse the old man, it was common for three or even four people to squeeze onto the bench seat of a pickup on the reservation, but after a minute he put it in gear, and the truck eased back onto the road and continued toward town, never topping thirty miles an hour.

When they reached Gallup, Jake slapped his hand on the top of the cab, and the old man pulled over to the sidewalk. Jake hopped out, poked his head in the window, and said his thanks. The man said something back in Navajo, and the woman made a kind gesture with her hand. Jake nodded, and then walked to the Copper Street Pub. He ordered steak and eggs and a red beer, which was just a Bud Light draw topped off with tomato juice. Cally wasn't working. He ate, had another red beer, and left.

Outside, he looked up and down the street but nothing much registered. He checked his phone and it had a strong signal, but he found himself reluctant to call Yazzie. He was too drained to explain everything. Explain himself. He figured there was some rule against going to the office while on administrative leave, but he went anyway. He was surprised that the door was unlocked and Mary was at her desk.

"You're not supposed to be here."

"Is there some rule?"

"It's in the Bureau's regulations."

"Can I just go upstairs and check my fantasy team?"

She stared at him for a long time without saying anything and he figured this was her way of letting him into his office without any proof that she had. He took the stairs gingerly and slipped into his office. His team had somehow fallen to fifth place in just two days. He shut down the computer and looked around his office. He tore down his map of Indian Country with the crime scenes marked with thumbtacks, and folded it up, and stuck it in a binder holding the forensic files and coroner reports. He started toward the door and then stopped. He riffled through his desk drawer until he found the lighter with the rainbow decal, that he'd found under the shadow of Shiprock, at the scene of the second murder. The murder of the girl. He put the lighter in his pocket and locked the office door behind him.

At the bottom of the stairs he had to stand directly in front of Mary before she would look him in the eye.

"Hey, can you give me a jump?"

"I bet you say that to all the girls."

TWENTY-SIX

Mary drove Jake in her late nineties Chevy Malibu up the mountain to Jake's burnt out trailer. He used her jumper cables to start his truck, feeling tremendous relief when the big V8 roared to life. He revved the engine to make sure it was charged enough not to crap out on him, and then pulled a wide arc through the little field in front of what had been his house, and back out to the road to town. He drove to the Walmart on the outskirts of Gallup and bought a four man car camping tent, foam sleeping pad, thick flannel lined army green sleeping bag, a bag of Kingston charcoal, lighter fluid, Johnsonville bratwurst, a case of Busch Light, a cylinder of beef jerky, and two cartons of 9mm ammo. He bought a pack of Winston Lights at the register.

He wheeled his shopping cart to his truck and loaded the supplies in the bed. He turned the ignition and cracked a Busch Light. He fiddled with the radio until a Kenny Chesney song came on he could tolerate. He lit a cigarette and finished his beer watching the Walmart parking lot. It was full of Indians from the reservation. They shuffled across the asphalt in no hurry, some taking the time to gather in their surroundings, locate the mountains and orient themselves with the four directions, taking in the size of the parking lot and the big box store beyond, couples holding hands and families in town for a day of entertainment at the air conditioned superstore. Jake crushed the empty beer can on the dashboard and tossed it into the bed of the pickup. He belched and threw the truck into gear.

It was early evening by the time he made it back to his trailer, and the mosquitos were out. He set up the tent inside of the trailer where his old bedroom had been. Two full days of unobstructed New Mexico sun had dried out the water and fire retardant the volunteer firefighters had used to put out the fire, and the winds had carried away much of the smell of burnt industrial building materials. The roof was gone and the sliding plexiglass door was no more, but the hundred mile view was still there.

He kicked away some yellowed buffalo grass and range cactus behind his house and poured out a small pile of charcoal into the small hole he'd dug, and doused it with lighter fluid. He used the murdered girl's lighter to set it ablaze. He dragged a lawn chair to the fire and drank beers while the briquettes burnt off their chemical skin and rendered coals suitable for cooking food. He snapped off a pine bough from the nearest tree and shaved it down to a barkless skewer with his pocket knife. He stuck three brats onto the skewer and dangled them over the fire for a good fifteen minutes until the casings split and the juicy innards bubbled greasy liquid into the fire, kicking up the flames. When the sausage had blackened on the outside, he flicked them onto a newspaper, trying not to burn his fingers. He pounded a beer and watched the stars. The wind kicked up and howled through the pines. He listened to the sound of the wind coming off the mountains, but it told him nothing. The stars became fuzzy and then seemed to duck, blink, and weave over the valley below. When the brats cooled some he wrapped the newspaper around them to dry away as much grease as possible. He ate them with his fingers in between swigs of beer and then tossed the grease soaked newspaper onto the coals. The newspaper simmered and then burst into flames and sent embers up in a spiral into the sky that fanned out over the trees and into the valley below. Jake watched the embers flutter and fade away.

TWENTY-SEVEN

He woke up drenched in sweat. The tent was hot and stuffy. It was late enough in the morning that the sun was overhead and sunlight shown directly onto the tent. He unzipped all the flaps to let in some air but the walls of the trailer blocked any breeze. He threw on his jeans and went outside. There was an old hand pump spigot that drew up well water that had been on the property long before the trailer had been dragged there. He ducked his head under the spigot. The water was cold. It stung and took his breath away but he held his head under for a long time anyway.

He cupped his hands and drank as much water as he could, and then he walked back behind the house and blew on the coals from last night's fire until they smoldered awake, and he placed some dried grass and sticks on top and eventually snapped off branches from a nearby downed pinion, until he had a good sized camp fire. He took the two remaining brats out of the fridge. There was no power but the fridge still worked as a cooler. He cooked the two brats over the fire and ate them sitting in the lawn chair with a beer. He'd been problem solving in his subconscious, something he did better than with his conscious mind, because since he had woken up he realized what should have been obvious before but wasn't—he was targeted. Of course he was targeted. It couldn't have been coincidence. Five arsons was a lot, but there were three hundred thousand people on the Navajo Nation. Old Joe was probably not a coincidence either, that had been a message to him. For the first time he was truly happy he'd killed the mohawk man. Before he'd been conflicted and in shock. But who even knew he was on the case? He kept a low profile. Yazzie knew, so did Bradley and Yance, the Gallup detective. There was Mitch, his douchey ASAC. Mary of course knew everything and everyone. The more he thought about it, everybody seemed to know everything on the rez. Still, he felt he must have stirred something up with the shooting at Shiprock. But how would methheads find out where he lived so fast? Could they identify him, track him down and retaliate in less than 24 hours without help? Which brought him back to Bradley. Why was Bradley at that doublewide trailer if he wasn't working the case?

He heard gravel crunching under tires. He sprung out of the lawn chair and raced to his bedroom, and careful hopped through the shattered plexiglass door, avoiding the sharp broken edges still wedged in the frame, and grabbed the Glock out of the tent. He checked that it was loaded and went to the front window as he heard a car door slam. He saw a blond ponytail on a wispy girl digging in the back seat of an old Nissan Sentra. Cally. He ran back to the tent and hid the gun under his pillow but he didn't have time to throw on a shirt before she was standing in his living room.

"Wow, I like what you've done with this place."

Jake dug his hands in his pockets and rocked back on his heels. Cally looked him up and down and then looked away self-consciously. She held out a tin foil covered tray. He approached cautiously, bare feet on the debris covered floor, and took the tray.

"Chicken enchiladas."

"Thanks."

He looked around for a place to set it down but all his furniture was burnt up or had been trampled to splinters by the firefighters.

"I feel like taking my enchiladas back. This is clearly no place for them."

"Don't, I will provide a good home for your babies."

Jake put the tray in the fridge. Cally wrinkled her nose. The refrigerator was already beginning to smell funky without electricity.

"Wow, you've really gone caveman." She reached out and touched his seven day beard. He felt his head tingle.

"How...don't take this the wrong way...but how did you know where I live?"

"Mary thought you might need some looking after."

"Huh...man, I can't figure Mary."

"You overthink things."

"Yeah, you're probably right...you want a beer?"

"No thanks. Listen, you can't stay here. You can't live like this."

"I've lived in worse."

Cally gave him a look, sharp eyebrows and a smirk.

"Okay, maybe not this bad, but I did live in a basement walkout in a row house in Georgetown. Do you know what happens to those things when it rains?"

"I can ask my mom if you can stay with us?"

Now it was his turn to give her a look.

"Okay, that sounded bad...lemme take you out for dinner then."

"Alright."

TWENTY-EIGHT

Two days later Jake was summoned to Albuquerque for another meeting with the Office of Professional Responsibility. Cally had snuck him into her mother's house so he could shower, and he had on jeans and a flannel shirt, freshly washed from the laundromat. The investigators had taken great interest in the affairs earlier in the day in question, and his state of mind at the time of the shooting. Rather than one of the interrogation rooms, this time he sat in a regular office, calendar from the annual fall hot air balloon festival on the wall, pictures of the kids on the desk, coffee cup full of pens, any one of which he could have buried straight into the investigator's jugular. He felt this was a good sign.

"Agent Keller, you told us that you saw a man with a mohawk looking at you the day of the shooting."

"Yes."

"And this was the same man you killed?"

"Yes."

"And you knew this at the time that you killed him?"

"Yes."

"But by your own account of the events of that night you were never closer than fifty feet from the man, and it was pitch black outside."

"Yes...well my house was on fire and that provided some light."

"But you were over a hundred yards away from your house when you killed the man."

"If you say so."

"It's your say so, Jake, that we're interested in."

"Yeah, I get that."

"So you told us when we interviewed you before that you saw the mohawk, in profile, turning toward you, when you discharged your weapon."

"Yeah."

"So did you see the man's face, see that it was the same man you saw earlier in the day, or did you only fire when you saw his mohawk?"

"I fired because he had just shot at me, and burnt my house down, and was turning to shoot at me again, I don't think it matters that he had a mohawk."

"That's what we're trying to figure out, Jake, that's what we're trying to understand..."

Driving back to Gallup Jake's phone vibrated fiercely in his jeans pocket. He dug deeply into his pocket to get his phone out, which required him to put his foot on the gas and gun it up to ninety.

"Yeah."

"Agent Keller."

"Yeah?"

"This is your ASAC."

Silence while the seams in the highway asphalt made rhythmic noises.

"Hey, Mitch."

Silence while the voice on the other end of the line gathered and regathered itself.

"I have good news and bad news."

"I'm not in the mood for games, Mitch."

"Okay, Agent. The Office of Professional Responsibility is concerned that you killed that man for personal reasons, prejudice against Indians or whatever. Personally, I don't pry too much into a man's personal politics. OPR is also concerned about your drinking the night of the incident. But you were off duty and in your home at the time of the incident. OPR is clearing you."

"Thanks, Mitch. Saying I'm prejudiced against Indians is the stupidest thing I've ever heard, since I'm married to an Indian, but whatever."

"Didn't know you were still married, Agent. It was the mohawk."

"But Navajos don't have mohawks."

"I don't split hairs, Agent Keller."

"So what's the bad news?"

"I have your application to the Bureau sitting here in front of me."

"So."

"You checked a box on this application, under penalty of perjury, that you had never taken any illegal substances."

"So."

"During your interrogation you admitted to marijuana use in college. It was verified during your lie detector test."

"So?"

"Agent Keller, you're fired."

BOOK II

TWENTY-NINE

Iraq — June 23, 2003

It was a Monday, not that anyone knew or cared except for Hargrove who was counting Mondays, and only Mondays, because he had exactly four more before he would rotate home, to Delta, Colorado, a little town on the Animas River. The other five members of the squad would probably re-up, but not Hargrove. He'd had enough.

Alpha squad was set up on a sandy berm, triangulated from Bravo squad and Charlie squad, covering Highway 1 for a caravan of semi-trucks headed to Baghdad that was already three hours late. Hargrove was on his belly in the sand, his sight trained on some unfixed point in the desert. Miller and Zapata were sitting on their helmets smoking cigarettes and bitching about the caravan and how the semi drivers made ten thousand dollars a month driving for KBR while they made barely two grand a month covering their asses. Hernandez, the squad leader, lay on his back next to Hargrove with his eyes closed. He wasn't asleep, but he knew Hargrove wasn't taking any chances so the safest place to relax was next to him. Denton was taking a shit behind a sand dune, the fourth one of the day. Hernandez kept count of Denton's shits because a command memo required reporting of any precursors to heat stroke or dehydration and so far Hernandez was crushing his evals and he meant to keep it that way. His dailies were spectacular and if his ratings kept up he was in for a mandatory grade-up promotion. An extra five grand a year automatic. It wasn't that Hernandez didn't care if Denton had heat stroke or dehydration or diarrhea or whatever, he just knew that whether he did or didn't was out of his control and the important thing was that he not get blamed for not detecting it and reporting it up the chain. The only member of his squad that he couldn't account for his precise location was PFC Bradley, a skinny Indian who joined up after 911 and was already on his second tour, the first being in Afghanistan. Bradley liked to keep on the fringe of the unit, which Hernandez didn't mind, it meant early warning, someone was keeping a look out.

"What the fuck is that?" Hargrove spoke to himself, barely a whisper but Hernandez heard it.

"What?"

Hargrove was silent for a few too many seconds.

"I don't know."

Hernandez opened his eyes.

"What do you mean, you don't know. Is it the convoy?"

"No, I don't think so." Hargrove said slowly, thoughtfully, looking through his scope.

"Well, what is it?"

"Looks like a dust cloud."

"But not the convoy?"

"No, unless it's driving from the west."

"From the west? There's no road from the west."

"I know. That's why I don't know what it is. It's not on the road."

Hernandez sat up.

"Alright, lemme see."

Hargrove handed over his sniper rifle. Hernandez held it up to his right eye and peered through the scope. It took him a moment to orient himself.

"What the fuck is that?"

"Exactly."

Hargrove could see it now without the scope. He shaded his eyes with his hand. It was brown haze clearly above the ground that seemed to be rising with every passing second. Hernandez handed the rifle back to Hargrove and held his hands to his forehead like binoculars. They both watched as the brown haze rose off the sandscape as if the horizon itself had shifted upward.

"Shit."

"What?" Tension in Hargrove's voice. The last thing he wanted at the end of his tour was some new horror.

"Sandstorm."

They watched as the approaching brown wall rose to what must have been a thousand feet as they could now judge depth perception against distant sand dunes that were swallowed up.

"Cover!" Hernandez yelled. Miller and Zapata responded by flattening themselves on the ground, scattering their helmets and smokes and then regathering them and holding their hands over their heads. Denton shuffled up the dune holding his trousers and dove into the sand next to Hargrove. The wall of sand blotted out the sun and towered above them. They watched as Bravo squad disappeared into the sandstorm. The dark title wave of billowing sand and wind crossed the highway and overtook Charlie squad. Hernandez wanted to yell some order to his squad but nothing came to mind. He just watched as the world turned black and they were scoured with angry earth.

<u>THIRTY</u>

Hargrove and Hernandez watched as a wall of sand and rock crested upon them like an avalanche launching off a cliff. It was suddenly dark as a moonless night in a raging typhoon. Hernandez yelled again for his troops to cover but he couldn't even hear his own harshly barked order over the deafening roar. Hargrove had his hands over his ears trying to block out the sand. Miller and Zapata disappeared before his eyes. A shape that might have been Denton was already half buried in sand. He clenched his teeth and felt grit and chipped enamel. He tried to spit but the insides of his cheeks filled with sand the instant he parted his lips. He curled into the fetal position, one hand over his helmet to shield as much of his face as he could and the other hand holding onto Hargrove's left boot so he could at least account for one of his soldiers.

Time stretched until it lost all definition. Hernandez felt nothing but the scorching wind on his back and the current of sand running over him in rivulets. He kept his eyes closed. Minutes could have passed, or hours, or eons. At some point he saw his girls, his five year old holding onto his chin with two little hands on the sides of his face scrunching up her nose and saying, "silly daddy, silly daddy"...as he lay in bed next to his wife, his youngest climbing on top of him saying "sodry, sodry,

sodry...I sodry" every time she dug a tiny elbow or knee into his stomach or put a hand into his face trying to brace herself on top of his rolling and undulating frame..."Its fine sweet girl, you don't have to say I'm sorry," but still she wriggled on top of him, stepping on his adam's apple and poking him in the eye crawling to a comfortable spot on his chest to lay her head, apologizing all the way, "sodry, sodry, I sodry," and he thought, could I be asleep? Was that possible?

He felt a rough hand shaking his shoulder. He tried to open his eyes but they felt sealed shut. He heard a voice, far away, muffled. He pulled an arm out of the sand and then he felt a moist heat in his ear, someone yelling so close to his ear that he felt three day stubble on his cheek. It tickled.

"The convoy. Sir, the convoy."

It was Bradley. Hernandez forced open his eyelids with his thumb. His vision registered a whirl of dirt. The pressure on his shoulder increased and he actually felt himself being yanked free from a sand drift and spun around. Bradley was there in his face. Indian features despite the close cropped hair. Bradley's eyes were stern, piercing.

"The convoy's under attack! They're using the sandstorm as cover," Bradley yelled.

Hernandez felt his hot breath in his face. The world was brown. He couldn't see but a few feet in front of him, but it was something at least. His right hand was still clenching Hargrove's boot and he pulled himself on top of the man and slapped him into action, pulling Hargrove into a sitting position. They rallied Denton and stumbled arm in arm against the wind to Miller and Zapata.

Even over the screaming of the wind they heard the pop, pop,

pop, of semi-automatic gunfire, and wandered toward the sound. Dim yellow ovals that could have been headlights appeared like apparitions and faded in and out thought the blasting sand. They advanced side by side with their weapons drawn, spinning with the orange and white flashes of concussion grenades and RPGs, careful not to fire since anyone they might shoot could be their own. Suddenly the ground shook with a huge explosion, a giant mushroom cloud momentarily cut through the sandstorm, the orange flame twisting with the wind and whipping in circles like a whirlpool on fire. They all hit the deck or were blown to the ground. They heard the sound of shrapnel in the air along with the sand. One of the KBR tanker trucks had been hit.

The next few minutes were a matter of perception. Both of Hernandez's arms up to the elbows were buried deep in the sand. He pulled his arms up and was happy to see both his hands still attached. He felt naked without his weapon. Like waking from the reoccurring dream he'd had ever since his first daughter was born, the one where he lost her, just seeing her one second and then the next she's out of sight, and he felt that she was close, but even though she was close, she was gone and he couldn't know if he'd ever find her or see her again. He spun in a circle pushing aside the sand until he felt something solid. It was a boot. He felt a moment of horror looking inside, expecting to find a severed foot with the bone jutting out and tendons twisting in the wind, but it was empty. He heard a groan and saw Hargrove rolling on his side. Hernandez tossed him the boot.

The wind intensified and Hernandez rallied his troops to their feet and toward the sound of gunfire. The constant roar of the sandstorm enveloped them in a heavy blanket of noise. They rushed forward, holding hands at times to stay together. The sound of explosions, bullets, and the screams of the wounded reverberated all around them, but they couldn't make contact with another living soul. Eventually the sounds of war grew dimmer. Still they carried onward.

Night fell. They could tell only because the wall of brown surrounding them turned black. The sand pelted them relentlessly. Communications had been down since the sandstorm started. The satellite phone and internet link were hopeless. After some hours, Hernandez put a hand on each of their shoulders and told them it was time to stop. Each man set down their gear and made a nest in the sand to wait for the storm to end or for morning to come. There was no point continuing forward. They were lost.

THIRTY-ONE

A low haze clung to the dunes, rolling over the sand in wisping waves. Hernandez rubbed his eyes not sure what he was seeing, not sure night was over and he had survived. The haze wasn't smoke and the sandstorm was over. It looked to him like all the souls of all the dead the desert held over the millennia had crept to the surface to float around. It burnt off as soon as the sun cleared the horizon revealing nothing but an expanse of unbroken sand as far as the eye could see.

"Get the fuck up," Hernandez yelled. A few forms in the sand shifted and half buried bodies emerged. All six were accounted for. The men shook sand from the folds of their fatigues and emptied their boots as best they could. They lit cigarettes, cupping their hands against a meandering breeze. They looked around and couldn't believe what they saw. No road or landmark of any kind. Just dunes.

"We are fucked."

"Cut that shit, Denton. Hargrove, try the sats," Hernandez said barely above a whisper, stroking the stubble on his chin, and squinting into the distance. Hargrove tried the satellite phone, but he could hear the rattle of sand inside the hard plastic casing, and knew it wouldn't work. The GPS wouldn't even power up.

"Go figure," Hargrove moaned.

"Alright, quit your bitching," Hernandez said calmly. "Compasses."

All six men took their compasses from their packs and set about watching the needles spin.

"What the fuck?"

"Anyone know which direction we came from?" The men looked about at the sea of sand, some staring at the endless sky. A dune looked familiar to Hernandez, but then he shook his head like wiping a slate clean. They all looked the same.

"Bradley?"

"North by north west, sir."

"How far?"

"Impossible to tell, sir. But couldn't be more than ten clicks."

"How do you know?"

"Slow going in the sand. Postholing all night. I'm judging by our time and pace, sir."

"Okay. So which way?"

"North by north west, sir."

"Back the way we came?"

"Don't know where anything else is, sir."

"Anybody else?"

The men were still spinning circles, some on their second cigarette, amazed anyone could find their bearings without GPS, glad somebody had, willing to believe somebody had.

"Aight, north by north west it is, until we find a road."

Hernandez ordered them to eat an MRE and then did a water check. They had roughly a liter per man. They started walking, using the sun as the reference point for their compasses since the dunes seemed to be always shifting, but Bradley was the only one Hernandez had any confidence in to constantly adjust for the sun's movement across the sky and steer their direction accordingly. They walked for an hour with no change in the landscape. Their second hour became their third. When the sun was high overhead they stopped and spread the desert camouflaged ponchos the army had seen fit to give them over their heads and made makeshift tents. They took sips of water and smoked cigarettes for an hour and then set out again.

Their boots were heavy in the sand. They walked to sunset. Hernandez figured they'd walked five clicks in the morning and five in the afternoon. But there was still no sign of the road, or any road. They sat in a semicircle as the wind blew sand over their heads and the orange orb of the sun grew in size to a giant's an angry red eye, unblinking as it sunk to the horizon. The eye of the devil. Hernandez ordered them to eat another MRE and conserve their water. When the sun was set he cursed himself for realizing too late that they should have been traveling at night the whole time. The stars came out. Millions of them. Billions of them. The men had never seen stars like this. The sky so black and the stars so bright they could see the contours of the dunes by the light of the Milky Way. There was no moon.

THIRTY-TWO

The sun rose over the dunes. Hernandez shaded his eyes and looked at his men. They were out of water. They should have run across Highway 1, but they hadn't. Bradley had navigated by the stars during the night, infinitely better than using the sun as a guide. Now, Bradley was as tired and confused as the rest of them. He looked at his compass and muttered about witches. Denton was feverish. His diarrhea hadn't let up and had worsened over the night, which was entirely predictable, and Hernandez couldn't help but think about how to write it up, even though another part of him couldn't care less about reports anymore. He thought more and more about his daughters. He could feel his five year old's soft hands feeling the stubble on the sides of his face.

"You are so hairy daddy, like a lion. Are you a lion, daddy?"

"Yes, I am a lion."

She caressed his face again.

"Mommy, why did you decide to marry a lion?"

Hernandez looked at his wife, her beautiful brown skin as smooth as the wind blown desert sand. She shrugged her bare shoulders.

"Because I fell in love with a lion, mi hija."

Hernandez refocused and just saw dunes. It was midday and

the sun was high. He saw Miller go down and Zapata fall to his knees in the sand trying to help him up. The two men got to their feet with Bradley's help and trudged onward. Hernandez ordered his men to drink their urine, or at least piss on their shirts and then put them on again to get the evaporative cooling effect. The shirts were dry again in minutes. They had all shed their body armor, except for Hargrove who was too close to getting out and feared getting shot more than heat stroke.

In the afternoon Denton collapsed and didn't get back up. They rolled him onto his back and brushed the sand from his mouth. They propped their rifles and machine guns in the sand and spread a poncho over them to make a crude tent to provide Denton some shade. His temperature was a hundred and five and his respirations were shallow. They wiped his forehead with piss rags.

Denton died sometime during the night. They wrapped his body in the poncho and buried it in the sand with the broken GPS and a dead cell phone, figuring military intelligence or spooks from some other agency would have the technology to pick up a signal from one of the devices somehow and locate the body. They disassembled Denton's M16, since no one was going to carry it, and made a cross out of parts with duct tape and planted it in the sand to mark the grave. They had discussed carrying the body, but none of them could conceive of actually doing it. Denton was dead, and they wanted the best chance to live. None said it, but they all thought it.

The men stood around the shallow grave and smoked cigarettes. They sky was black. Cherries glowed red and lit their faces when they took drags. The smoke disappeared into the stars. Hernandez said a few words. Hargrove had a lump in his throat, like an apple was lodged in his windpipe. He'd been with Denton through basic training and felt like crying but was too stunned and dehydrated for tears so he was left with choking, his emotions manifest as a physical pain, an expanding mass in his esophagus. Hernandez said a few more words in Spanish and crossed himself and then they started walking, not wanting to waste the dark coolness of night.

They trudged one foot in front of the other. The desert spread out before them. The stars ran to the horizon. The men felt themselves winding down, running out of time, adrift on the dunes like abandoned ships pushed along by the waves. Even Bradley walked with his head down, watching his feet, no longer scanning the skyline. When he finally looked up, he stopped walking and stood still. His mouth was too dry for speech. He wasn't sure he could hear his own dusty voice over the droning buzz in his head anyway. He held up his arm with his fist clenched but none of the men saw him. They just kept walking in whatever direction they were heading. Bradley ignored them and crouched down. He took out his sniper riffle and looked through the scope. There was no moon but the infinite stars provided plenty of light for his night vision goggles. It was a slim chance, but something about the unbroken desert wasn't right. The spacing of the dunes seemed wrong. Manipulated somehow. There seemed to be a consistently spaced gap. He tried to do some calculations in his head, judging the angle of the gap, but his mind was a wall of static. Pounding, feverish, loud, static. But just eyeballing it he could tell the gap was uniform. And nature hates uniformity.

A road. Or at least something manmade, Bradley thought. He shouldered his rifle and trot across the desert, his boots kicking sand up into his eyes. One by one he caught up to each man and shook them out of their thirst crazed stupors. He frantically gestured toward the direction of the line in the sand and sprinted off to the next man. The closer he got to the gap in the dunes the more he was sure it was manmade. He looked for power lines but could see nothing above ground. He crested a dune and there it was below him, a thin but straight road.

It wasn't asphalt, more like hard packed dirt, perhaps once coated with oil to congeal it and tamp down the dust. The men stayed on the dunes above. They leaned on each other in a circle. Those who still could, smoked cigarettes. After some hushed debate they agreed the road had to be in use or it would have been washed over and buried by the desert. Besides, no one could imagine walking onward. They would wait. Wait for anything. Hope the road would provide. Hernandez, Hargrove, Miller and Zapata hunkered down on top of a dune, their weapons within arm's reach. Bradley scouted a couple hundred yards down the road toward the east and disappeared from view.

Just as a thin band of black sky was beginning to turn blue, and some of the multitude of stars faded into the heavens, Bradley's voice crackled over a walkie-talkie on Hernandez's shoulder.

"Lights."

"What kind."

"Headlights."

"What kind."

"Can't tell."

"How many."

"One."

Hernandez signaled with his fingers for Hargrove, Miller and Zapata to get into position. The men sighted their M-16s on the road below, fingers on triggers, safeties off. Dehydration made their breathing ragged and their fingers shake. They wanted to kill, kill for water, kill for the hope of water. Hernandez slapped each man's helmet and told them to get a grip. Remember their training. Their movements ceased and they focused on controlling their breathing. The air was still. They could hear the slightest breeze and feel the grainlets of sand that blew across their faces as they eyed down their sights. They felt themselves sink into the sand. A minute later they heard the whine of a small engine, probably four cylinder.

Bradley saw right away that it was a civilian vehicle, not that that necessarily meant shit. A late twentieth century Renault sedan side-saddled down the narrow semi-improved dirt road across the desert, shimmying from side to side as it seemed in a hurry to get to its destination on outmatched tires. Bradley adjusted the scope on his rifle and saw that the driver was the sole occupant. He radioed to Hernandez.

"Car. Solo driver. No militia."

He listened with his hand over the com but only heard static. He watched the headlights disappear into the valley of the dunes.

Hernandez saw the headlights first and held up his fist. He heard the sound of the engine rev as the Renault's bald tires lost traction on patches of wind blown sand. A second passed in which he may have thought or he may have not. And then Hernandez brought his fist down and Miller, Zapata, and Hargrove let loose with the M-16s, aiming low at the tires at first, and then into the driver's side window. The Renault swerved as the tires exploded and the car fishtailed and then drifted off the road and rolled down the embankment of a sand dune. The headlights strobed one time illuminating the reflective startled eyes of some tiny desert creature and then went dark in a plume of displaced sand.

The men scrambled down from their position and onto the road as fast as they could, Zapata sliding on his belly and using his M-16 as a rudder. They could hardly contain shouts of excitement as they sprinted down the road. Water was close, they could smell it. Had to be. They jumped into the deep sand on the other side of the road where the Renault lay overturned with its rear wheels still spinning. Liquid ran out onto the sand making a dark, damp circle. Zapata put his face in it and came up coughing and spitting out sand. Gasoline. Miller and Hargrove were using their gun butts to breakout the remaining shards of glass in the driver's side window. A body was awkwardly contorted around the steering wheel, a bullet hole where an eye should have been, and the top half of the driver's forehead embedded in the windshield. The corpse wore a suit and tie.

They could see a thermos on the floor next to a weathered brown leather briefcase. They pried the driver's side door open with their guns, kicking the bent metal with their combat boots. Miller and Hargrove frantically pulled the dead man out of the car, the broken bones splintering and popping through the skin as they pulled. The head was wedged in the windshield and Hargrove had to use a half nelson choke hold around the dead man's neck to pull him free, leaving the bloody scalp lodged in the glass.

When the shredded corpse was yanked free from the interior and left crumpled and leaking face down in the desert sand, the men tore the inside of the car apart looking for water. Bradley jogged up, looking dismayed, in disbelief that they hadn't managed to stop the vehicle without destroying it. It was, after

THIRTY-THREE

They'd driven less than ten clicks when Hargrove slammed on the brakes and angled the Land Cruiser into the shadow of a sand dune. There was an object glinting in the sun just above the horizon, past a low rise. Hargrove, Miller, and Zapata stayed with the Land Cruiser and Hernandez and Bradley crawled up the rise on their bellies to scout it out. Hernandez looked through his binoculars and Bradley used the scope on his rifle. Below them, the road ended at a gate to an installation surrounded by a fourteen foot chain link fence topped with razor wire. The square security fence guarded a lone structure, a small cinderblock building. There were no guards. There was no movement of any kind.

"Black site?" Hernandez whispered.

"Yeah, but not one of ours."

"I'm guessing what's going on there is going on below ground."

Bradley trained his scope on the low cinderblock building. "One door, steel. Going to be a tough entry. Have to go in hard."

"What if we draw them out?"

"That could work. Better than banging our heads against that steel door."

They watched for another twenty minutes but saw no movement. The installation looked abandoned. But obviously it wasn't. The men with the briefcases proved that.

The Land Cruiser drove up the gate and stopped. There was only one occupant. A driver behind the wheel. Hargrove. He honked the horn and waited. He grimaced as he waited, feeling the intense heat now that the vehicle was standing still. He glanced nervously at his helmet and his M16 on the floor in front of the passenger seat. He checked the rearview mirror and saw empty desert. But he knew the squad was there somewhere. Bradley would have his sights on him right now, with his sniper riffle, alert for the slightest motion.

A minute passed. Nothing. Hargrove thought about checking the gate. Maybe it wasn't locked and whoever these drivers were, they were supposed to open the gate themselves. But he was afraid to get out of the truck. Too close to discharge. Too close to Delta, Colorado. He could feel the fresh mountain air, hear the sound of the creek running over rocks. The smell of a cooler full of beer and fish bait. Another minute passed. He looked pleadingly in the mirrors but saw nothing. No instructions. He was on his own.

He honked the horn again and immediately the metal door of the concrete hut opened and two men hustled out to the gate with machine guns slung over their shoulders. Hargrove kept his head down, just barely above the steering wheel. One of the soldiers worked a switch and the metal gate began to roll back. The other squinted at the Land Cruiser, shielding his eyes with his hand like a visor. The soldier seemed to sense something he didn't like and began to say something to the other one when both their heads exploded. A second later Hargrove heard the reports from Bradley's sniper rifle. The two headless men dropped like unformed clay let loose on a pottery wheel.

Hargrove exhaled and clutched his chest. Sweat dripped off his nose and brow and landed in big drops on his lap. He checked the rear view mirrors. Miller and Zapata had come out of nowhere and were sprinting past the Land Cruiser and through the gate, Hernandez and Bradley just behind them, sand flowing off of their fatigues like contrails as their legs pumped up and down. He grabbed his M-16 off the floorboard and set his helmet, pounding it tight with his fist, and pushed open the driver's side door with his shoulder and stood behind it, with his weapon sighted on the square cinder block building, covering the others.

Miller and Zapata reached the building and flattened themselves against the concrete on either side of the metal door. Hernandez and Bradley caught up to them as Hargrove scanned the fence line and beyond for any signs of life, but there were none. Just the sound of the desert wind and the sand running across razor wire. Hargrove listened to the sound of his own breathing for ten seconds, studied the perimeter again and the blue sky beyond, and then ran toward the building.

Miller tried the metal door. The dead men had left it unlocked. No one expects they are going to die. Hernandez went in first with Zapata on his hip, and then Bradley with his sniper rifle shouldered and his side arm held tight with both hands. Miller went in last, waiting for Hargrove and then leaving him topside to guard the rear.

The door opened to five flights of narrow steps with metal railings and flickering florescent lights mounted to the walls. The four men advanced as they were trained, quietly and in control. At the bottom of the stairs there was a thick metal door.

Remarkably, the door had a thin rectangular glass window, criss-crossed with a grid of reinforced wire. Two on either side of the door, they peeked in and saw tall stainless steel columns running fluid in a maze of tubes through thick white compressed resin. Hernandez held up two fingers and pointed to the left and the right. They took turns looking through the window and saw four Iraqi soldiers in fatigues with kalashnikovs and a half dozen men in white lab coats with clipboards checking the gauges on the columns.

Hernandez gingerly tried the round metal doorknob. He couldn't believe it turned. The Iraqis must simply have never conceived that this facility would be discovered this way, by a group of foot soldiers in one of their workers' vehicles. They must have believed if the facility was ever discovered they would know by the bunker-buster dropped from thirty thousand feet, in which case their reaction time wouldn't matter much.

Miller opened the door slowly and Hernandez and Zapata slid fully into the room before they were noticed, and by then it was too late. Hernandez put two bullets in each of the soldiers on the left side of the room and Zapata did the same to the two on the right. The soldiers never even got their fingers on their triggers before they were sent sprawling onto the floor. The roar of the weapons reverberated around the bunker along with bullets that entered and existed bodies and ricocheted off the stainless steel tables, chairs, and columns, and sent the men in lab coats running in all directions. Miller was through the door and emptied a clip into the lab coats gunning down four of them, their white coats splattered with ballooning red circles where they had been hit. The gunite floor quickly became slick with rivers of blood that ran to a drain. The floor was designed to handle such messes.

Two lab coats avoided the initial slaughter as their colleagues absorbed bullets in front of them. They ran toward the back of the room. Hernandez, Miller, Zapata, and Bradley worked their way to the back of the room, hiding behind two hundred gallon Nalgene tanks and the resin filled columns, some now leaking the thick white resin where they had been punctured by gunfire. They assumed the men were arming themselves and were taking no chances. But when they'd worked their way to the back of the room they found the two men cowering against a back wall with no exit, next to an eyewash station and an industrial grade ventilation hood, with their hands up and arms outstretched, jabbering in some language none of the squad understood.

The standoff only lasted seconds. One of the men made some motion in the direction of lab equipment and Hernandez shot him in the head. Hernandez turned to the other man who started shouting "WMD! WMD!"

"WD 40? What's he saying? Why do we need that?" Miller mouthed.

"Fuck if I know," Zapata said, who followed Hernandez's lead and trained his M-16 on the man, who kept shouting "WMD" in heavily accented English.

"WMD. Weapons of Mass Destruction," Bradley said calmly, and then addressed the man, who was still wearing his protective eye goggles and looked very much like a scientist. "Do you know where they are at? Is that what you're making here, in this facility?"

"I...I know...I know all..." the man struggled through panic.

Hernandez cocked his side arm. "Fuck this."

"No, wait," Bradley said. "This guy's useful. Important. WMD is what this war is all about."

"I thought it was about oil," Miller said.

"I don't give a fuck what it's about," Hernandez spat, "we're taking their water, their food, and their coms, and getting the fuck out of here."

Hernandez started to press down on the trigger when he was shot three times in the chest and blown back against one of the huge Nalgene tanks, slumping to the floor in a sitting position. Miller and Zapata turned to Bradley, hardly believing that his smoking gun had taken out their squad leader.

"What the fuck," Miller croaked and turned the barrel of his gun toward Bradley. "Never trusted you."

Bradley dove behind a column as Miller and Zapata fired at him, spraying bullets across the lab. Bradley rolled onto the floor and put a bullet into each of their heads. When he stood up, the scientist was rubbing his head, shaved bald.

"Tenk you, tenk you," he said in broken English. It was the worst sound Bradley had ever heard.

Hernandez watched himself bleed out. He knew it was over. They were too far from rescue even if Bradley let him live. His eyes focused on his dusty combat boots. All he thought was—silly daddy, silly daddy.

THIRTY-FOUR

The Navajo Nation — The Present

The late morning sun poured through the large front window of the Copper Street Pub and warmed Jake's back. He was hunched over a green chile burrito with one hand clutched around a frosty mug of beer and the other thumbing the pages of the Gallup Independent. Slowly, the smell of Hatch green chiles was overcome by the soft scent of a perfume he'd come to recognize, and knew Cally was reading over his shoulder. The newspaper's front page story was about three bodies found charred and locked in a van on the reservation. Burned to death.

"Do you think it's related?" Cally faced him and leaned her back against the bar, sipping lemonade through a straw.

"Not my problem anymore."

Cally arched an eyebrow and then gave him a half smile and squinted. He thought her eyes looked green-gray today.

"Hum...I thought you shot the guy..."

"Easy. You know what they say about opinions."

"They're like assholes?"

"Yup. And you are one."

Cally put her hand up to her cheek. "My word!"

Jake shoveled in the last of the burrito and washed it down with the rest of his beer. "Gotta run. Gonna pick up my personal effects."

Jake tipped the bill of his baseball cap at Cally.

"Ma'am."

She winked at him.

"Sir."

THIRTY-FIVE

The walk from the Copper Street to his office should have felt different, as it was almost certainly his last, but it didn't. He opened the door and the bell jingled. Mary was at her desk. She looked up from her computer maybe a fraction quicker than in the past.

"Well, if it isn't Cheech. Or should I say Chong?"

"I didn't get fired for that."

"That's not what I heard."

"I got fired for lying about it."

"Well, if you really needed to smoke you should have just gone to the doctor. Mary pulled out a canister of joints from her handbag. I get mine from a doctor in Flagstaff...medicinal."

"Jesus Mary, put those away."

"It's medicine. Jeez, what kind of stoner are you?"

"I'm not. And New Mexico doesn't have a medical marijuana law."

"I know. Duh? I just said I got these in Flagstaff, Arizona."

"I'm just gonna get my stuff."

Mary shrugged.

Jake went upstairs to collect his personal effects, but quickly realized he didn't have any. There was a photo of Aimee in a halter top and jeans, looking over one shoulder at the camera, smiling. He thought about taking more case files, but he'd already taken the important stuff when he was placed on administrative leave. And there was no need to get Mary in trouble.

He bounded down the stairs with the photo in hand. Mary didn't even attempt to click away from TMZ. She spoke without looking up. "Listen. You should fight this. File an EEOC complaint. Call the union. You'd win an administrative appeal. I've seen people win with less."

"Thanks. But Mary, I don't know what I'm doing out here."

Mary crossed her hands and settled them in her lap. "Jake, all that matters is who you are doing out here."

Jake laughed, "Don't ever change, Mary."

He walked back to his truck. He was wearing sandals instead of his cowboy boots. The wind blew pebbles that stung his feet. He drove the F-150 slowly through town. He had nowhere to go. The streets seemed unusually empty. Blue sky and brown mountains.

To the north and east—across from Old 66 and New I-40— were red cliffs, curved like a fit woman's legs from shin to knee and just as smooth. The cliffs ran up to the big mountains, the trailing edge of the Rockies. The shape of the cliffs reminded him of a row of cheerleaders squeezed together on bleachers knee to knee, their firm tan legs touching. They reminded him of Aimee. "I'm loosing it," he thought.

Eventually he drove home, easing the truck down the rutted driveway, listening to the crunch of gravel under tire, and finally bringing it to rest next to the burnt out trailer. He walked through the destruction inside, sidestepped his tent, and righted a lawn chair that had blown over, and sat down in front of the hundred mile view. Cally didn't come by and his phone didn't ring. He kept looking at it hoping for a Washington, D.C. area code to pop up, but he couldn't will his ex-wife to call. He'd never been able to will her to do anything.

THIRTY-SIX

Jake woke to the sound of an engine and crept low into the remnants of the living room with the loaded Glock tight in his grip and peaked through the empty smashed out window frame. It was Yazzie's Silverado pickup, his off-duty vehicle. Jake snuck back to his tent, stashed the Glock, and put on some underwear.

By the time he came out to greet him, Yazzie stood in the destroyed kitchen picking something off of his boots like he'd just stepped in dog shit. Yazzie surveyed the damage. The trailer looked like one of the burnt-out meth labs that scarred the reservation. He was glad he was wearing his shitkickers. Then he surveyed Jake. The fire damage was old, the smell of smoke was gone, but the empty beer cans were fresh, and there were dozens of them. Jake looked like he'd just woken up but that didn't mean he was sober. Yazzie decided that he would do the driving.

"Come on let's go. I'm driving."

"Where we going."

"Hunting."

Jake squinted his eyes and seemed to think about this, perhaps wondering if this was some kind of rouse. An intervention.

"Bird or deer."

"Bird."

"Where's Emily?"

Emily was Yazzie's bird dog, a yellow lab / rez dog mix that would have been a pointer if she had the temperament, but she was too hyper, and only good for flushing. Yazzie named her Emily because it was such a quintessential white person's name and he never grew tired of saying, "Emily get over here you bitch!"

"Emily is in the truck. Do you think I'd let her in this shithole? She would probably get hepatitis, or tetanus, or syphilis or something."

Jake thought about that. He looked around but focused on nothing. "Well, I certainly couldn't rule that out. Wouldn't insure against it."

"Put some damn pants on."

"Okay."

THIRTY-SEVEN

Jake rode shotgun with Emily drooling on his shoulder as Yazzie drove the Silverado south on Navajo Route 28 toward Zuni and then west out of the foothills down into the flatlands. Yazzie eased the groaning Silverado along a dry wash and then onto open country, and parked behind a stand of palo verde. Emily clawed Jake half to pieces in excitement trying to fling herself out of the truck. She sprawled onto the dry, cracked earth and spun her paws for a moment showering the truck with dust and stones before gaining traction. She immediately spun circles around and in between the thin green palo verde trunks and startled three doves resting in the thorned and spindly branches of the trees. The spooked birds flew to safety long before Jake and Yazzie had even taken their shotguns out of their cases. Yazzie used a Winchester Super X3 20 gauge semi-automatic to hunt doves which Jake regarded as overkill and somehow the opposite of what he thought a Navajo would use. The gun was light with a wide spread and, most egregiously, semi-auto—it was almost unfair to the little emblems of peace that dumbly just wanted to live another day. Jake himself used a Maverick Model 88 Pump 20 gauge that he'd bought on sale for a hundred and forty-nine dollars at the Walmart. He knew that prejudging what a Navajo would use to hunt doves was vaguely racist, or rather he knew that he'd been out on the reservation long enough to know that he didn't know what was racist.

Jake had a beer stuffed in each of his front jeans pockets and he opened one and looked up at the sun. The sun looked back. They started walking the desert, Yazzie with shotgun at the ready, Jake with his gun resting across his shoulders hooked behind his elbows like a crucifix.

Emily blindly charged into a corpse of russian olives, adroitly dodging yucca and assorted cacti milliseconds before being impaled, and flushed out half a dozen doves that had congregated around a small spring hidden by bramble and a large blackbrush acacia. Doves are migratory birds, usually shot at some point in their long journeys from winter grounds to summer, or vice versa, by hunters holed up in camouflaged blinds. But having grown up on the reservation, Yazzie had a few tricks up his sleeve and knew where they liked to congregate, around the scant dribs and drabs of water to be found in the high desert. Yazzie's semi-automatic Winchester roared in a haze of smoke and ejected shells and five doves dropped from the sky. The last dove flapped away with palpable agitation, gaining elevation. Jake lifted his sunglasses and squinted at the bird and then lowered them again. He unslung his shotgun with what seemed like great effort. He aimed high at the blue sky at nothing perceptible and pulled the trigger. The shotgun let out a thundering boom. The boom echoed off the mountains and seconds later the bird dipped down as if encountering a strong wind, flew a little longer, and then spiraled to the ground. Jake had aimed in a high arch to compensate for the great distance and his birdshot had rained down on the dove from above.

"Neat trick."

"Thanks. Too bad that skill doesn't put food on the table."

"How do you mean? It just did."

"I mean, I need a job."

Yazzie reloaded, taking a moment to pick the flakes of red shell casing out of the chamber. Emily chased down the dead birds with her nose to the ground in a zigzagging pattern and brought them back to Yazzie, one at a time.

"So, you're not going back east."

Jake looked perplexed. "Hell no. Why would I do that?"

THIRTY-EIGHT

Bagram Airfield, Afghanistan — July 1, 2003

Hargrove sat on a folding metal chair outside of a glass enclosed office in a bunker made of concrete block. The air base had the feel of a hastily put together boiler room full of fly by night stock traders—scattered paper, telephones, ill-fitting furniture, and too many people for the space. After a time he was called into the office where he sat on another metal folding chair. A colonel in desert fatigues sat behind a desk, two men in dark suits flanked the colonel and a contractor in body armer dangling an unlit cigarette from his lower lip cradled an M-16. Hargrove didn't look directly at any of the men. Instead he looked out the window, some plastic blast resistant polymer, poorly installed and flexing against a strong wind, scraping the cinderblocks and causing a trail of dust to leak down to the floor. Outside there were sprawling rows of gray concrete bunkers, blast walls, and watchtowers with spaces of brown dirt in between. Beyond the outer most wall and turreted gun nests was more brown running to infinity. The sky was a shade of blue that reminded him of gray. Silver razor wire glinted from an unseen sun.

Hargrove braced himself for a long debrief, but he was only asked one question, over and over again, in various forms. Did he know what happened in the underground bunker. Not what happened. But did he know what happened. He said he did not know. He hadn't ever gone underground. His orders were to stay topside. He never spoke to Bradley or to the Iraqi scientist he brought back with him. He didn't know how his friends died, who killed them, or why.

They didn't ask him about the ambush of the KBR trucks on Highway 1, or about getting lost in the desert, or how they'd lost their communications and couldn't get help. How even their compasses didn't work. They didn't ask about losing Denton to the heat and dehydration. Or where his body was. They didn't ask about the civilians they killed, or even about how they found the Iraqi black site. They just wanted to make sure he really knew as little as he actually did.

When they were satisfied, the colonel picked a blue folder off of his desk and made a show of leafing through it. The colonel leaned back in his chair and noted that Hargrove had three weeks left in his deployment, and asked what he wanted to do now. Hargrove again looked out of the window. Green tents and camouflage netting covering clapboard barracks flapped and pulled at their anchors. The wind reached some critical velocity where it sent the desert dirt swirling airborne with a low howling sound, pelting the gray buildings and running through a squad of soldiers marching dutifully in formation across the brown ground. The sky was faceless.

At the same time, 30,000 feet above the Indian ocean, Bradley was strapped into a jump seat in the cargo hold of a C130, feeling the reverberations from the droning engines coursing through his chest. He felt sick. It had been three days since he was airlifted out of the desert, three days since he'd killed his friends. In spite of exhaustion, dehydration, and a healthy dose of Trazodone added to an IV bag administering saline solution, he hadn't slept. Every time he shut his eyes he saw Hernandez slumped on the floor of the lab, whispering to himself as he bled out.

He had been interrogated over two eight hour sessions at an undisclosed location. He admitted everything. He told them how they'd killed the civilians when they didn't have to. How he couldn't watch another unarmed man executed, not one that might know where the WMDs were hidden, so they could stop the threat. So they could protect the Great White Father. So he could return home with honor, having done his part to uphold the Treaty and defend the United States from its enemies. So the war could end.

They told him the man he saved knew nothing. Bradley didn't believe it. Couldn't believe it. They would never tell him what the man knew. Why would they? Still, he almost wretched. They watched his face as they told him. There were a lot of men in the room. Most wore sunglasses.

They went over his relationship with each man in the squad in excruciating detail, taking turns, always a fresh interrogator. Was it personal with the squad? Was it personal with Hernandez? He told them he respected Hernandez, loved him even, at least as much as he could love a white man.

"Hernandez was Mexican," the sunglasses said.

"You know what I mean," he replied.

"That's right, you're a real deal Indian. The genuine article." The sunglasses pursued that angle for a while but it petered out quickly, as no one knew enough about Indians to sustain an in-depth line of questioning.

After another sleepless night he was brought into a bright

room with a stainless steel table and chairs and a long one way mirror. The walls, ceiling, and floor were all painted the same beige color. He was left alone for some length of time. How does one tell time in an empty room with no clock? He was achieving a trance-like state, not unlike when he was fourteen years old and his father sent him alone into the Chuskas to hunt and forage for himself. When he felt himself transcending the very nature of consciousness, the door opened and in walked the man with the bald head. His head was newly shaved, even though it seemed incredible that they would have given him a razor. The harsh florescent light overhead reflected off of his shiny head like a halo. Bradley felt his vision blur, like it was difficult to look at the man. To really see him. He was out of focus. Bradley wondered if he was really there. If he had ever really been there. The man walked up to Bradley, faced him, and extended his hand, palm up. Bradley would not shake hands. He did not nod, smile or make any gesture of acknowledgment. He did not move at all. He stood perfectly still, starring at the man as if he was an apparition. A skinwalker.

Eventually the man with the bald head dropped his hand and the two men stood there watching each other for nearly an hour. Finally, the door opened again and sunglasses came into the room. They had been watching from behind the one-way glass, observing how the men would react to each other.

"PFC Bradley, this man's going stateside," Sunglasses spoke. "We can't afford another friendly fire incident right now, so you are going to keep your mouth shut and you won't spend the rest of your life at Leavenworth."

Bradley said nothing. He felt like he was going to pass out. The bald man in front of him kept dematerializing.

"And the best part, PFC Bradley, the best part is you are going to babysit him for us. We may still have a use for him. And you. You can keep each other quiet. Wait for orders."

"And my family?" The shaved head said it to Bradley, but he was talking to the others.

"We're getting them out right now."

The Iraqi smiled, for the first time showing any expression, and turned to the men in the room and shook their hands. The men laughed, as if there was an ongoing inside joke, and led them to the tarmac. The C130 was waiting.

In the years later, when Bradley reflected back on that moment, he figured the men had laughed because they thought it was funny to pluck a towel-head from the Iraqi desert only to drop him in another desert ten thousand miles away.

THIRTY-NINE

Gallup, New Mexico — The Present

Jake sat at the bar at the Copper Street Pub with the want ad section of the classifieds from the Gallup Independent spread out in front of him. He'd circled one listing with a pink highlighter he found in a glass full of pens and bottle openers behind the bar. Cally slouched over the bar next to him. Her perfume announced her approach. He tried to remember when she'd first started wearing it.

"Doorman at the American? Really? Interesting choice."

"Beats Home Depot."

"That's a sketchy bar."

"Most bars are, aren't they?"

"No. This one's not."

"Well, you're a good influence on this place."

"Uh huh. Didn't one of the murders happen there, at the American? Coincidence?"

"Could be."

She edged closer so their arms were touching as she scanned the job listings. Her blond hair dangled over her half of the newspaper.

"Look, here's one perfect for you."

"Tanning salon?"

"They would love you there. Besides, it's safe. I worry about you."

"Why are there so many tanning salons around here? It's not like folks need more sun."

"Everyone loves a good tan. People go on spring break you know, even at Navajo Community College."

"I'll never understand this place."

"Nope, you won't."

"You want a home cooked meal tonight?"

"What are we having?"

"Dove."

FORTY

Jake drove to Cally's house in the evening and cooked a dozen doves in an aluminum tray he bought at the Walmart to minimize the mess and the cleaning afterward, four a piece for Cally, Cally's mother Miriam, and himself. Once cleaned, the birds were tiny, but four provided enough meat for a meal. He rendered some fat first to grease the pan, and then broiled the birds in the oven with potatoes, carrots, celery, and onion, and a healthy dose of salt and pepper. Miriam smelled beer on Jake and she gave him the stinkeye whenever she could, but there was something disarming about him. Besides, she believed her daughter when she said there was nothing going on between them. Mostly believed her anyway.

After dinner Cally washed the dishes as Miriam sat at the dining room table nursing a glass of white wine with Jake, who drank a can of beer he had apparently brought with him. Classy, she thought.

"So you're unemployed?"

Jake scratched his burgeoning beard. "Yeah, I guess I am. Weird. I haven't been unemployed since I was thirteen years old."

Miriam took a sip of wine and dabbed the corner of her mouth with a paper napkin. "I didn't mean it like that, I mean, I heard what happened. Heck the whole town heard. Didn't sound like you got a fair shake."

"Mary thinks I should fight it...I hear you know Mary."

"Oh yes, I know Mary...and Aimee."

"Aimee...yeah."

"Yeah...Aimee."

Jake nodded. It was his honesty that was disarming, Miriam thought. He was an open book. One with all the pages dogeared or torn. She could see what her daughter saw in him, and decide to redouble her efforts to not like him.

"But I'm not going to fight it. I did what they say I did."

"You murdered that man?" Miriam whispered it, but she could feel Cally shooting her a look from the kitchen.

"No, I was cleared of that. It was pot. Not really pot—lying about it."

"That doesn't seem like you."

"It was the only way to work for the FBI. Everyone lies on those applications."

"Well, it wasn't right."

"No, ma'am. It wasn't."

"Jake, you ready?" Cally interrupted. "Movie starts at eight, that's the late show around here, would you believe it?"

"Sure." Jake slammed the rest of this beer in big gulps set the empty can down on the table a little too hard.

"Thank you for dinner, Jake."

"You're welcome, ma'am."

Cally drove them to the movie theater in her 1996 Nissan Sentra. The sky seemed unusually dark and the town was quiet. There were less than a dozen people at the movies, couples mostly, speaking in whispers, keeping to themselves. Jake bought two tickets to a horror movie Cally wanted to see. Jake had no interest in it, but he didn't care. It just felt good to be with her. To be with someone.

The theater was pitch black inside. Without sight, his other senses came alive. Her perfume just made him feel good. He tried to remember where he recognized it from, who it reminded him of. He felt a little electricity sitting next to her, their arms almost touching. Halfway through the movie it started raining and the sound of the downpour on the tin roof of the theater completely drowned out the sound to the movie. Jake snuggled next to her. It was cold in the theater, and they could smell the dampness from the rain. His right arm intertwined with her left arm on her side of the armrest. Jake played with her fingertips and watched her face as she watched the silent actors move around the screen. She looked straight ahead, just the traces of a smile.

FORTY-ONE

The next day he went to the American to talk to the manager about the doorman job advertised in the paper. Chuck, the manager, was from Boston. Gallup, like most places in the West, was full of people from somewhere else. Chuck had been managing the bar since he'd left Dorchester a decade ago and spoke with an accent that had only grown stronger over time. It was dark inside. There were a handful of customers, mostly in the corners. Chuck looked him over with bleary, red rimmed eyes.

"So you're ex-law enforcement, yeah?"

"That's right."

"You're sure you're ex?"

"What does that mean."

"It means I know all the undercovers around here. We have a good relationship with Gallup PD. We help each other out. I don't care what you've heard about this place, but we watch each other's backs around here."

"Yeah, I'm ex. I got fired. Is that a problem for you?"

"No, I heard you shot that psycho. Good for you. I'm sure he had it coming. Too bad those chicken shits in DC fired you for it. Just weird you want this job."

"We all need work. Got bills to pay."

"We all fall on hard times, kid. You work the door, maybe a bartending shift opens up. We'll see how it goes."

"Thanks."

"Just be here at nine."

FORTY-TWO

Jake walked into the American at eight-thirty. The place was half-full, the jukebox played Hank Williams III's rendition of "Punch, Fight, Fuck" at full volume. He felt like everyone stared at him as he came in. Maybe they knew who he was. Maybe they didn't. Maybe they all knew each other and didn't like strangers.

Chuck was nowhere to be seen. Jake introduced himself to the bartenders. Max, a three hundred pound Samoan, and Phil, the only black man he'd seen in Gallup.

"You're the new guy?" Phil said extending his knuckles.

"Yeah." Jake gave him a fist bump.

Good, we need help, glad that piece of shit Chuck hired someone. Max slung out a giant meaty arm drawing Jake halfway across the bar and held him to his sweaty breast. Phil lined up three shot glasses on the bar and filled a metal mixing cup with ice and Stolichnaya Orange. He used the strainer and leaked out three shots. The bartenders clinked glasses and then touched them to the bar and took their shots. Jake hesitated for a second and then followed suit, grimacing slightly as the vodka hit the back of his mouth.

"Heard you shot a dude," Phil said. "That's good, we need that around here."

"Well, I'm not armed."

"You should be dude."

"Yeah, be a lot cooler if you did." Max said, open faced smile, meat sweats.

They pointed Jake to a bar stool beside the door. Just card everybody, they told him, and have our back when the yokels want to fight. The dented metal door to the American opened up to a narrow passageway where there was once a ticket booth. Jake sat on his barstool where the passageway opened to the bar, that way he had the chance to eyeball people for a few steps as they entered, and before they got too close to him. From nine to eleven nearly everyone who came in had an attitude, mostly regulars, indignant about being carded. A few tried to ingratiate themselves with him, perceiving some future benefit. They were the exception.

There were four nine-foot pool tables between the bar and the dance floor. The early hours of the night were punctuated by the crack of tightly racked balls being broken by heavily chalked cues with torque behind them. Later in the night it was too crowded for effective pool games. The pool tables were a source of fights, a table bumped during a shot or a gut shot from a zealously drawn back cue. Or sometimes people just looked for a fight, and the vagaries of a game played for money without a referee was a perfect set up. Those betting on pool at the American needed to gauge wisely whether there was any real chance of collection.

Every half-hour or so Phil or Max called Jake over for a shot. Always Stoli O chilled, glasses clinked together and tapped on the bar before imbibed. There was no band that night, but the place was still mostly full by midnight, and Jake had to thread his way through a crowd to get back to his bar stool by the door. He was feeling pretty good. Yes, I am, he thought. A good, consistent amount of vodka will do that.

It was dark inside, the overhead pool table lights and neon beer signs providing most of the light. The bar area was carpeted and it smelled like wet dog. Jake was glad it was dark.

At one a.m. a fight started that Jake couldn't stop. Jake was hunched on his bar stool listening to "One More Saturday Night" banging on the jukebox when he noticed a giant of a man in a flannel shirt with the sleeves cut off choking out a little guy in a black hoodie with a pool cue dangling limply from one hand. Phil and Max called the little guy Squirm, he was barely five-foot-two, but he'd drank at least a dozen vodka cranberries since Jake's shift had started, and was some kind of pool hustler, from what he could tell. Squirm was also a heroin junkie but that didn't seem to be slowing him down at the moment. Phil was shouting at Jake and pointing at the junkie being choked out. Giant hands completely encircled Squirm's neck and his face was tomato red. His legs kicked furiously but he never let go of his pool cue, an expensive custom job with a silver and turquoise inlaid shaft. Jake grabbed the big man's wrists but they were locked onto Squirm's neck like a pit bull's jaws. Next he leapt onto the giant's back and applied a half-nelson but it was like trying to strangle a rock, or a lodge pole pine. The man shook off Jake and dropped Squirm to the floor. It occurred to Jake that this was what the man might have been waiting for. Choking out a junkie wasn't really sporting. They ducked into some kind of wrestling stance and the crowd, which had been watching with amusement, formed into an actual circle and began clapping hands. The big man smiled. Jake dove for a meaty leg and applied pressure on the knee hoping to cripple

153

the man, but he was just too damn big. When Jake finally popped the knee, the man went to the floor, but he did so with as much of his body weight as possible directly on Jake's sternum. Jake felt the air forced out of him. One ham-hoc paw pressed his head into the carpet in an awkward angle. The carpet felt wet and sticky on his face. He smelled mildew, stale beer and man sweat. The big man laid his weight on him. He felt the man's belt buckle dig into his thigh. Insult to injury. His vision became a river of purple and green bubbles as the last of the oxygen in his blood was consumed and was replaced by gasps of nothing. The crowd made an audible "oh" sound and seemed to release and step back, and then Jake saw with the last of his sight two sets of arms around the giant's shoulders pulling him back. Max and Phil were there, pulling the redneck up long enough for Jake to crawl out from under his girth. The man jumped back into a ninja pose. The crowd moved further back, placing tables and chairs between themselves and the spectacle. The man squared up with Jake, Max and Phil, looking at each in turn and grinning madly.

Jake caught his breath, controlling his adrenaline. He looked around the bar and it dawned on him that this was a certain amount of theater. He righted himself and jutted his chin out at the gigantic roughneck.

"Hey man, leave now and we won't call the cops."

This seemed to please the big man. He grinned and had blood in his teeth. Somehow his lip had been cut during the fracas even though he'd gotten the better of everybody. He saluted the bar staff, looked at the crowd, and picked up his jean jacket off the back of a bar stool and walked out the door, pulling up the collar on his way out.

"Shots for the bar!" Phil shouted and the crowd roared. They slapped Jake on the back and piled to the bar for weak kamikazes that Max and Phil poured for everyone—a drop of well vodka, triple sec and sour mix that cost the bar about ten cents. Squirm was nowhere to be seen. The tips that night were tremendous. They always got the best tips on nights with a good fight, Max explained.

At one forty-five Phil called last call, and at two a.m. Jake went around taking drinks out of people's hands and telling them to get the fuck out the bar. After he'd forced the last customer out, he locked the door and Max showed him how to clean up and shut everything down while Phil counted the till and put the night's receipts in the office safe. After the mats were pulled and mopped, the well ice melted down and sinks bleached, the fruit caddy with the lemons, limes, cherries and olives put back in the walk-in cooler, the tables wiped, ashtrays collected, pool cues hung back in the racks, beer signs and video games turned off, and the last of the mugs, pitchers and glasses - shot, pint, and rocks - were washed, they sat at the corner of the bar smoking cigarettes and drinking beer while Phil counted out the tips. The bartenders took home about a hundred and twenty bucks each. They tipped Jake out forty.

Jake asked Max and Phil how they'd ended up in Gallup since they seemed out of place in the town of cowboys and indians. They'd both been recruited to play football at the University of New Mexico in Albuquerque. Phil had washed out his freshman year and been cut from the team. Without actually saying it, he alluded to dealing to drug-hungry frat boys using his contacts back in Chicago before needing to leave town. Max was a starting offensive lineman for the Lobos for three years before blowing out his knee, shoulder, and just about everything else. Now he'd blowed up to a good three hundred and fifty pounds. With no family in the mainland U.S., and nothing going on in Albuquerque, he eventually followed his buddy to Gallup. Jake thought there was more going on, he was surprised they'd been as candid with him as they had, but then again, they'd already gone to war together against a giant redneck and were a dozen shots in.

Phil talked Jake into shooting pool for ten bucks a game.

"Don't do it," Max said. Things started badly when Phil racked for nine-ball, nine balls in a diamond shape instead of the full rack of balls Jake was used to for eight-ball, the standard game everyone plays as a kid.

"What the fuck is that."

Phil laughed. "We only play nine-ball here, son. For real, they only play nine-ball everywhere. Isn't that right, Max?"

Max nodded and grinned, wiping the sweat from his eyes. He was always sweaty. "Dude, you're about to get rolled."

Jake lost the forty bucks he'd made in four straight games of nine-ball. Max watched, eating from a paper plate full of Lays potato chips covered in chile con carne from the bottom of the walk-in cooler that he'd reheated in the microwave and topped with mayonnaise. As soon as he sunk the nine ball for the last time Phil immediately felt bad and tried to give the money back but Jake wouldn't have it. He'd lost fair and square. Instead, Phil offered to buy breakfast. They took Phil's Audi Coupe to Bill's Diner on the end of Main Street with a view of the Interstate, Jake wedged in the backseat. Outside the sun was rising and the sky was periwinkle blue at the edges. Jake marveled at the red cliffs on the other side of the Interstate, glowing in the sunrise. The cheerleaders' knees. They ordered the most expensive breakfast on the menu at Bill's Diner, the steak and eggs, and ate with their sunglasses on. Jake felt the ranchers and early rising old-timers viewing them with suspicion, possibly disgust. He liked the feeling.

Max doused his steak and eggs with hot sauce and salt. Phil hunched over his plate, elbows wide, and looked around the diner. The locals looked away or turned back to their coffees when Phil caught their attention. Phil grinned at Jake.

"These people aren't used to black people."

"Or Samoans."

"What are you talking about, you're native."

"Native Samoan."

"Still. These people understand you and your tribal shit."

"Understand this." Max flipped him the bird and laughed so loud it echoed off the walls of the boxcar diner.

The waitress came over and filled their coffee cups. She didn't seem the least bit bothered by their foolishness. To the contrary, she laughed and shook her head at Max as he showed her the middle finger he was holding up for Phil's benefit. She was the same waitress who'd served Jake when he'd had mutton stew with Yazzie a little more than a week ago, but she didn't seem to recognize him now. He was glad he was wearing sunglasses so she didn't have to see how red his eyes were.

Max had a slice of flan topped with whipped cream for dessert and Phil paid the tab, as promised. He left a twenty on the table for the waitress.

Phil eased the Audi back to the American where Jake's pickup was parked in the alley behind the bar, not far from the grease stain that had been the music agent from Milwaukee. Murder victim number four.

They all man-hugged, half handshake half chest bump, and Jake got in his truck and started the engine. The NPR station was on the radio. He shut it off. He watched the Audi do a three-point turn and gun out of the alley in his rear view mirror. He took a deep breath and rolled down his window to exhale. He knew he was still too drunk to drive but didn't know what he could do about it, and not sure he cared.

He took the couple turns through downtown onto Old 66 and drove the speed limit up the mountain to his trailer. He collapsed into his tent wondering what the hell just happened.

FORTY-THREE

Pinon, Arizona — December 27, 2003

The man with the shaved head paces in the one bedroom apartment. The carpet is just a thin film over floor boards, a series of ruts and rows mere millimeters high, fraying, leaving little balls of fuzz and fibrous long strands like kinked hair stuck to a dying skull. His feet are bare. People here do not take off their shoes when they enter a home. He will never get used to that.

Cold air rushes in under the door and stings his feet. His toes are numb. He has laid a towel on the floor to plug the gap, but still the cold comes in. He paces with his hands behind his back and stops in front of the large front window. The sky is overcast, diffusely bright, and he squints at the washed out landscape. Snow flakes fall slowly from the sky and are whipped by the wind as they reach ground, pushed into the ripples in the earth, sluiced, caught in eddies around the rusty playground equipment in the center courtyard of the two story Section 8 housing project.

He watches a smattering of birds peck at the ground. They have wide scooped beaks, like long upside down shovels jutting off of their heads. Quail, he thinks. He's been reading. That's all there is to do. There is a TV sitting on a cardboard box in the corner of the living room but it doesn't get any channels. Sometimes he leaves the static on for light. His family has not arrived. He has not heard from them at all. He used to think compulsively about them, about his children, but he knows now. Now he wills himself not to think about them. He knows. When the wind gusts the quail hop to a different spot, ruffle their feathers, and peck at the ground some more, their heads clicking. Hop and peck. Peck and hop.

The government cheese has run out. It did not come this month. There is little to eat. Only the provisions Bradley brings every two weeks. And that is not food. Boxes of neon orange macaroni and cheese and styrofoam Ramen noodles. Cans of soup and Chef Boyardee ravioli and spaghetti and meatballs. Chile con carne. Something called Hamburger Helper, but with no hamburger. Sugar frosted cereal with a grinning cartoon tiger on the box. Cheez-Its. It is processed carbohydrates, salt, and fat pressed into various shapes. His stomach often cramps. Toilet paper is a problem. He uses newspaper and anything else he can find. Sometimes there is nothing he can do but wash himself with his hand in the shower. The cheap molded plastic floor of the shower dents and buckles under his feet. He has to stoop to get under the lime crusted shower head. He wonders what will happen when the shower stall cracks and springs a leak.

His feet are cold. He thinks about putting on socks but they have dried into hardened casts where he has hung them in the bathroom after washing them in the sink and he believes they will give him little relief. He paces again to the large front window and looks out. It is a strange town. It reminds him of a refugee camp. The streets are unpaved and haphazard. There are no businesses. Up the hill, at the entrance to the town, there is a large supermarket, a video rental store, and a gas station, but once you enter the town there are no stores of any kind.

There are a few pre-fabricated government buildings of some type. He knows because of the flags that fly out front. And there is a small library housed in a singlewide trailer run by Jesuits. Many people go to the library. But no one talks to the Jesuits. He walks to the library every day. All he does is read now. That is all there is to do. He is allowed to take home up to ten books at a time. He does not read English well. He is drawn to books with pictures. Books on plants and animals and natural landscapes with large, full page photographs. Books on the American West. Guide books. There is a book with black and white photos of America's National Parks that he renews every time it is due. The library has a large section on Native American history and he uses those books to practice his reading. He struggles with terms like manifest destiny, tribal sovereignty, and domestic dependent nation, but his reading is improving.

There is a knock at the door. It is a hollow sound. At first, he doesn't move. He is not expecting anyone. There is no one to expect. He has learned this. The knock comes again, louder. He resigns himself to inevitability. There is nowhere to run or hide out here, even if he still had the will.

The man at the door has a mohawk, narrow face and small eyes. His hands are buried in the pockets of a green army surplus jacket, Vietnam era. Little rice-like snowflakes blow past the man's boots onto the thin carpet. The mohawk sidesteps around the man with the shaved head and comes inside. He quickly walks the apartment, checking the kitchen and then poking his head into the bathroom and the bedroom and the small closet. The man with the shaved head shuts the door to keep out the cold. He does not feel particularly violated by this stranger's sudden intrusion for he does not truly think of the apartment as his home. It is just the place where he sleeps. Where he waits.

The mohawk walks to the large front window and peers as far as he can in either direction. When he is satisfied, he sits down in the center of the room, cross-legged on the floor. The man with the shaved head also sits down cross-legged so the two men are facing each other. The mohawk takes his hand out of the deep recesses of his jacket pocket. He holds a glass pipe. He lights the bottom with a lighter, brings the pipe to his lips, and rotates the bowl. White smoke blooms in the bowl and he inhales and then exhales it out into the room. The other man watches him. The two men watch each other. After a time the mohawk reclines back onto his elbows. He looks out the window, disinterested this time. Neither man has spoken.

The day grows dark. Shadows reach across the floor. Sometimes the mohawk appears to be sleeping. But he is not. The man with the shaved head realizes that he has seen the mohawk before. The two men have never spoken but he has noticed him before, on his walks to the library and the few times he has ventured up the hill to the supermarket to look at the food he cannot buy. Something searching about the mohawk. He is a man who scans faces.

The man with the shaved head speaks first. It has been hours. He does not know how this will end. If the mohawk will leave. If he should go to his bed and leave this man siting cross-legged on the floor. What will happen next. So, he speaks. He makes some grating, inconsistent sounds. His English has grown somehow worse, with no one to talk to. While his reading has improved, his speech has atrophied. He switches back to his native tongue to regain the rhythm of language. The mohawk rises back to a sitting position. His eyes seem to focus. He lights the pipe again, the flame casting orange on the walls. With an audience the man with the shaved head tries again to speak in English. He tries basic questions and pleasantries he learned long ago, but the mohawk shows no sign of reciprocating. He just stares at him blankly. His niceties left stillborn in the gap between them, the man with the shaved head returns to silence. The shadows are subsumed by the darkness of night. The front window is black. The two men can barely see each other. The man with the shaved head does not know what will happen. When this will end.

The mohawk's eyes glint like coal in moonlight. He is still awake. It feels as if time has slipped, but they are both still there, sitting on the floor. The man with the shaved head gathers himself and begins to speak again. This time he speaks slowly, with no intention of having a conversation. He tells the mohawk what he has learned from his books. The history of native peoples in this country. Not his country, but nonetheless, this is what he learned. What he knows. He starts from the beginning. He starts with Conquest. When he gets to the end, to the present, he starts again from the beginning. Occasionally the pipe sparks. That is how the man knows the mohawk is still there. They sit in darkness. He starts again from the beginning and ends again at the present. Dawn lightens the eastern sky to pale blue. Finally, the mohawk speaks.

"Is infinity real?"

"Yes."

"But how? How is there infinite space and time? Where the universe ends, how is there another one on the other side? And another after that, forever. It is against all human knowledge."

"Infinity is part of nature…it is against human understanding...but it is so."

"And the Holy People? The Holy People live forever, and the Earth People do not."

"Yes, the Holy People live forever, but we...we must die."

"Do not the Holy People go insane, living forever?"

"The Holy People...may be insane."

The mohawk nods. The pipe sparks and glows orange for an instant. Time passes. The room turns from soft blue, to white blue, to sharp yellow. There are large gaps in the blinds. They do not keep out light well. The mohawk speaks again.

"Were you sent here? To us?"

"Yes...I was...sent here...to this place. I did not choose."

"Are you a Shaman?"

FORTY-FOUR

The Navajo Nation — The Present

The tent was hot and humid, the inside coated by a film of condensation. Jake's head pounded, but strangely, not as bad as when he was drinking without a job. He crawled outside and judged from the sky that it was late afternoon. He had to be at the American in a couple of hours. It was Friday night. His shift started at six.

He washed himself off with ice cold well water and held his head under the spigot for as long as he could take it. He drank heavily from the spigot. He didn't know if the well water was safe to drink, but it was the only water he had. When his head had cleared a bit, he went inside the burnt out trailer and put last night's jeans back on, and his cowboy boots. He found a flannel shirt left over from college and ripped the sleeves off and put it on over a ribbed wife-beater undershirt. What would Aimee say if she could see me now, he laughed to himself.

He drove into town. As soon as he came off the mountain and into cell phone range his phone buzzed with a text message. It was from Cally.

Guess what? I'm getting my own place!!!!

He texted back, holding the steering wheel between his knees. Texting did not come naturally to him.

Cool.

Help me move?
When?
Sunday.
Sure, see you then.
 ;)

Jake squinted at his phone and tried to decipher what that meant. Then he got it. He spent another minute trying to decide if proper texting etiquette required a response, and decided that it did not. He rolled into town at dusk and parked in the alley behind the American at 5:30. Phil was behind the bar.

"What's up, Tex? Nice shirt."

"What, I'm trying to blend."

"Good luck, but we don't blend, son. You work at the American now. Just how it is."

Jake looked down at his getup. "Okay. Keep that in mind."

Phil poured out two shots of chilled Stoli O and they clinked shot glasses and then tapped the bar and bottomed up. The bar sold frozen Tombstone pizzas for eight dollars that cost two-fifty in bulk at Costco. Jake made himself one and took the stool at the corner of the bar. Phil poured him a tap beer and Jake ate and waited for his shift to start.

Regulars filtered in, pool players, and roughnecks getting off from their shifts in the fracking fields. At nine, a new bartender joined Phil behind the bar. Brad was a scruffy dude with salt and pepper hair who walked with a limp from an old injury he'd suffered from his time on a fishing boat in Alaska. He shook Jake's hand but eyed him suspiciously, although he appeared to have a lazy eye and maybe looked at everyone that way. Because it was Friday night, a waitress also came on at nine, a young girl named Stara with tattoos and dirty blond dreadlocks. She followed closely behind Brad. She introduced herself to Jake with a tight hug. She wore bib overalls with a Misfits T-shirt underneath, and it was impossible to tell whether she had a nice figure or not, but Jake guessed that she did. Phil poured four shots of Stoli O from the shaker. Brad made sure to stare at each of them with his crazy eye as if this was a solemn act, some sort of death pact. Jake thought he looked like a ship captain not quite past his prime, about to hunt the white whale.

Friday night was busy and the four of them worked non-stop, meeting often at the bar, communicating through a series of hand signals and head nods across the room when someone decided it was time for a shot. Chuck appeared for a couple of hours but spent most of the time in the office with the door locked. When Chuck was on the floor he sat at the corner of the bar and eyed staff and customer alike with contemptuous, bloodshot eyes. He left before midnight, skulking past Jake without acknowledging him.

Just before last call Phil came out from behind the bar and tapped Jake on the shoulder.

"Left something for you, in the office, under the rolodex."

Jake looked puzzled for a moment. Phil wiped his nose.

"Go. Now. Office. I'll watch the door for a minute."

Jake shrugged. The office was off of a cinderblock corridor on the way to the back alley guarded by a flimsy plywood door. It was a small room lit by a dingy yellow light bulb, only big enough for a desk, shelving with scant office supplies, and a square safe sitting on the concrete floor. Jake found the rolodex on the desk. He lifted it up. Underneath it was a small line of white crystals. Jake had never done hard drugs of any kind, but he'd grown up on TV and movies like anyone else. He took a dollar bill out of his wallet and rolled it up, held one nostril shut, and snorted the line. This was the way in. The way to go deeper undercover than the FBI would have ever let him.

The line he snorted burned more than he thought it should, more than it looked in the movies. He reeled, trying to figure out what was happening in his body, but then decided he didn't have time, Phil was watching the door, and it was last call. He flew out of the office and gained his stool by the door without remembering how. Phil gave only the slightest of grins and joined Brad back behind the bar.

Last call was a blur. The drunkards were ushered out, the doors locked, the glasses collected, mats pulled, ashtrays cleaned, pool tables swept, cues racked, beer signs switched off, and bar stools set atop the bar. Jake was aware that there were more than the four employees still in the bar—Brad, Phil, and Stara had let some friends stay and drink after the doors were locked—but he didn't pay any attention to it, except for one guy with a shaved head that he thought was looking at him too much, except Jake wasn't really sure because he wasn't looking anybody in the eye, not now—but what really consumed him was the Steely Dan playing on the juke box and who would play so much Steely Dan? Definitely wasn't Phil. Wasn't the guy with the shaved head. Must be Brad, or maybe Stara? But she seemed too young for Steely Dan. They should have all been too young for Steely Dan. Even Brad, who had an old presence but in reality probably wasn't over forty.

Jake played pool, badly, and lost most of the seventy bucks Phil and Brad had tipped him out. He sipped a beer, awkwardly, his swallowing mechanism wasn't functioning properly, and found Stara at his side.

"You okay?" she asked, her hand patting his back in a soothing motion.

"Yeah, I think so. Some strong coke huh?"

"Uh, that wasn't blow, that was meth."

"Shit."

"You snorted it?"

Jake nodded.

"All of it?"

Jake nodded again.

"Damn, that wasn't a nice thing to do. You should have smoked some, saved some. You'll be up for two days."

Jake shook his head and suddenly felt the room close in. It was dark with the neon beer lights shut off. The room was only lit by the overhead pool table lights and he couldn't make out the faces of the strangers in the bar. He needed to leave. Before he did, he eyed Phil nudging Brad with his elbow.

"He's buggin."

Brad screwed a trucker cap down low over his eyes.

"Yup, new guy's grippin' hardcore."

Jake pinballed off of the cinderblock corridor to the back alley and shouldered open the heavy firesafe door. Outside, the stars in the black night sky spun like a kaleidoscope. He felt with his key for the keyhole in the door of his truck until the jagged edge entered the slot, a rude penetration. He climbed inside and ran his hands lightly over the steering wheel, trying to control his heart rate with no success. He started the truck, afraid of its power. He drove through town dangerously below the speed limit, checking the rear view mirrors as often as he checked the road ahead. When he gained the mountains he breathed as much as of a sigh of relief as he could— his breaths were so rapid and shallow there wasn't much relief in an exhalation.

The sky was beginning to lighten when he reached the dirt road to his trailer. He didn't even attempt to sleep. He stripped naked and paced the trailer for most of the following day, paranoid, checking the windows every few minutes with his gun at his side. He tried to come down by drinking Jim Beam out of the bottle. As the whiskey took hold he gained his senses enough to realize that he needed to stay hydrated, and he made frequent furtive trips to the well spigot to drink and wash some of the sweat from his body. He could smell his own stink.

Night fell and he watched the sunset in the lawn chair looking out over the hundred mile view with the bottle of whiskey in his lap. He was grateful that he had the night off from working at the American. He couldn't work or even be seen in public. He wondered why anybody ever did meth. It was one of the worst experiences of his life.

FORTY-FIVE

At some point during the night, whiskey and Tylenol PM put him down. He woke Sunday morning and was relieved to feel vaguely like himself again. He hadn't eaten since the Tombstone pizza on Friday before his shift. He washed himself with a rag outside in the sunshine and the breeze. The ice cold water felt surprisingly good. He drove into town feeling somewhat reborn. He had survived.

He ate at Bill's Diner, glad no one from the American was there. As he pushed a slice of wheat toast around his plate to sop up the last of the runny yolks from his three eggs over easy, his phone vibrated with a text.

Are you ready?

It was Cally's number. Jake stared at the phone trying to figure out what he was supposed to be ready for. As if she heard him thinking, as if she knew he'd seen the text and was thinking, the phone buzzed again.

To help me move?
Jake immediately texted back.
Be there in 15.
;)

There is was again, that damn symbol. He thought it was cute, but it also unsettled him. It was too cute.

He left a ten dollar tip on the eight dollar tab, feeling it was expected of him now that he was seen as one of the American's crew. He drove the F-150 the six blocks to Cally's mom's house and parked behind Cally's old Nissan Sentra. The screen door banged open and Cally bounced down the porch stairs with her ponytail swinging and hugged Jake, barely able to contain her excitement.

"Ew, you're a little ripe." She relaxed her grip on him and looked him in the eye.

"Yeah, I know. Been a long couple of days." He smiled at her sheepishly.

"Just glad you're here with the pickup."

"Oh, so you're using me for my truck?"

"Yeah, and other things."

She turned the backside of her boy shorts to him and skipped back up the stairs into the house. Jake followed her inside, trying not to stare at her ass. It was dark inside the house and boxes were stacked in the living room. Cally's mother sat at the dining room table where they'd eaten dove, with a glass of Chablis in her hand. The leaf had been removed and the table was smaller now. Jake hadn't pegged Miriam as a day drinker. It dawned on him then that this was a big day in their lives. Perhaps one of the biggest.

"Ma'am."

"Jake."

She carefully set the glass of white wine down on the table. The shades were drawn and the room was dim, but the table still gleamed and smelled of lemon Pledge. Cally took a box and started loading up the truck. Jake picked up a box and was carrying it out the door when he felt Miriam's hand on his arm.

She didn't grab him, she just laid her palm gently on his bicep.

"Jake, I know you think you're a good guy. But what you think doesn't matter. If you hurt her, I will kill you."

FORTY-SIX

Jake worked the door at the American the nine to close shift Monday, Tuesday, and Wednesday, and the six to close shift on Thursday night. Each night he crept into Cally's apartment as the sky lavendered and fit his body next to hers under the sheets of her futon and relished the smell of her hair as he draped his arm around her sleeping body and closed his eyes. Each day she was gone before he woke up, working her day shifts at the Copper Street Pub.

Friday night he worked the door six to close with Phil, Max, Stara, and a second waitress named Sadie. Sadie was a rail thin blond with tattooed arm sleeves and a giant eagle tattoo across her back that seemed to flap its wings when she flexed her boney shoulder blades. He saw the look in her eyes and knew she was high on meth. He thought if he was ever going to do meth again, it would be tonight. He was on his fifth night in a row of working, playing the butt sniffing game with roughnecks and brawlers, and doing quarter-hour shots of Stoli O. The nights were blending together. So were the drunks. By midnight he was craving clarity. The kind that hard drugs gave, overruling alcohol, tiredness, boredom, hunger, conscience.

Friday night was hopping. It was three deep at the bar. Phil and Max slang drinks on cruise control, the beer spilling out over pint glasses with the chrome tap buried to the hilt, the liquor poured high and splashing out of the shot glass lined up like so many shallow bedpans. Jake's back hurt from hours on the barstool. Sadie brushed past him like a ghost in cheap perfume. He followed her to the bar where Max slid them two shots of vodka. Jake turned and Sadie was gone, slipped through the crowd back to her tables, and was replaced by Stara.

"My turn."

An innocent smile between the dreadlocks. Or maybe just honest. They did a shot of Stoli O with Phil who worked fast but never looked hurried.

"Good night. The yokels are paying. The drunks have cash. Must be the beginning of the month."

"I have no idea." Jake's vision blurred. Neon and bar lights shone off of sweaty faces. "Phil, you got anything?"

Phil got up close into Jake's face with a grin. "No, dude. That girl Sadie does though."

Jake pushed his way through bodies back to man his barstool by the door. Sadie came by with a tray full of Bud longnecks. He pulled her to him with a finger in her skirt hem.

"You got anything."

"Meet me in the walk-in."

Ten minutes later Jake lifted the handle and pushed open the heavy steel door to the walk-in cooler. Sadie had a glass pipe. Jake handed her the dead girl's blowtorch lighter. Her skinny arms shook. She lit the base of the pipe and rotated it for him as he pulled hard. He exhaled white smoke.

When Jake emerged from the walk-in Kid Rock's "Prodigal Son" was hammering full volume on the juke box. It was last call and he pushed people to the door. Anyone who caught his eyes moved out of the way. He cleared the bar and locked the door except for a half dozen people he'd never seen before that Phil and Max said could stay after hours. The only one he recognized was Squirm, who was trying to coax a drunk Indian into a game of nine-ball, the Indian in a faded black leather jacket wavering like a sapling in the wind.

It had been a good night and Phil counted the till, changed out tips, and did the deposit as Jake pulled the mats and cleaned the bar in a blur. Max made a Tombstone pizza. Those chosen to stay past closing time played pool and drank as the jukebox was loaded with dollars. Stara sat at the bar with a joint. She tried to hand it to Jake, but he waved it away. He wasn't interested in weed. He looked for Sadie, but she was gone.

Jake started drinking hard. He tried to join the one dollar / two dollar game of Texas hold'em at the end of the bar but he was too hopped up from the meth to sit still with the focus and patience the game required. Phil was dealing the cards with a stack of dollar bills on the bar in front of him. When the hand was done Jake waved him over to the office.

"Phil, do you know where to get some shit."

"Man, you're bad off, aren't you."

"Just been a long week, the nights are piling up," Jake shrugged.

"My connections are dry right now. But I know a place we can go. It's kind of a last resort though. Don't like to go out there myself."

Jake feigned thought, as if he was mulling over whether to go or not. But there was no decision. He'd had a taste. He knew coming down would be a bitch, but he needed more. At least tonight he did.

"Let's go."

By four in the morning they'd gotten everyone out of the bar and Phil and Jake were cruising north on State Route 491, past Ft. Defiance and Window Rock, until the highway straightened and Phil gunned the Audi up to 80 mph. Red rock mountains with green forests higher up loomed somewhere to the east, unseen in the darkness, but a presence to be felt nonetheless. To the west, open desert ran to the canyon lands and the old gods. The darkness closed in on the car and limited their world to just the scarred and weed grown highway. Yet, Jake felt like the journey was familiar, like he was experiencing déjà vu. Reality was intermittent, like the faded yellow center line running underneath the Audi at impossible speed.

After a time they turned left off the highway onto a dirt road. The night was moonless but Jake could still make out Shiprock by the black space without stars in the shape of a monolith. After a mile, Phil turned onto a jeep trail, the Audi bouncing and bottoming out. Jake got a sick feeling in his stomach. Sand scraped the underside of the car as Phil parked in front of a doublewide trailer, one Jake was well acquainted with.

FORTY-SEVEN

Phil told Jake to wait in the car while he went inside to score. The night was deathly still and quiet. Jake heard every footstep as Phil walked to the front door and knocked. The windows were covered from the inside with tin foil so the house looked completely dark. The door opened a crack exposing a shaft of light. There were clearly people awake inside. He doubted they ever slept.

He watched Phil disappear inside. He tried to keep his hands from twitching. As his eyes adjusted to the night he could make out the hole in the wooden fence where a shotgun blast had almost taken his head off. As the seconds ticked by and turned into minutes, he was worried something had gone wrong. He worried for Phil. He knew in his guts that this was an epicenter of evil, that the psychopaths who burned people alive were somehow connected to this place, but he didn't know how or why. He knew it had something to do with meth. His own soul had already been tainted, darkened. And he knew he wouldn't stop. Not now. Not yet.

The wait was excruciating. He rolled down the window and felt the cool air and listened to the night noises, the thorny knotted tangle of grasses and pebbled sands pushed about by the wind, the crickets and cicadas, the groaning of cactus.

The night's darkness was thick. He could barely make out the house, as if it had receded into the red cliff walls. Part of his brain told him that was impossible since the car hadn't moved. He squinted and the house reappeared. His vision was blurred. He wondered if meth did that to you, or the lack of meth. His fevered mind wanted another hit.

And then the door opened to a golden shaft of light and the sound of clinking bottles and people talking and Phil was shuffling back to the car, no more hurried or anxious than a trip back from the corner store. Phil held out two tiny zip lock baggies with a few millimeters of white crystals at the bottom.

"One for you, one for me." He handed one of the baggies to Jake.

"Thanks, what do I owe you?"

"Twenty."

Jake took a twenty dollar bill out of his wallet and gave it to Phil. He put the baggie in the coin pocket of his jeans.

"I didn't know it was so cheap."

"Why do you think everyone around here does it. You want to take a hit now?"

"No, I'll wait until I get home."

"Oh, you're one of those, huh? Do your shit alone, probably like to get all freaky and shit."

"No, I'm just getting a little paranoid out here."

"Shit, next you'll be seeing the Shadow People."

"Who are they?"

"Not who, what. They're the people you see out of the corner of your eye but when you look, they're gone. You haven't heard the tweakers talk—they can only be vanquished by fire and shit? I don't really believe it, but I was raised Catholic, so I know all about the devil. That shit can be real, so why not the Shadow

People? Maybe they're demons."

"Maybe we're demons."

"Speak for yourself." Phil started up the Audi and wheeled it around with one hand until the front heavy nose pointed toward Shiprock. He took the jeep trail going back faster this time.

"Maybe they're skinwalkers."

Phil laughed, his cheeks shiny green in the dashboard lights. "Now you're getting it."

FORTY-EIGHT

Judgement is the first human trait to go when one undergoes the transformation into a skinwalker. If not judgement, certainly restraint. Judgement may still be there, like a TV on mute, but it loses its weight, its importance. Its meaning. Jake knew what he was about to do was wrong. He just couldn't control himself. Not after that white smoke hit his lungs.

He left his truck at the American and walked the ten blocks to Cally's one bedroom apartment on Lead Street. The stars were beginning to fade into a periwinkle sky. He couldn't feel the cold.

Her apartment was a small adobe with a garden in the yard and a chair swing on the front porch. It already had her touches, a ladybug door knocker, potted tomato plant, mailbox painted with sunflowers. He went inside, letting his eyes adjust. The light was blue. The floor boards creaking loudly. He hunched over a coffee table and emptied his twenty sack onto a copy of US Weekly. Cally watched him from the doorway to the bedroom. She wore only a T-shirt that ended at her thighs. Her legs were long and smooth in the otherworldly pale morning light. Her hair looked white. He loaded a glass pipe and slowly drew a hit. It hit him in his chest and groin and spread out to his extremities. She said nothing.

He rose slowly and crossed the room until he was standing right in front of her, so close he could feel his molecules ionize and strain against his skin, drawn to her form. He put the pipe to her lips and she drew in a breath. She exhaled and gripped the door frame. She let out a low hum, a quiet moan, and let her head drop onto his shoulder. She inched closer to him until her nipples brushed against his chest through the thin fabric of her worn T-shirt. He let his fingers trace a path down her arm to her hip and thigh. He sunk to his knees and wrapped his arms around her legs, soft and firm at the same time. He ran his hands down her calves and ankles and knelt, as if in prayer, and placed a kiss on each bare foot. Her toenails were painted yellow. He ran his thumb over each lacquered nail feeling the shape. She looked down at him and smiled. He rose until his mouth was next to hers and put his hand on her jawline. He let it drop to her neck and squeezed ever so slightly and she sucked in a breath and rocked back and forth involuntarily, her hair falling in her face, until his lips opened her mouth and they kissed deeply, pressing their bodies tightly together. It was their first kiss.

Her arms around his neck, he backed her into the bedroom until they fell on top of the futon. She looked at him with a mix of want and confusion. He lightly kissed her ear, running the curve from top to lobe, and then grazed her neck with soft kisses, getting lost in the nape of her neck, getting lost in her smell, the supple taughtness of her skin, and let his mouth explore every part of her. He wanted to eat her, devour her. He laid his full weight on her. She clawed at him, drawing him in and wanting to hurt him. She smelled like peaches.

FORTY-NINE

They were up for two days and nights fucking and smoking and when the twenty sack was gone and the glass bowl cooked until no chemical fumes were left, Jake took to drinking Jim Beam and Cally locked herself in her bedroom pacing and cursing at herself and picking at her cuticles. She'd missed work. Not even called in. She'd never done that before. She wrapped herself in a blanket and thought about cutting herself. She wasn't a cutter, but she now understood why some people did it. How the act of cutting her own flesh might change things. Might cut through the fog. Might bring clarity. Might bring her back to herself.

When she finally came out of the bedroom and joined Jake on the living room floor she had dark circles under her eyes and looked much older than nineteen. He handed her the bottle and she took a pull. She let him hold her.

"I'm so sorry."

"I'm a big girl."

"You are now." He smiled.

"Shut up, asshole." She elbowed him in the ribs. "You think I've never done that before?"

"You've done *that* before?"

"Well, not like *that*."

"I don't think anyone's ever done *that* before."

"It was pretty spectacular."

"It was crazy."

"You're crazy."

"I know."

"I don't want someone crazy."

"I know."

"I missed work and I didn't even call in. That's not me."

"I know."

"I guess we're just like everybody else around here now."

"We are not."

She looked at him. Her eyes were green-grey in the dawn light. "Okay. I want to be alone now."

"Okay."

Jake walked back to the American to get his truck. He was sore all over his body. He didn't know if was from the marathon sex or severe dehydration and mineral depletion. They hadn't eaten a thing during the bender, but he wasn't hungry. He drove up the mountain to his trailer, grateful for every second he wasn't pulled over. He hadn't been back to the burnt out trailer in a week, and he was struck by the devastation. How did he lose so much so fast? It wasn't funny anymore.

The smell of rain was in the air. The wind gusted and a flap from one of the trailer's remaining walls had come loose and torn a hole in his tent. It took half a roll of duct tape to repair. He took a lukewarm beer out of the non-functioning fridge and brought it out to the lawn chair and the hundred mile view. He noticed a voicemail on his phone that must have recorded when he was in town, sometime during the last three days. Or maybe the last week. He'd stopped checking for emails and voicemails at some point, he wasn't sure when. His fantasy baseball team had been left rudderless, abandoned, and was probably mutinying. The voicemail was from Aimee, wanting to know why he hadn't signed the divorce papers yet. She wanted to see him when she came to town for the Pow Wow. He deleted it. He looked out over a darkening sky. The wind blew hard. He lit a cigarette and watched lightning strike the valley below.

FIFTY

Fall turned quickly to winter that year. The smell of mesquite from wood fires hovering over the old pueblos and reservation towns, the cold wind rattling the mobile homes and loose window panes in Section 8 housing and slicing through thread bare clothes. Across the Big Reservation the sheep skin parkas, wool blankets, and Raiders jackets with oversized hoods came out and stayed out until spring.

Jake woke one morning to a layer of frost on his tent. He shook off the chill with a hit from the glass pipe and went out into the woods to gather firewood. He picked yellowed grass and twigs kept dry by the low boughs from the young pines near the trailer to use for kindling. He cleared a space next to the tent in front of where the plexiglass door used to be and set about building a fire. He balled up some toilet paper, set the kindling on top of it, and propped up the sticks he'd gathered in a tee-pee formation. He lit the toilet paper and watched the dry grass contort and crinkle and the smoke begin to rise. He crouched next to the fire with his hands outstretched, trying to get feeling back in his fingers, numb from the cold. He imagined he looked like a caveman, or a particularly unskilled settler from the nineteenth century, waiting to be attacked by Indians.

He put a frying pan over the fire and attempted to crack

open two eggs but they'd frozen during the night, the insides a yellow crystallized paste. One of the eggs had a red blotch the size of a marble in the yolk, a little chicken fetus. The Navajos would think it was another sign, a bad one. Jake scooped out the slushy goop with his finger, flicked into the frying pan, and watched it sizzle.

After he ate and dressed he started his truck and blasted the heat. His passenger side window had been smashed weeks ago, Jake didn't know by who. He had yet to replace it. The cold wind whistled through the cab as he drove down off the mountain. Coming into town he was struck by how different everything looked to him now, how different the town felt before. He'd been working at the American for almost three months, and when he saw people he saw them as their petty crimes, the drugs they did, their schemes and hustles, or their drudgery. Everyone in town knew he ran with the crew at the American, and everywhere they went they got hooked up—free drinks, free tickets, the best tables. They all tipped well and were remembered. But Jake knew deep down they weren't really liked. In that way, maybe it wasn't that different from being an FBI agent.

Jake parked his truck in the alley behind the bar and took a hit off the pipe. He got out and faced the cold wind. It felt good. The cold cleared the mind he was continually clouding. He took another hit off the pipe and went to work.

FIFTY-ONE

The man with the shaved head walks along the shoulder of the road and onto a dirt turn out where a van is parked. His gait is slow, languid. He is in no hurry. When he reaches the van a skinny kid in a tank top and jeans opens the cargo doors and smoke billows out. Three smoldering bodies lie on the floor of the van, bound and gagged. One is clearly a corpse, the other two wriggle and scream under their gags. Their skin is charred black. They are bald, their scalps bubble. He lowers the gag on one of the survivors and the person, it is impossible to tell anymore if it is a man or a woman, immediately begins ranting in Spanish—"we will cut off your balls and stuff them down your throat—have you seen the videos on the internet of what the Sinaloa cartel does to people like you? You'll be famous—your soldiers will puke and beg to join us when they see what we will do to you."

The Shaman crouches down and puts his lips to its burnt ear and whispers. "We are very similar, me and you, but you haven't seen what I've seen."

He walks back to the road where a new Dodge Ram is idling on the shoulder. He returns carrying a tool box with the same slow, methodical walk, heel to toe in his cowboy boots. All the time in the world. He sets down the heavy tool box inside the back of the van and groans a little as he ducks inside, his arthritis acting up, his joints never quite the same after that first cold winter on the reservation.

He checks to see if the burnt thing is still alive. It is. He leans in close so it can hear.

"Nail gun or power drill? We are quite skilled with both."

FIFTY-TWO

The nights were one long night. That's how it felt in the bar. Especially in the short dark days of winter. When the metal door shut, time stopped. Like a purgatory, one with beer, music, and pool.

Jake was bartending. He hardly ever worked the door anymore. It was Calcutta night at the American. The bar sponsored a pool tournament and the staff as well as some locals bid on the players and took a share of the purse if their player won. There were sixteen entrants, half were locals with virtually no chance to win, and Max bought them all for a dollar a piece. There were a few local hustlers and a couple of old guys who knew their way around the pool table that went for up to ten bucks each. Phil put a twenty on an out-of-town hustler because the guy wore a black Stetson and a silver bolo tie. Jake bought Squirm for fifteen dollars.

Squirm blanked a retired postal worker five games to none, who Stara had bet on because she liked his beard, and continued to cruise through the early rounds. Brad played in the tournament and had bet on himself for five bucks. He limped around the table glaring at the competition, leaning low on the felt, chalking his cue with anger and vengeance. He took a shot of Stoli O with Jake after each round. He lost in the semi-finals to a local kid who wasn't even old enough to drink, but was let in to play pool because he was something of a nine-ball prodigy, and Chuck thought he could train the boy to be a professional someday, or at least a half-decent hustler.

Squirm and the Stetson made it to the final round, a best of seven. A crowd of thirty or so ringed the pool table, and Chuck played "Eye of the Tiger" on the jukebox to build the drama, but before the match began Squirm shot up in the bathroom and came out barely conscious, leaning on his enamel inlaid pool cue like a walking stick. He scratched on the break and nearly nodded off on the pool table and the crowd booed and threw their drinks at him. He laid down under the table and went to sleep.

"Yeah bitches," Phil pounded fists with the stranger in the Stetson. They split the five hundred dollar prize.

Disgusted, Jake went out back to break down beer and liquor boxes. He stacked the flattened cardboard and filled a recycle bin. As he turned to leave he noticed a figure in a dark hoodie hunched in a stairwell across the alley. He waited a moment and then saw a spark and the glow of glass. Jake approached cautiously.

"You holding?"

The hood covered the man's eyes but a dingy toothed smile cut through the murky darkness. "Trade you head for a hit."

"What? No...Jesus fucking Christ!" Jake stomped off to the sound of laughter echoing through the alley. Back inside he was struck by the warmth and the dank smell of mungy carpet and stale cigarette smoke. The air felt thick, humid. The walls were sweating.

A man with a shaved head sat at the end of the bar. Jake took

191

a shot of vodka by himself and washed some glasses in the sink. He felt the man watching him. Jake went to the far corner of the bar and lit a cigarette. Phil and Stara made their way over to say a few words to the man. Jake noticed that everyone in the bar either steered clear of the man or gave him some kind of acknowledgement. Everyone. Something about the man reminded him of the mohawk man he'd shot and killed and lost his job over. The man bent forward with his head low on the bar and stared through his whiskey right at Jake. That's not why I lost my job, he thought. I lost it because Mitch is a douche. He took a long drag and stared back at the man. That's not why I lost my job, he thought. I lost it because I lied. The man drank his whiskey in one slow smooth swallow and then tapped his empty shot glass on the bar. Jake ignored him. That's not why I lost my job, he thought. I lost it because I had to. The man slammed his shot glass down harder, so hard customers turned their heads. That's not why I lost my job. I lost it because I wanted to. To become this. Phil, Brad, Max, even Stara looked over at Jake tending bar, waiting for him to serve the man. Jake snuffed out his cigarette slowly, deliberately. He blew smoke out his nose as he walked down the bar and stood in front of the man. The man tightened his grip on his empty shot glass. He looked coldly at Jake. Flecks of red in otherwise brown, almond shaped eyes. Jake waited for the man to speak first. He could feel the contempt. It felt good.

"Shot."

"Of?"

"Jack."

Jake pulled a bottle of Jack Daniels out of the well and filled the shot glass in the man's hand to the rim until the meniscus broke and wet the webbing between the man's thumb and forefinger. The man looked down at the honey colored liquor and when he looked up the redness seemed to have spread to the whites of his eyes. He looked about ready to bleed tears.

"How is your girl?"

Jake suppressed a sudden urge to smack him in the mouth.

"None of your business."

"Maybe it is."

"She's just a college kid. She better not be your business."

"Not that one. The federal agent."

"What about her?"

"She's done well for herself, I hear. They say she is a big star in Washington, D.C. A rising star."

The man smiled. His words slithered. As much as Jake's impulse control was shattered, the urge to break the man's face was tempered by fascination. His skin was the color of sand. His appearance seemed to be shifting, like dunes blown by the wind. It was a weird affect. Jake couldn't put his finger on what he was seeing. On what was real.

"I wouldn't know about that."

"It is good. I like for the local girls to do well. But she should not come back to the reservation."

"Why not."

"Because she is not like us, is she?"

Jake cocked his head. Who is this guy? What is he?

"Like us." The man turned up his palm revealing a small baggie of crystal meth. The bag seemed to slide across the bar toward Jake. "Do what is right."

Jake went to palm the baggie, but as he did the man grabbed his hand in an unnaturally quick motion. "Do it here. Now."

Jake stared at him. "Here?"

"Here."

"Or I don't get it?"

"Or you don't get anything. Ever."

Jake tapped a pile of white crystals out onto the bar. He took a straw from the bar set-up that also held the napkins, coasters, and stir sticks. He took the paper wrapping off of the straw and cut the straw in half with the knife that he used to cut limes. He could feel the patrons watching him. The pool tables had gone quiet. He glared around the room and everyone looked away. He held one nostril shut and snorted up the little mound of white on the bar.

"I said Goddamn!"

Jake rubbed his nose. The man laughed. Jake pinched his nostrils together and surveyed the bar, but no one would meet his gaze. They knew the American had hit a new low. They all had.

FIFTY-THREE

The bar cleared out unusually early that night. Last call was a breeze. The mats were pulled, neon turned off, tables brushed, and the till counted and the bank deposit bag slipped into the safe by two-thirty. Jake was high as a kite.

It was just the staff. No after-hours guests. Stara begged off and slipped back to Brad's RV to fire up the propane heater and smoke a joint and bury herself under blankets until morning would bring new warmth. Phil, Brad, and Max sat with Jake drinking Pacificos and shots of Stoli O, looking forlorn, like they didn't want to be there but were afraid to leave.

"Hey, I know of a party," Jake said. His eyes were bloodshot and glassy.

"Any girls gonna be there?"

"I know of at least one."

"That's good enough for me," Max said. "Shit that's better than a lot of the parties in this town."

Jake took a bottle of Stoli O from the walk-in cooler and left forty dollars in the office to cover it. They locked the doors and headed out into the night. The cold air livened the senses and gave them a new energy. They bounded off each other like pinballs as they weaved down Lead Street. Jake stopped them in front of Cally's apartment. All the lights were out and it was quiet, the only sound came from the wind rushing down off the mesas, rattling the street signs and moaning in the trees.

"This don't look like no party."

"Don't worry, it will."

Jake knocked on the door. The boys crowded behind him, filling the small porch. After a minute a light came on in the back bedroom. A chain lock slid in its sleeve and a deadbolt clicked back and the door opened. Cally stood there in a nightshirt, a sleepy smile on her face, dismayed but not altogether surprised. Her legs were bare and she shivered in the cold. She surveyed the men and shook her head.

"Well, come on in."

Phil and Brad gave each other pissed off looks but Max burst through the door without hesitation and filled the small living room with his barrel chest and ear-to-ear smile and boisterous laugh. Cally texted her friends and soon Drake was on the stereo and there was a good group of girls partying. Cally sat on Jake's lap in the corner, passing the bottle of Stoli O with Phil and Brad as the big Samoan occupied the center of the room, sandwiched by two high school girls, twerking. They ignored the sweat pouring off him or just thought it was funny. Cally took a picture with her phone of Max rubbing his nipples as the two girls grinded on him, and sent it out on Instagram with the caption—*Bartenders from the American partying at my house!*—and by six a.m. there was a full fledged rager at her place.

The small house was packed with bodies dancing. Phil and Brad had left at some point, but Max was still the center of gravity, the kids circling him, drawn to him. Jake felt a young Navajo staring at him. The kid was thin with long braids and copper skin leaning in the doorway to the kitchen. Jake's skin itched. He struggled to suppress the urge to jump up and wrap his hands around the kid's slender neck and strangle the life out of him, smash his head into the cabinets and drag the limp, helpless body outside and slam it on the pavement. And then he realized the boy wasn't staring at him, he was staring at Cally. Jake couldn't blame him. She was gorgeous. He kissed her on her neck and picked her up and set her on the couch. She read his eyes.

"Go."

"I'll see you soon."

"I know."

Jake pushed his way outside feeling like he was about to puke. His hands shook as he lit a cigarette for the walk back to his truck parked at the American. It was cold inside the truck. The wind whipped through the broken window. He used his left hand to hold his right hand steady as he tried to fit the key into the ignition. The truck started and he exhaled his relief. Thank God for the little things. The little things were huge. Heat. Transportation. Freedom. The steering wheel was cold in his hands. He crept the truck through town, feeling lighter with every inch of Old 66 behind him. He gained the mountain and lit another cigarette, feeling the early morning sun on his face.

As he reached the top of the ridgeline he glanced in the rear view mirror and was startled to see a large pickup truck riding his ass. The chrome grill of a jacked-up Ford dually entirely filled the mirror. He could make out a black cowboy hat and mirrored aviator sunglasses. Bradley.

Jake took his foot off the gas, trying to figure out what the Navajo Tribal Police Chief was up to. As he did so a blue siren lit up the dually's dashboard. That fat fuck's pulling me over,

Jake said to himself. An impulse to jam the accelerator to the
floorboard momentarily flooded his mind until he seized control
of himself and eased the truck onto the shoulder.

Bradley got out of his truck and walked slowly up to the
driver's side window, his considerable belly riding a mammoth
silver and turquoise belt buckle like a bear on a tricycle. Jake
lowered the window.

"Hey, Chief, did I—"

"Get out."

Jake looked into the mirrored sunglasses and saw a greasy
scraggly bearded burnout looking back at him. It was his own
reflection. He barely recognized it. Then he noticed Bradley's
hand move to his sidearm and slide back the safety. Jake put his
hands high on the steering wheel where Bradley could see them.

"Take it easy."

"Get out."

Jake cautiously moved one hand to the door handle and
opened the door. He got one leg on the ground and was ducking
his head to get out of the truck when Bradley brought his fist
down on Jake's nose. Jake flew back into the open door and
Bradley punched him in the gut on the rebound, and then
unleashed a right cross that sent Jake sprawling to the asphalt.
Bradley kicked him in the ribs until he rolled off the road and
onto the dirt shoulder. Bradley crouched low with his hands
on his jeans as Jake coughed out a mouthful of blood.

"Your presence is no longer welcome on the reservation."

FIFTY-FOUR

Jake drew into the fetal position. He waited until he heard the cowboy boots clomp back down the pavement and the big dually fire up and drive away before he rolled over and pushed himself up to his knees. He lifted his head and looked at the cloudless blue sky. He felt something loose in his mouth and spat out a tooth.

He dusted himself off and drove back to his trailer. Yazzie's Tahoe was parked in front. Jake's head began to pound.

"Honey, I'm home!" Jake slammed the screen door behind him.

"I'm out here, sweetheart." Yazzie was drinking a beer in Jake's lawn chair behind the trailer. He wore a plaid shirt unbuttoned to the navel, taking in the sun. He handed Jake a beer. Jake popped it open and plopped down in the brittle yellow grass with his legs spread out before him like an old toothless bear that could no longer ride a tricycle.

"Jesus, you look worse than usual. Who's handy work?"

"You won't believe it. Your boss's."

"Bradley?"

"Yup. Pulled me over. We had a talk. Apparently, I am no longer welcome in the Navajo Nation."

"Strange. Bradley hasn't pulled anyone over in years."

"It was like he was waiting for me. Stopped me just as I got onto the rez."

"That sounds like solid police work. Not like Bradley. He just pushes paper these days."

"Good guys don't like me. Bad guys don't trust me."

"Who says the cops are the good guys."

Jake adjusted his jaw. He held the beer to his face and then drained it in a series of gulps, letting the foam run over his chin. Yazzie handed him another out of a twelve pack of Busch Light.

"Listen, I might need some equipment."

"I left my glass pipe at home."

"Very funny. I mean for the investigation."

"Investigation?"

"You don't think I'm doing all this for the fun of it, do you?"

Yazzie lowered his black Ray-Bans and looked hard at him. "No, it doesn't look like you're having fun, but with you, it is hard to tell. It's like that thing with your ex, it's like you enjoy the punishment."

"Speaking of, the king of the tweakers threatened her life if she comes back to the reservation."

"That so? I hear she'll be here next month. Coming for the Pow Wow."

"Really? Who told you that?"

"See, there you go. You like the punishment. You should not worry so much about who she talks to these days."

"Just concerned for her safety."

"You should be concerned for your own safety."

"Too late for that."

FIFTY-FIVE

Pain from a beating is different than other kinds of pain. The welts and bruises and swelling were placed there intentionally, and so too their continued existence are intentional, a lingering insult. Every time Jake touched his nose he saw the blow coming, and in his mind he dodged right and countered with an upper cut to Bradley's chin. But that's not what happened. Thoughts are malleable, the past is not.

He drank the rest of Yazzie's beer and used the ice from his cooler to calm the angry redness in his swollen nose and ease the ache of his blackened ribs. He was able to sleep. The meth he'd snorted at the bar should have kept him up for days but the beating and the beer had taken the fight out of him.

In the morning he woke up hungry, which was a good sign. He didn't have any food but he wasn't ready to go to town yet, to face people. He built a small fire, wrapped himself in his fetid sleeping back, and smoked cigarettes until midday. The radio in the F-150 said the high would be 56 degrees. Since it didn't look like it was getting any warmer, Jake bathed in the ice cold well water and dressed quickly by the fire.

At sunset he drove down the mountain and parked on a seldom used BLM road on the outskirts of town, but within cell range. He called the American.

"American."

"Max?"

"Yeah, this Jake?"

"Yeah."

"Good party the other night, dog."

"Yeah, was Cally alright? After I left, I mean."

"Dude, your girl is fine."

"She's not my girl."

"I saw with my own eyes, dog. You're crazy. You should lock that down or she won't be yours."

"Well, is she okay? I mean, did everyone leave her place okay?"

"Yeah, you know I wouldn't let anything happen to one of my people."

"She's one of your people?"

"You're one of my people. That makes her one of my people. You know this."

"Thanks. I was fucked up that night."

"Yeah you were. So was your girl."

"What do you mean?"

"She was smoking a little."

"Glass?"

"Shit yeah. Listen, I think Chuck wants to fire you over snorting crystal on the bar the other night, but he's afraid to cuz you were with the Shaman."

"I was?"

"Yeah, that dude who gave you the shit is the Shaman, man."

"No shit. Who the fuck is he?"

"He runs everything here. You probably get your shit from him, you just don't know it. Listen, I gotta go."

"Who are you working with tonight?"

"Brad. Phil's off."

"Cool, thanks. Later, Max."

"Late."

Jake lit a smoke and exhaled out the shattered window of the truck but a stiff breeze pushed the smoke back inside. Out the windshield waved a field of yellow grasses just sprout from the earth, clinging to it with baby hands, blown hard by the wind howling off the Chuskas. He revved the engine to get some more heat in the cab. He thought about Cally and felt a knot in his stomach. But it could have been splintered ribs. He wanted desperately to check in on Cally, but he needed to pump Phil for information, and since they both had the night off, he had to try. He dialed Phil's number. After seven rings a voice answered.

"Yeah."

"Phil, it's Jake."

"Hey Tony Montana. That's my new name for you now. You're a scarface motherfucker. Snorting a mound of white off of the bar—you fucking cock-a-roaches!"

"What? That's not me, dude. Anyway, you want to get fucked up? You owe me dinner at least after stealing the Calcutta."

"That two-fifty is mine fair and square, son. You're the one who bet on Squirm."

"He would have won if he hadn't shot up and nodded out."

"No doubt he's the best. Once I saw Squirm hustle this local hustler named Apple. Now, Apple played everyday, but he know Squirm would whoop his ass straight up. But Squirm is desperate for money, probably needed his fix. So Squirm says he'll use a mop instead of a pool cue. Apple says no. Squirm says he'll soak the mob in the bucket so it's good and wet. Apple says no. Squirm says he'll play one handed. Apple says no. Squirm says he'll play one-handed, left handed. Finally Apple agreed. Squirm ran the table off the break. Apple never got to take a shot. Squirm beat him one handed, left handed, with a wet mop."

"I knew he was the best."

"But you never bet on a junkie."

FIFTY-SIX

The old Nissan Sentra's door was rusty, and in the cold weather, it stuck on its hinges halfway open, so Cally had to leverage all of her one hundred and ten pounds to get it to shut. The car was a piece of shit, but it was her piece of shit, and she loved it. It was midday, but the streets of Gallup were empty. Perhaps the people were at their jobs, inside, warm, in front of desks with computers and printers, answering phones, but Cally assumed the people were all holed up in their bedrooms smoking glass. It's what everyone did now, all she could conceive of everyone doing now, at this moment in time.

The Sentra drove like a big go-cart. Press one peddle and the car moved. Press another and it stopped. She wheeled through the barren streets, neck craned upward, watching the gray sky through the tinted stripe at the top edge of the windshield. Bald tires padded over wind swept road-crew sand and dead leaves. She parked in front of her house, gently nudging the curb with the sides of her tires. She turned the tangle of keys in the ignition to the left, and the engine died. She listened to the quiet. She watched her house for movement inside, but there was none.

She hurried out of the car and checked her surroundings to make sure nothing had changed, nothing had snuck up on her. The street was still empty. The branches of a leafless cottonwood clacked overhead with the wind. She clutched her handbag, a Coach bag Miriam had bought her for Christmas last year, under her arm like a football, and walked briskly up to her front porch, head down, bracing herself against the wind, and whatever waited for her inside. The porch steps creaked underfoot. She fumbled with her keys until she got the right one in the lock, and then realized the door was open, and was dumbfounded that she had been in such a panic when she had ran out of the house that she would have left without locking the door.

Pull off the Band-Aid, she thought. She entered the house quickly. It was dark inside, blinds drawn, winter sun low on the horizon. And cold. She checked the house—the kitchen, the bedroom, the bathroom—all empty. She exhaled. It was cold enough inside the house to see her breath. She checked the thermostat on the wall by the door to the bedroom. The heat was switched off. She wondered who'd done that. She hurried to the front door and triple locked it with the key, the dead bolt, and the chain. She set her purse on the coffee table and dug inside for the twenty sack she'd just bought and the glass pipe. She tapped some crystals into the pipe. Her hand shook as she did it. She lit the pipe and held in the smoke for a long time. When she exhaled, the room seemed warmer, but smaller somehow. She paced through the house, the rooms ever shrinking. She caught her refection in the bathroom mirror, eyes wild, hair stringy, sweatshirt frayed and wet with something. She went back out to the living room and took another hit. Just as she was about to exhale, something moved out of the corner of her eye. There was something in the house. Something moving in the living room wall. She jumped in her seat, swiveling toward the movement, but there was nothing there. She blew smoke out into the small rectangular room. Through the white cloud she tried to refocus. It was quiet except for the sound of the wind whistling through poorly caulked window frames. She sat very still, with her hands in her lap, clutching the pipe. Shallow breaths. A few seconds passed, and then a minute. Long enough to think about taking another hit. And then something moved on the far wall. In the far wall. She barely saw it, in her peripheral vision, but it was there. The Shadow People had come. They were real. And they were here.

She recoiled and dropped the pipe. It bounced on the floor, spilling burnt chemicals. She went after it by reflex, reaching around the coffee table, grasping for the pipe as it rolled under the couch. She was down on her hands and knees, fingers outstretched, feeling under the couch, her fingernails scraping the hardwood floor, looking back up at the room around her in terror, when she saw a shadow seep across the wall. It had a vaguely human form, with two arms and two legs. She could see where the edge of the shadow's head met the wall, smooth, as if it had no hair. It moved slowly, as a shadow driven by sunlight might, its limbs lengthening and shortening with each slight change in degree, but in a walking motion, a walking dream. And she was sure that was what it was, a dream, a tweaker's dream. Until it stopped moving across the wall, turned its head, and looked back at her. She opened her mouth to scream. The shadow oscillated between worlds, its limbs shaking and contorting, the outline darkening, solidifying. A man with a bald head and almond eyes seemed to come out of the living room wall, arms outspread, reaching toward her. As it materialized, the eyes shade red against the darkness. It looked down at her, on her hands and knees, and smiled.

Just like a dream, she screamed but nothing came out. She felt her throat strain and crack, and yet she heard nothing but supersonic silence. She flew to her feet and to the door, clawing at the locks, tearing at window blind, leaving scrapes with teal nail polish embedded in the house paint. She ripped the door open and ran to the Sentra, leaving the door unlocked, wondering if she'd done this before.

FIFTY-SEVEN

Cattleman's was the only bona fide steakhouse in Gallup. Phil and Jake sat at the bar and ordered sixteen ounce ribeye steaks that came sizzling on butcher block cutting boards. The place was dark and smokey, seemingly lit by a sepia glow emanating from the whiskey bottles behind the bar. Jake drank wine, a California Cab, smooth and silky but heavy on the tongue. The wine immediately calmed him. He felt warm inside. The steak, poached in butter, was almost too salty and decadent. He didn't eat much anymore and had to adjust to the intensity of flavor. He knew he had crossed over. His body needed certain things now. Drink first, the itch for the pipe would soon follow. But for now, the wine glass felt satisfying in his hand. This is how the devil drinks blood, he thought.

Phil picked up the tab out of his Calcutta winnings, leaving a hundred dollar bill on the bar for the meal and a fifty for the bartender. The night was dark and moonless and full of possibility. They walked to the Gallup Grill, a long low fort-like adobe with shafts of firelight glowing from slat windows with Spanish wrought iron bars. They ordered whiskeys and watched the fourth quarter of the Broncos game on a first generation flat-screen, more than a few years out of date, as Phil flirted with the Navajo bartender, a leggy brunette in skinny jeans and cowboy boots in a Peyton Manning tank top. She bought their next two rounds, knowing Phil would get her back the next time a good country band played at the American. The Broncos beat the Chiefs and they took turns hugging the bartender and then headed back out into the cold.

They drove Phil's Audi to the Shalimar, a rundown dancehall where drunk couples held each other up to cumbias. Phil disappeared to a dark corner table while Jake leaned back against the bar with a whiskey and a cigarette. Red, green, and yellow lights pulsed with the music on the dance floor. The pine wood bar, stained black, was strung with Christmas lights and candles. Contrast with the cold outside, it was warm inside, hypnotic. A Mexican couple walked past arm in arm. The man tipped his hat at Jake, the woman laid her head on the man's shoulder. The song ended and the crowd, entirely hispanic and Navajo, filtered to their tables and the men to the bar. Jake did a shot of tequila with the group of men around him, and prepared to do a second when Phil motioned that it was time to go.

When they got in the car, Phil tuned the satellite radio station to Hip Hop Nation and cranked it up. "I can't listen to the twangy shit they play on the radio around here, man. Gotta beam my shit in from outer space."

"I kinda like country now. You know, country music today would have been called rock and roll a few years back."

"Hate that shit too. For me, music begins in 1993. Listen, wanna get some shit?"

Jake pretended like he was thinking about it, but he knew he did. "Do we have to go all the way out to Shiprock? Those some weird motherfuckers."

"Nobody else around right now. I checked. What do you

think we were doing at the Shalimar?"

"I loved that place."

"Mexican guy who hangs out there usually has a little, cheap too, but he was all wigged out. Said he's out of the game."

"There's no one else?"

"Used to go to a guy named Jimmy Kills Back, but he left town after skinwalkers got his grandfather."

"Skinwalkers."

"That's what they say, have to be some kind of evil to set an old man on fire like that."

FIFTY-EIGHT

The Audi cleared the city lights and plod the desolate road to Shiprock. The interstitial times between craving and actual drug procurement were always anxious, bewildering, free will surrendered, a conveyor belt that may or may not drop off a cliff, but the soupy darkness of State Route 491 cutting due north on the Big Reservation added to the vast sense of purgatory, of nowhereness.

Phil chewed the inside of his lower lip and moved his head to Lil Wayne, bass rattling the interior. Jake had business to take his mind off the purgatory. He thought about the last conversation he had with Old Joe, not long before he was murdered. Jake had asked him why skinwalkers went after people. Joseph had said that sometimes, they attack people close to one they were after, that it was worse that way. Jake had asked Old Joe out of idle curiosity at the time. But now the puzzle was coming together. He texted Yazzie:

2nd murder, grl @ Shiprock, any drug connection?

His phone lit up his face. The screen reflected in all the windows. Beyond that, blackness. Less than a minute passed before Yazzie texted back:

Been over this. She was clean.

Not her. Anyone close to her? They burned her as a warning to someone.

"You texting your girl?" Phil said, taking one hand off the wheel to look over at Jake. "Man, she fine. A young'n, but she fine."

"She's not my girl, but, I know. Gotta check on her later. Don't like her smoking glass."

"No doubt, that shit will ruin bitches."

The phone vibrated with a text from Yazzie:

I will check on it.

Jake turned off the phone and put it in the front pocket of his jeans. He looked out the window but it was so dark all he saw was the reflection of dashboard lights and shadows of mesas and mountains where the darkness was thicker, more profound. Phil slowed the Audi to a speed unnatural for it as they made the turn onto the dirt road in the night shade of Shiprock. Even from a distance they could tell there was something different about the doublewide trailer. Headlights crisscrossed the desert. Pickups and rusted out hand-me-down cars were parked at all angles in front of the compound. Beyond the wooden fence, flames danced up the red cliff face behind the house.

The door to the doublewide was open. Jake noticed that it was reinforced with two deadbolts and three steel bars that slid back into welded casings. They pushed their way through a crowd of tweakers to the backyard, drawn by a huge bonfire and wild, half-naked people. Embers shot up to the sky. The flames licked the sandstone wall towering five hundred feet up to the top of a mesa. Across the fire, Jake saw the Shaman, his bald head pulsing sweat, eyes locked on him, following his every move. The Shaman lowered his brow until he was staring at Jake with just the whites of his eyes. And then he began to speak. Over the blazing fire and splintering wood and contorting bodies his voice was clear. Calm. Venomous.

"The Shadow People...they know now not to challenge us...they know what we can do to them...this war will be won someday..." The Shaman hissed, his words echoing off the sandstone in a reverberating whisper that his followers felt swirling deep inside. The crowd made a semicircle around him as he continued to speak in a whisper that rose and fell with the flames. Several young men took running starts and jumped through the bonfire, landing on the other side and rolling in the dirt to put out their burning clothes. A girl in baggy jeans, a Raiders jacket, and a knit cap pulled low over her eyes threw grain alcohol onto the fire and it leapt up high into the dark night sky. The Shaman kept speaking, his words weaving a fabric that cloaked the night, understood for their texture rather than their meaning.

"I ain't listening to this shit anymore," Jake said, turning to go, feeling the Shaman's eyes bore a hole through his back as he did so.

"Yeah," Phil said quietly. "I bought two twenty sacks, let's go."

They walked through the trailer toward the front door. Jake stopped. On a battered old couch in the center of the room a girl was absently giving head to a tweaker with scabby skin and a spider web neck tattoo, grinning over a scraggly mustache revealing a missing front tooth. Jake recognized the girl. She was a pretty brunette, sophomore in high school, one of the girls dancing with Max at Cally's house. Her head was in the guy's lap, her ass in the air, the guy running his finger over her ass crack on the outside of her skinny jeans. Jake stood over them. She looked up at him, cock still in her mouth, only the vaguest hint of recognition. Jake reached down and picked her up in one motion.

"Hey asshole, wait your turn!" The tweaker said tucking away his flaccid penis. Jake set the girl down and she immediately fell over. He took a step toward the tweaker and punched downward, rotating his shoulder and throwing his weight into it, and splintered the guy's nose. He set his knee on the guy's chest and let his fists go, left right left right left right. He felt an orbital bone crack and teeth give way. Blood splattered onto the grimy couch. Phil pulled Jake off and shoved him toward the door. Jake fought free and knocked two skinny kids down who stood between him and the girl. He picked her up and slung her over his shoulder. They reached the front door amid shouts and chaos. They ran to the Audi as people stumbled out of the house after them. The Audi roared to life and Phil floored it, dirt spraying in headlights blinding everyone in a cloud of grit. The Audi careened into open desert, bouncing over rocks and small cacti and bottoming out as it regained the jeep trail to the dirt road back to State Route 491.

"Jesus, don't get these guys against me, man! Can't you see they're fucking crazy?" Phil punched the steering wheel. "This is a small place, you a mad dog, you a wrecking ball, you gotta get a grip or you're gonna wind up in a ditch with bugs crawling out of your eyes."

"Don't be dramatic," Jake said, checking on the girl in the back seat. She was curled up in the fetal position, eyes unblinking.

"Fuck, it's probably too late. You should leave town. Fuck, I should leave town."

"Maybe you should."

State Route 491 was empty. The Audi tore over the blacktop at over a 100 mph. There were no headlights in the rear view mirror. Phil drove to where Jake's truck was parked back at

Cattleman's. The girl was sitting up now, wild eyed.

"Get in the truck."

She did as she was told. Jake moved to get out of the Audi, but Phil grabbed his arm. He popped the glove box and dug out a nickel plated Beretta 9mm. The handle gleamed in the street light.

"You should take this. I'm gonna take a leave of absence. Go back to Chicago for a couple of weeks. Let this shit die down."

Jake picked up the gun and watched it glow green in the stereo light. He put it back in the glove box. "You forget, six months ago I was a federal agent. I got my own piece."

"Yeah, I do forget that about you. I can see why they fired your ass."

"I wasn't always this way."

"Yes, you were. You just didn't know it until opportunity presented itself."

Jake smiled. He got out of the car and leaned in the window. "Take care of yourself, Phil."

Phil shook his head and held up two fingers. "Deuces."

The Audi peeled out and hit I-40 headed east. Jake drove the girl to Cally's house. She answered the door in sweat pants and a hoodie, her straw colored hair limp and greasy. She took the girl's hand and led her inside, but she made Jake wait at the door. She looked up at him, green eyes searching his face.

"Go home. Jake."

He slumped against the door frame. He was tired. His fists hurt.

"Look, I just want you to know—"

"Don't. You're a sexy bitch Jake, but I can't do this right now...I feel...so grimy, and...depleted."

She hugged herself against the cold, the wind cutting across the porch, the porch swing creaking and scraping against the side of the house. He put her head in his chest and she let him hold her.

"Who would have thought, of all the people to do *this* to me, it would be you."

FIFTY-NINE

He stood on the porch long after Cally went back inside and the lights in her apartment went off. Back in the F-150, he looked up and down the street and checked the mirrors, but the street was empty. A few parked pickups, houses dark, traffic lights blinking red. He lit a cigarette and put the truck in gear. He stayed on Lead Street until it ended at pasture land. A skinny horse stared at him and then went back to eating the weeds growing along a barbed wire fence.

He followed a dirt road until it intersected with Navajo Route 28. The tires spun their way up onto the pavement and he started up the mountain. Immediately, headlights appeared in his rear view. Through the open window he could hear a large engine growl and knew there was a truck behind him. It was coming fast. Jake floored it and his own Hemi roared to life as the F-150 lurched forward. But it was too late. As he took the first sweeping turn up the ridge line an old Chevy Blazer, a K5, made of cast iron and heavy as a tank, pulled along side him and turned sharply into the F-150, crushing the left front wheel well. The metal bent inward shredding the tire and bending the front axel. The front end collapsed sending sparks down the road. The back end swung around as the truck fishtailed and plowed into a low ditch and then bounced through it and down a steep, grassy field, managing to stay upright long enough to mow over a sapling and slam into a pine tree.

Jake had blood in his eyes. He wiped his brow. The blood felt like grease. Forty yards up the side of the hill the K5 Blazer was idling on the road. He saw a figure move through the headlights holding a big stick. Jake unclicked his seat belt and used his shirt to wipe his face. When he looked back up he saw a muzzle flash and he threw himself onto the passenger seat as buckshot pelted the driver's side door. Jake felt frantically around under the passenger seat where he kept the Glock hidden, now that he had to. There was another boom and the back end of the truck was rocked by a shotgun blast. Somewhere, he smelled gasoline. The Glock wasn't where he left it. The passenger door was propped open by the splintered stump of a pine tree and Jake wedged himself onto the ground. There was a blast aimed at the undercarriage and Jake's leg was hit by dirt, weeds and ricocheted buckshot. Still on the ground, Jake reached his arm into the cab and felt along the floorboard, over empty beer cans, gatorade bottles, and cigarette packs until he felt the Glock. The collision had knocked it out of its hiding place and wedged it under the floor mat. He grabbed it and pulled himself up so he was looking over the hood. Less than ten feet away a man had a shotgun pointed at him. Jake put his back to the door as the man fired. The blast tore the side mirror off just above Jake's ear. He heard the shotgun's pump action and rose up with the Glock, putting three in the man's torso before he could get another shot off.

Jake limped around the truck's crushed and steaming grill and cantilevered himself up the hill. The gun shook in his hand. The man was dead. White guy, tattoo of the sun on his adam's apple with a red dot in the center where one of the bullets had passed straight through his throat. Even in the darkness, Jake could tell it was not the guy he'd given the beat down to at the doublewide. The shootout had been all reflex but now his adrenaline spiked. His heart hammered in his chest. The man had been waiting for him. How many others were waiting for him? Jake looked up the hill to the parked Blazer, engine running, red taillights casting the tall grass by the roadside in a devilish glow. He looked down the mountainside at his wrecked truck, teetering on a stand of thin white pines, and then beyond that to a hundred yards of hardscrabble scree dropping to the desolate valley below. His instinct was to run, but he couldn't. The skin up his left leg was red and raw, scraped clean from ankle to knee by the buckshot, his jeans tattered and dangling like blinds in an open window.

He saw the lights before he heard the sirens, coming up Navajo 28, taking the ridgeline at full speed. How are they here so fast? Had to be close by to begin with. Too close.

Jake took the twenty sack of crystal Phil had bought for him at the doublewide out of the coin pocket of his jeans, and wiped any prints off it with his shirt, squeezing the bag between his thumb and forefinger. He put the baggie in the dead man's pocket. He fought his way up the mountainside, grabbing onto weeds and stunted little saplings to help pull himself up. He reached the road just as the first police car arrived. He let go of the Glock and threw his hands in the air, limping backwards onto the shoulder, making sure he was visible in the idling Blazer's headlights.

A lone officer got out of the patrol car. A big man in a cowboy hat. Jake couldn't make out the man's face, backlight by the cruiser's spotlight, but his walk was familiar. Jake squinted and shielded his eyes with his hand. The light was blinding. Red and Blue alternated off of a large silver belt buckle. Bradley.

Bradley drew his sidearm out of his holster and trained it on Jake. Jake spread his arms wide and raised them even higher into the air.

"It was self-defense."

Jake reached his arms outward slightly and lowered them a little, showing his palms. Far in the distance they could hear other sirens approaching. Bradley looked at the stream of blue lights climbing the ridge line, and then back at Jake.

"So is this."

Bradley widened his stance, gripped the gun with both hands, and shot Jake in the chest.

BOOK III

SIXTY

Yazzie awoke at quarter to five in the morning. His alarm was set for five a.m. but he hadn't needed it in years. He always woke up at this time. The bed was warm. His wife was asleep. Her back was turned toward him, her hair swept over the pillow. He eased out of bed and picked up a gray Army Football sweatshirt off the floor and put it on. He wore it for exactly a half hour everyday, in between getting up and showering. His wife despised clothes left on the floor, just as she would not tolerate an unmade bed, but after seventeen years of marriage she had accepted that the sweatshirt could stay on the floor between uses. In marriage, you pick your battles.

It was dark in the room. It would be dark at this time in the morning until mid-summer. He shuffled from the bedroom to the kitchen and turned on the light. He started a pot of coffee and set a frying pan on the stovetop to heat up for bacon and eggs. He walked down the hallway to his son's room and gently knocked on the door. He listened for a few seconds, not expecting to hear anything, he would come back and knock harder when breakfast was ready, but he loved those few seconds. Every time he thought of his son it felt like those few seconds. The boy was perfect. He was safe. He would be fed soon.

He didn't make breakfast for his wife. She worked at the

Bureau of Indian Affairs Agency in Crownpoint, a forty-mile, thirty minute drive from their home outside of Window Rock, but this was her telework day so he wouldn't dare wake her up. He set eight strips of bacon on the frying pan and poured himself a cup of coffee. He turned on the police scanner but he couldn't hear it over the sizzling bacon. There was frost on the window panes. He warmed his hands on the coffee mug and watched the first light of dawn. He fished out the bacon with a fork and set the curling strips to dry on a paper towel and then cracked four eggs into the pan to cook in the bacon grease. When breakfast was ready, he divvied up the bacon and eggs on two plates for him and his son, and washed the pan in warm water so the smell of grease wouldn't saturate the whole house. It was quiet again in the kitchen except for the crackling of the scanner. He looked down the hall at his son's door. Sometimes, when he was just about to wake him, he became afraid. Not for the usual reasons, but because the boy was so good, almost in high school and still a sweet kid, respectful, smart. Yazzie's heart was full, bursting. Not with pride, because he was not a prideful man, but with joy. And it made him afraid. So much so that it hurt.

The scanner called for more units on Navajo Route 28, mile marker 7. Yazzie set down the mug. He knew that was close to Jake's trailer. He did not believe in coincidence. Instead of waking the boy, Yazzie crept into his bedroom and put his hand on his wife's shoulder. She made a soft noise and eventually responded by putting her hand on his.

"I made you breakfast."

SIXTY-ONE

Navajo Route 28 mile marker 7 was easy to find. Yazzie parked his Tahoe behind a long line of emergency vehicles. He walked up the road with his hands in his jacket pockets and his shoulders hunched against the morning chill. He stopped Darrell Begay, a young tribal police officer, one of the few who wore his hair long and unbraided. Most tribal police had close cropped hair, veterans like Yazzie, who never gave up the routine of a buzz cut every two weeks. Down the hillside a half dozen officers were stooped over, searching for evidence and planting little flags. Another group was carrying a body bag on a stretcher into a waiting ambulance. Yazzie recognized Jake's pickup, shot up and battered, crashed into a small corpse of white pines halfway down the mountainside.

"Who's in the bag?"

Darrell gathered his hair in his hands and smoothed it back. "White guy. Gunshot wound."

Yazzie pat Darrell on the back. It was a strange gesture for him, and he didn't know why he did it. He supposed he did it for himself. He wasn't surprised Jake was dead, the glass pipe kills everybody in the end, but he was saddened.

He walked up the road to the ambulance as they loaded the body inside. Yazzie knew the paramedics well. He asked for a moment and the paramedics went around the side of the truck for a cigarette. He pulled back the zipper. But he did not recognize the dead man.

SIXTY-TWO

Jake only had one thought: Aimee was there. He could sense her, no, smell her. One time he felt a hand on his cheek, and he knew she was there. For a time there was numbness. A blurry world without sight. Not darkness, more like a red hazy glow, womblike, consciousness cocooned and distant. But Aimee was there. That singular thought was a nugget to hold onto, at once familiar and comforting and yet perplexing and unexpected. *Why is she here? Where am I?*

Fear. Fear and panic as he tried to fight through the layers of coma. He fought with his mind. His body would not move. Or if it was moving he couldn't feel it. There were shadows now, moving in the room, he felt that he was in a room, not outside or in some netherworld. The air was too stagnant to be outdoors, antiseptic. The shadows gained some definition as the background lightened to orange, crisscrossed with branches of veins and capillaries, the insides of his eyelids, like a road map placed over a slide projector.

When he finally opened his eyes, Aimee was there, just as he'd known she would be. She had come back. And she looked... pissed. Her mouth was a tight line, her high cheek bones indented where her jaw muscles flexed from clenching her teeth. Her hair was a jet black curtain on both sides of her face, like gleaming armor. Her tan skin had lost much of its color, gone ashen from either the east coast winter or her mood. She wore a tight black blazer over a black pencil skirt and tights. She looked like she was here for business.

"Jesus, you really went to pieces in a hurry."

Jake wasn't sure if he was dreaming this. It was her voice, and she looked as he remembered her, except that she needed more sun. But don't dreams always seem real when they are happening? She walked over to him, the sound of her heels echoing around the sterile room, and took his hand. Her hand was smooth and cool. It was her touch. He tried to speak, but realized he didn't know what to say. He was fairly sure he could speak, but now that she was actually here, nothing he'd wanted to say seemed to fit anymore. She saw the bewilderment in his eyes and made a shushing sound.

"You know, you're no good to my lawyer if you're dead."

He squeezed her hand hard. As he did he noticed the hospital gown, the oversized sleeve running back on itself. The door to the room opened. Jake found he could tilt his head forward. It was Cally. She held a bouquet of flowers in a glass vase. She looked like she had just gotten out of the shower, hair pulled neatly back in a pony tail, track suit and UGGs. The dark circles under her eyes were gone. She stopped when she saw Aimee.

Aimee put her hand on Jake's forehead.

"I gotta go, Jake. I'm glad you're alive." She grabbed her purse, an oversized black leather bag that looked more like a briefcase, and stopped in front of Cally on her way out. "Take care of him."

Cally nodded, avoiding her eyes for as long as she could. But when she finally looked Aimee in the eye she didn't see anger, just a palpable seriousness.

After Aimee left the hospital room, Cally couldn't set the vase down fast enough and nearly knocked it over before rushing to Jake and showering his face with kisses. She held onto his hands, and wiped away a tear, which made her smile and laugh a little, giddy with relief. She searched his face, but he was already back asleep.

SIXTY-THREE

When he awoke again, Mary and Cally were in the room. Cally wore jeans and a sweater, her hair had been done in loose curls, her eyes were bright and clear, her lips pink. She was clearly off of meth. He realized he was too. He wondered how long he'd been out.

Mary brought a basket of fry bread. He supposed it was the smell that had woken him up, the warm bread out of place in the astringent room. Or maybe it was a familiar perfume that thread its way through his dreams. Now he was awake, and in serious pain. He found he could move, but he dared not. The slightest twitch sent lightning bolts of pain throughout his body. He felt like his chest had been split open, and then realized that it probably had been. He looked under this hospital gown and saw a jagged line of raised stitches. Blood and some clear viscous liquid leaked out between the seams and ran down his stomach in orange streaks. A drainage tube leaked a yellowy liquid into a gauze pad.

"Holy shit."

"Oh, it's not that bad." Mary was the first to notice him awake. She rang for the doctor, as she was told to do once he woke.

"Jake!" Cally clapped her hands together when she saw him up and went to his side. She picked up his hand and held it to her. "You're going to be okay."

"What happened?"

"You got shot, dummy. I was so worried. We all were."

"All?"

"Well, me and Mary, and my mom even, if you can believe that. Officer Yazzie was here for a while. And Aimee came as soon as she heard." Cally let the words sink in, she thought he might have been so doped up after the surgery that he didn't remember seeing her before.

Jake nodded and winced in pain.

"Your friends from the bar came to visit. See?" She pointed to a eighteen year old bottle of scotch, Macallan, with a red bow stuck onto it that had been left on the nightstand. Classy. "Do you remember who shot you?"

"No. I don't think so."

The door swung open and a doctor came into the room carrying a clipboard. Doctor Patel was a small man in a crisp shirt and sweater vest under his white lab coat. He had immigrated from Delhi decades ago to work for Indian Health Services, the only health care provider hiring doctors from India at the time. For the last two decades he had privileges at Rehoboth McKinley Christian Hospital, and was the region's most highly regarded surgeon.

"Mr. Keller, how are you today?"

Jake looked up at him dumbly.

"So, you've been shot in the chest. I will tell you this, Mr. Keller, it is good to see you up and about. You can talk, yes?"

"Uh huh, but it hurts."

"Of course it hurts. You had a tube down your throat for twelve hours of surgery. Not an easy job. But, here you are. Okay. I'm

233

sure you have many questions, so, here is what happened. You...
were...very lucky." Doctor Patel spoke with his hands, looking
over his glasses for emphasis, a barely suppressed smile causing
him double chins. "I tell you this, man, you were lucky. The
bullet lodged in your sternum. Instead of shattering your breast
bone, sending bone fragments all over the place, puncturing vital
organs, your heart, I mean your heart is right there man...the
bullet stuck there." Doctor Patel pointed at the slash of sutured
skin with a jabbing motion, his finger so close to the wound
Jake felt the hole in his chest pulsate. "So, we took it out. The
breast bone was split almost in two, so we used a little metal
plate and screws to put it back together. You can move, yes?"

"Uh, uh. Hurts too much."

"Of course it hurts, You've been shot. That's going to hurt.
But you must move. You—and I can tell you this—you cannot
sit there, you must get up and start walking as soon as you can."
Doctor Patel bobbed his head emphatically. "Move, you must."

"Okay."

"You, get him up and about." Doctor Patel wagged a long
finger at Mary and Cally, and then he turned back to Jake.
"Okay. You are doing really good. Eat some of that fry bread. I
am sure it is very good. I will see you soon." The doctor patted
Jake on the leg and left in a hurry.

"He seems nice."

"He's the best." Mary unfolded the cloth over the basket of
fry bread and brought a piece over to Jake in a napkin and set
it in his hand. "Eat."

Jake lifted the bread to his mouth with the smallest incre-
mental movements possible. "It's good. Thank you, Mary."

"I also brought you this." Mary produced a joint and set it

on the bedside tray next to a thermos of ice water with a long straw and a plastic cup of red jello.

Jake nodded.

"I'm kidding, it's a joke. You shouldn't be smoking."

"No, I'll take it," Jake said laughing weakly. The movement was excruciating. He tucked the joint under his pillow. He ate a nibble of fry bread, chewing slowly. Cally wiped crumbs and drool from the corner of his mouth. He found her eyes, sea green today. He held onto her wrist.

"Thought you were done with me."

"I don't think of people like that. I'm never done with them. Besides, you have the good pills now." She shook a bottle of oxycontin that she found on the night tray. He looked at her and raised an eyebrow.

"Go ahead, take two," she said. "But no more."

"Thanks."

She kissed him softly on the lips. "Me and you are going to do a some physical therapy later."

"Jeez, I'm still here you know." Mary coughed. "Take it easy on an old lady will you? Going to make me blush."

SIXTY-FOUR

Visiting hours ended and Cally and Mary left for the night. Less than a minute later Yazzie appeared. Jake figured he must have been waiting for the women to leave.

"You been lingering out there all day?"

"Hardly left the hospital since they brought you in."

"No shit? You're like my guardian angel."

"I'm too ugly to be an angel."

"No, you are beautiful."

"Are you going to ask me to the prom? Because I believe Cally would be upset. You were supposed to double date with her friend who's dating the starting quarterback."

"Fuck you."

"That's no way to talk to an angel."

"Seriously, I mean I know you care, but—"

"Whoever shot you is going to finish the job. I was at the crime scene. Two shooters, run off the road, this was a hit." Yazzie shook his head and lowered his voice. "They could be back any second."

"Jesus man, can I just be happy to be alive for now?"

"Be happy all you want. But we gotta get you out of here."

"It was Bradley."

"What?"

"Bradley shot me."

Yazzie let that sink in for minute. His hand unconsciously checked his holster to make sure his sidearm was there. He cinched up his jeans and sat down on a folding chair hunched over with his hands on his knees.

"It's worse than I thought then."

"What do you really know about Bradley?"

"When he was a young patrol officer with the tribal police he was very good. This is back before we had any of the resources we do now. You rode alone then, in some beat up Crown Vic they probably picked up at a county auction for a couple grand. The people did not like the police much. Took your life into your hands almost every day. He was good. Level headed. The muckity-mucks on the Tribal Council eyed him for management even then. When 9-11 happened he signed up right away, upholding the treaty."

"Wait, what?"

"Upholding our end of the treaty with the United States. To defend each other against our enemies. That's why so many Indians join the army, it's our treaty obligation to defend the United States. You don't think we go to war for fun, do you?"

"And how's that working out for you."

"It is sort of a one-sided deal, I admit. We haven't been attacked by the Apache in over a century, so perhaps we no longer need protection from them. Anyway, Bradley comes back from Iraq and he's highly decorated, you never seen so many medals. Just so happened Chief Betell retired that year, and next thing you know, Bradley's made Chief of Police. Gets fat and lazy. End of story."

The door to the room swung open. A man in a black suit

and a bland blue tie walked in holding creds. Yazzie again felt his fingers involuntarily drift to his holster to reassure himself the weapon was there. The man introduced himself as Agent Colton with the FBI. Jake had never seen him before or heard the name, but he knew he was out of D.C. Nobody in New Mexico wore a black suit, except to a funeral.

Agent Colton sized up Yazzie and held out his hand. "Do you mind waiting outside while I interview the witness."

"Don't you mean interview the victim?"

"Agent, I mean Mr. Keller, can be the victim all he wants, I'm only interested in the witness part."

Yazzie and Jake looked at each other. Jake unfurled his tongue and let it loll out of the side of his mouth.

"I will be right outside." Yazzie sidestepped the suit and waited in the hallway. Agent Colton questioned Jake for twenty minutes but he got nothing. Jake drooled on himself and did his best to be brain damaged. At one point he farted and shifted onto his side so the hospital gown rode up and left his balls hanging out, which he scratched.

After Colton flipped his notebook shut and left, Jake asked Yazzie to call Aimee and find out what was going on. A half hour later she texted directly to Jake's phone:

I'm the only FBI in Gallup. That guy's not FBI.

SIXTY-FIVE

Twenty minutes later Cally pulled up to the service entrance of the hospital in her Nissan Sentra and let the engine idle. Yazzie slipped cowboy boots on Jake's feet and eased him upright and out of bed. He helped Jake step into a pair of jeans and get his arms through the sleeves of a flannel shirt and button it over his stitches. Yazzie held Jake under his shoulder as he took baby steps down the hallway and to the elevator. The night nurse looked up from her desk disapprovingly and Yazzie told her that Jake just wanted to get some air. There was no law against it. Jake inched along with each step. He took tiny steps because any jostling was excruciating, but by the time he got outside, he was able to walk on his own, his body loosened up and grown used to the pain.

The night was dark and cold. Cally got out of the Sentra, her cheeks rosy, she could see her breath, white against the blackness. She gently hugged him, barely touching, and handed him her car keys. She popped the Sentra's trunk and pulled out an old black cowhide duster. She helped him put the long coat on over his loose fitting clothes that already stuck to the gauze over his wounds. It cut the cold and hid his damaged condition.

"It was my dad's. Been hanging in the mud room closet at my mom's house for like ten years."

"I like it. This is going to be my new look. Thank you."

"You're sure I can't come with you?"

"No, safer if you don't know where I am. I'll be in touch."

Yazzie pulled his truck up alongside Cally's car and put the Mossberg in the back seat of the Sentra. They helped Jake lower himself behind the wheel of Cally's car. He grimaced, waved, found the lone rock station on the radio, and drove off. Yazzie watched Cally's face as the Sentra's red taillights, dull from winter dirt and grime, disappeared down the hill into town. She pulled the faux fur lined hood of her jacket up over her long hair. She crossed her arms and exhaled deeply, her breath lit up by hospital lights, wrapping her head in an etherial glow. At nineteen, she was only four years older than his son, but he knew they might as well have been four decades apart in age. His son, home, asleep in bed after practicing most of the night for his dance at the upcoming the Contest Pow Wow.

Cally turned to face Yazzie and nodded to the direction Jake had driven.

"Do you think he'll be okay?"

"If the past is any indication, he will not."

Yazzie suddenly felt bad that perhaps he had been too harsh, that she wouldn't get the humor, but Cally smiled quickly, her eyes bright.

"Yeah, you're probably right."

"I didn't mean anything."

"You're just being honest. That boy does get himself into some trouble."

"Some he looks for, some looks for him."

"Can I get a ride home? My mom's not working tonight or I'd ask her, not that she'd be pleased that I helped Jake fly the coop."

"There is no way that Miriam could understand what is going on here, and she doesn't need to know."

Yazzie walked Cally to his Silverado, thinking that he didn't understand what was going on here either. Bradley had always struck him as odd, his ascension to Chief of Police followed by his rapid slide into apathy. One would have thought a younger man such as he would have been more driven to help the reservation. To help the Dine. But Bradley quickly grew to resemble the politicians that cared more about casino money and the perks it could get them than improving the lives of the People.

Cally opened the heavy passenger side door and climbed onto the bench seat and Yazzie started up the truck. The Navajo Nation public radio station was on the in-dash stereo. The station usually broadcast news and local events but at this time of night it was devoted to traditional music. The sound of Navajo singing and drumming filled the cab. Yazzie turned the volume down, but not all the way off.

Yazzie eased the truck down the hill and turned onto Lead Street. He spoke over the high voices rising and falling to a solitary drum.

"This may seem out of place, and, it is not my place to say so, but I assume you have heard of a vision quest."

"Sure, everyone has."

"It is kind of a cliché in Western culture," Yazzie nodded with a chuckle. "But the point is, I think, it is good to get out and look around. It opens the mind."

"Is this your way of telling me I should get out of town?"

"Well, not forever."

"Funny thing, a little while back an application for ASU showed up in my mailbox."

"You didn't send for it?"

"Nope."

"A sign, then."

"Oh, my Mom probably drove by and stuck it in my mailbox. I know it wasn't Jake, he's too damn selfish for something like that."

"Well, it wasn't me. I swear."

"You were low on my list of suspects. But thanks, maybe it is a sign."

"Are you going to fill it out?"

"I already started."

The Silverado's brakes squealed as Yazzie stopped in front of Cally's little rented house on Lead Street. He waited until she unlocked the front door, closed it behind her, and turned off the porch light before he put the extra-cab into gear. The wind kicked up and a river of dust blew across the road. By the time he hit State Route 264 West the wind was blowing steadily, rocking the big truck on its springs. The night was moonless and sticky black. He turned onto Navajo Route 12 North toward Window Rock and felt an unfamiliar prick of apprehension. No, it was fear. The few hairs on his arms and neck stood up and he felt them against the fine weave of his checkered Western shirt. He could see nothing beyond the headlights. The land seemed to have changed, as if he no longer recognized the reservation. He needed to find out what he could about Bradley. And it could cost him everything.

Window Rock was dark. There were no streetlights. Only the glow of interior lights behind curtains in the oddly spaced houses and the occasional porch light gave away the town. Yazzie parked at the Tribal Court Complex at the base of the rock formation which gave the town its name. He leaned on the Silverado's heavy door and swung it open, bracing it against the wind with his shoulder, and faced the Navajo Tribal Police Headquarters. Outside, mesquite trees whipped back and forth and the cottonwoods rustled. Blowing sand stung his face. At the right speed, the wind tuned the trees and a low moan swept across the land. It was black where the cliffs blocked the sky, but stars shown through a massive natural hole in the mountain, Window Rock, as if a pocket of stars were floating down to earth, untethered from the heavens. Nearby, horses snorted and bristled at the weather. The air was feathered with sage and some spice he couldn't quite place, cinnamon perhaps.

He turned up his jacket collar and walked past the courthouse to the police station. He pulled open the heavy, century-old wooden door and nodded to the duty officer, Dennis Johns, a good-looking kid that Yazzie had helped recruit. Johns was absently listening to the crackle from dispatch, leaning back in his swivel chair with his legs propped up on a desk. He dropped his boots to the ground and sat upright at attention when Yazzie walked in. Yazzie wished he hadn't. He didn't want to be noticed, remembered. He walked past the kid to the back suite of glass enclosed offices, where the detectives worked. It was dark and he flicked on the light switch. The overhead fluorescents blinked on one at a time, some more stubbornly than others, illuminating cubicles, file cabinets and boxes of documents stacked to the ceiling. The place seemed deserted. Yazzie tossed his keys on his desk and turned on his computer. He settled heavily into his seat. He let a minute pass and then peaked down the hallway to see if Johns was watching. The doorway was empty. He thought he could make out the kid's shadow, legs back propped up on the front desk. Yazzie quietly rose and walked gingerly on the old floorboards to the back corner office. Bradley's office. The shade was pulled down but he could tell it was dark behind the glass door. He looked over his shoulder one last time and cupped his hand on the door knob. He held his breath and gently applied pressure. It turned. The door was unlocked.

SIXTY-SIX

Jake watched Yazzie and Cally in the rear view mirror as he drove away from the hospital and felt his throat constrict and his adam's apple ache. He didn't know if it was the pills, the trauma, or the exhaustion, but he felt as if he might cry. He'd known them for a relatively short time, and yet he felt more connected to them than he'd felt to anyone in years. He beat back the emotion. He had to focus on the task at hand. Staying alive. It would be just his luck to finally fit into the place, only to die.

He drove to the Walmart on the outskirts of the west side of Gallup. Working the clutch produced a spur of pain and turning the wheel felt like being sawed in half. He walked slowly across the huge store parking lot a half step at a time, his arms crossed in front of him keeping the heavy leather coat from being blown open by the strong wind. The Walmart glowed white light from the wall of front windows, making the sky blacker and the stars disappear. The parking lot was mostly empty. The Walmart never closed.

The automatic door opened and he was pushed inside by the wind at his back. It was bright inside, artificial and overexposed, like the hospital's emergency room or the gates of Heaven. He shuffled inside, conscious of the fluids leaking from where the drains had been, wet gauze, crusted bed clothes. A greeter in a blue vest, round and bald, nodded in his direction but stopped short of actually greeting him, perceiving the uselessness in the gesture, the possible insult. The answer to "how are you doing today sir?", could not possibly be good.

His eyes were stung by the florescent light reflecting off of the gleaming floor like a burning halo. Pain killers, blood loss, adrenaline. His vision blurred. The place was unnaturally bright. All the shiny products were cast in a fuzzy nimbus around the edges. He used a shopping cart like a walker. It steadied him and he leaned over it as he plowed the aisles like some deranged farmer. Contorted grimace and drool. He saw Shadow People. Movement in the corner of his eye. But when he looked it was a cardboard cutout of Peyton Manning or a pyramid of beer. A bin overflowing with five dollar DVDs. Sometimes it was a person. An old woman in a housecoat and curlers running insomniac errands in the early morning hours, a reservation Indian eyeing him cautiously, weary of the evil stink surrounding him, a tweaker with a 40 ounce of St. Ides malt liquor and a box of Pampers Pull Ups. Jake squinted at the tweaker. The tweaker stopped and looked at Jake with a screwed up stare. The tweaker cocked his hat to the side and side-stepped to a different aisle, jeans too short and riding up over his ankles. Jake turned the cart with great effort, leaning to the side to arc a turn in the opposite direction. The shopping cart wheels squeaked and one rattled perpendicularly, now just a broken rudder.

Jake hurried now, ignoring the pain. He bought a first aid kit, an extra roll of gauze, a bottle of iodine, sewing kit, field binoculars, two cartons of shotgun shells, canister of beef jerky, box of Apple Jacks, Pop Tarts, Goldfish, Winston Lights, some cheap clothes and a handle of Jim Beam. The check out lanes were empty. When he was sure the tweaker wasn't in sight he rushed the cart to a check out counter. The clerk had a shaved head and a soul patch. At least two-fifty. Mouth breather. The clerk said nothing and somehow ran the items over the scanner while never taking his eyes off Jake, head tilted back, looking down at him through his eyelids, a spider web tattooed between his thumb and forefinger. Jake paid with a credit card and backed the cart toward the exit. The clerk watched him go, expression unchanged, head back and half buried in bulbous neck. Jake stopped near the customer service desk and used the ATM machine, taking out his daily limit of four hundred dollars in two installments of two hundred. He felt them watching. But there was nothing he could do.

Outside, the air smelled of burnt mesquite and dry pines. The wind was cold in his face. He crossed the parking lot looking over his shoulder. The Nissan Sentra was where he left it. He shoved the grocery bags into the back seat and started the car. He cranked the heater and watched the Walmart entrance. The car rocked in the wind. The Walmart's automatic sliding glass doors opened and closed sporadically, triggered by the gusting wind, but nobody came or went. Only ghosts were out tonight. After several minutes the dashboard vents blew air with the faintest twinge of warmth. He guided the Sentra out of the parking lot, the headlights illuminated night ghouls and spawned long shadows, revealing just how much darkness was out there.

The Walmart was off a frontage road alongside the Interstate. Jake's eyes darted between the rearview and side mirrors looking for anyone following him, anything suspicious. But the whole town was suspicious. At night, the buildings looked rundown or abandoned. No lights. Boarded up windows and chain link fences, the only sound from the wind across the plains and the big rigs on I-40. His pupils dilated from painkillers and post-surgery muscle relaxers, all the looking around made him nauseous, the few lights against the black night leaving streaks on his corneas, tracers that smeared across the windshield when he tried to focus on the road.

He hit I-40, did a mental coin flip, and chose east. He planned to drive as randomly as he could for as long as he could and then find a motel that took cash. Tweakers, cops, spooks—he didn't know who was hunting him, maybe they all were, but the best way to hide was to be off the grid and unpredictable. He needed to buy time, avoid his would be killers long enough to find out what was going on. He took the I-40 onramp in a long painful arc that made his stitches buckle and then floored the Sentra. It took awhile but the little Nissan topped out at seventy miles per hour, the four cylinder whining into the desert. It felt like light speed, the nothingness beyond the conical headlight glow was like a tunnel, and he was a horse with blinders. A semi blew past him doing ninety. The truck's wake wobbled the Sentra. Past Church Rock, the highway gained in elevation and the Sentra slowed to sixty.

"Shit," Jake yelled at the radio and pounded the steering wheel. He was more afraid of going too slow than too fast. More conspicuous. Twenty miles outside of Gallup, the Sentra crested the Continental Divide and started picking up speed again on the downhill. A set of headlights was behind him. Most passed him without hesitation. This one did not.

He eased up slightly on the gas peddle and the Sentra immediately slowed to under sixty. The headlights stayed the same distance behind. He got off I-40 at Thoreau. The headlights followed. The off ramp ran to a stop sign, a red and white blur, glowing like neon in the high beams, stark against the dark night. Jake squinted hard and was able to make out a rusted road sign with an arrow pointing to the left that read State Route 371. He took the left and followed the road through a narrow tunnel under the interstate, boxed in with the car right behind him. State Route 371 crossed the Transwestern Pipeline and skirted the four block by four block grid that made up Thoreau, a small reservation town, all dark except for flood lights outside the St. Bonaventure Indian Mission and School. It was a boarding school but it looked like a prison. A series of rectangular aluminum sided modules visible behind a high chain link fence that was ringed with barbed wire and angled outward at the top. Beyond the school there was a cluster of oddly arranged identical government issue houses, similarly fenced in. Outside of town, the two lane black top straightened. Jake kept it slow on the straightaway, gauging the distance of the lights behind him. He dug for his phone and took out the SIM card, bracing it against the wheel as he fought with it, and put it in the inside pocket of the duster. A quarter mile out from for a sharp curve that took the road up into the mountains above Thoreau, Jake put the gas peddle to the floor. The Sentra geared down into third and the tach jumped to over four thousand RMP. It wasn't much of a boost but enough so that the Sentra was going sixty when it hit the curve. The bald tires drifted, clung, and slid as the car accelerated up the mountain. The sound of screeching tires echoed through the canyon. The headlights behind him momentarily disappeared. The road slungshot back the other way around an outcropping of rocks where the road used to go a half century ago, before the BIA dynamited a straighter and wider cut. Jake pulled the emergency break and the back wheels locked up and the Sentra skidded off the shoulder onto the old dirt path that looped around the outcropped rock formation. The Sentra bounced, hit a rock that smashed out the left front headlight, and then nosed into the slope, up mountain. Every bump and pitch shot through his nerves, blunted far more by adrenaline than the oxycontin. He breathed hard and listened for the engine from the car following him. But all he heard was the hammering of his own heart and all he saw was dust in the lone headlight. He waited half a minute and then drove back out to Route 371 and turned south, back to Thoreau. He kept checking the rear view, but saw nothing.

Instead of getting back on the Interstate, he took the frontage road alongside the railroad tracks east for a dozen miles. Halfway to the town Grants he turned north on Indian Service Rte 481. The road turned to gravel and then dirt. The path climbed up into the mountains, deep into the reservation. Mt. Taylor loomed overhead, the southern most of the four sacred peaks. He slowed to twenty miles an hour, feeling through the ruts and avoiding the biggest rocks in the road. It was so dark he could have been teetering on the edge of a cliff and he wouldn't have known it. There were mountains. Shapes. He passed a mine, trussled conveyor belts and hulking slag piles lit by phantasmal flood lights that revealed a half eaten mountain before the road curved around a bend and the curtain of night fell once more.

He traveled in a northern direction, taking other BIA and tribal service roads as he crossed them. There were no lights. Occasionally he passed trailers and hogans, compounds with quonset huts, rusted machinery and old school buses, clapboard shacks and outbuildings, dogs giving chase and nipping at the wheels. At County Road 509 there was a stop sign. Jake carefully eased himself out of the car. Every muscle felt cramped, frozen, his body dead set against unfurling into an upright position. The road was empty. The stop sign banged against its post. Overhead, an ocean of stars. The night air was cold, cleansing. He inhaled as deep as his surgically repaired chest would allow, trying to clear the hospital stench, real or imagined, that followed him everywhere. He slowly spun around in a circle, letting the wind blow away the smell of sickness and death. Mountains made silhouettes in the stars against the moonless night sky.

He got back into the car and watched the stop sign bend and twist in the wind, as if it was trying to flap away from its pole. He made a left onto the county road. The road was paved and the smooth ride was a relief. Relief lasted only minutes as the road quickly intersected with the busier four-lane Highway 550. He got the Sentra up to seventy, cursing at himself, conspicuous now, traveling on a main road in an easily describable car with a headlight out. But he needed miles behind him. He drove past Bloomfield and Aztec, avoiding the main route through Farmington, and crossed the border into Colorado. He had left the Navajo Nation, crossed most of the Jicarilla Apache reservation, and was now on Southern Ute land. It grew colder and began to snow. The ice quickly piled up on the windshield wiper blades. Vision was reduced to mere yards. Oncoming traffic blinded him and barreled by inches away. He summited a nameless mountain pass deep in the woods. A green and white road sign read, Ignacio, pop 235. He stopped at a lone traffic light flashing red. There was a small Spanish mission at the far end of a weed grown town square. All the shops on First Street were closed. The gas station lights were out.

On the far edge of town a green neon motel sign illuminated big meandering snowflakes. An arrow pointed at some pine trees. An eight unit dogleg motel fronted the highway out of town. Jake wrapped himself in the duster and went into the office. There was no one at the desk but a TV was on in a back room. A grey haired man in a knit cap and wool sweater emerged from the back room holding a Bud Light tallboy in a gloved hand. Jake paid forty dollars cash for Unit Number 6 on the corner. He parked the Sentra around the side of the motel behind a large propane tank.

The room was musty. The electric baseboard heater rattled to life and blew dust around. It took three trips to bring his supplies inside, moving slower each time. He loaded the Mossberg and laid it on the nightstand next to the bed. He unscrewed the cap on the plastic handle of Walmart whiskey and turned on the TV. He felt suddenly tired, kept awake only by pain. He took two oxycontin with a glass of whiskey. It would work. The room would work. He fumbled with the curtains, trying to close any gaps. He had run farther than any containment zone a law enforcement agency would erect, and erratic enough to make the odds of finding him in a concerted search, remote. After all, he could have gone in any direction and gotten as far as California, Mexico, or Texas. If he stayed off the grid he figured he was hid. For now.

SIXTY-SEVEN

Light shown through gaps in the curtains. It was daytime. Jake crept to the curtain and parted it with two fingers. Outside, it was snowing lightly. His room faced the two-lane highway, empty in both directions. He craned his neck to check out the rest of the motel and saw only one other vehicle parked in front of Unit Number 2, an SUV with a roof top luggage carrier. He hobbled into the bathroom and set out his first aid kit and other medical supplies. He was shot eight days ago but was unconscious for at least half that time. He needed a bath.

He filled the tub with warm water and added a splash of iodine. He was moving better now, each movement still caused stabbing pain, but he no longer felt like he was about to split apart at any moment, a bag of blood and bones with a broken support structure, collapsing in on itself. He took his antibiotics and two oxycontin and lowered himself into the tub in agony. He gently washed, the water turning a murky rust color. When he was done all the motel towels were orange and it looked like he'd murdered someone, or quartered a large animal, but he felt better than he had in a week. Maybe better than he had in a month, now that the meth was out of his system.

He dressed and hid the Mossberg under the leather duster and carried it to the Sentra, mostly hidden behind the two hundred and fifty gallon propane tank. He walked back to the motel office and tried to smile politely at the drunk grey haired man behind the desk as he paid cash for two more nights.

He took Highway 172 through Ignacio, driving the speed limit, not seeing anything out of order, to Highway 160. He followed 160 west to Durango, fully alert now for state police, any kind of law enforcement, any kind of anything. In downtown Durango a Marriott hotel anchored Main Street on the east side. Jake drove into the underground garage below the hotel and parked the Sentra in one of the valet spots behind a gleaming black Mercedes SUV. He turned up his jacket collar to cover his neck, ears and jawline, and jack-stepped up the ramp to Main Street, the cold biting his face. The street was wide and it channeled a strong wind coming off Red Mountain Pass, chilled by fourteen thousand foot mountains and the tundra high above the tree line.

Main Street had a frontier town feel, shops with big glass display windows, brick buildings with wooden signs, old west storefronts. He spotted a pay phone. There was a tavern across the street. He went inside and sat at a long polished oak bar where he had a view of the phone and the street through the front window, the view only partially obscured by hand painted letters on the glass and taped up flyers for bands and beer specials. He ordered a beer and a cheeseburger and watched people come and go on the street.

When he was ready he walked outside to the pay phone and wedged himself inside the glass booth. He put the phone to his ear, paced in a tiny circle checking the traffic up and down the street, and called Aimee.

"Agent Begay."

Jake put his head on the glass slat and felt the wind against the phone booth. The sound of her voice still stopped him cold.

"What happened to Agent Keller?"

"He got fired, as far as I know."

"That's not what I meant."

"I know what you meant."

"When did you go back to using Begay?"

"Jake, we don't have time for this. I was worried about you. I am worried about you. I normally wouldn't say this, but you did the right thing by going underground. Something's going on here."

"What do you know?"

"So, I tried to pull our file on the Shaman, as you call him. Nothing. I mean, the FBI doesn't even have a file open on him. That's weird, right? I mean, for someone moving that much methamphetamine, and with such a recognizable alias. So, I searched our databases on the big movers in the southwest, the Mexican cartels, Sinaloa, the Zetas."

"You did all this?"

"Well, I had an intern do it. Anyway, the Shaman is referenced in a bunch of transcripts of wires, some interviews, some jailhouse calls, but nothing before 2004. I mean, the Shaman does not exist before 2004, maybe 2003 at the earliest. Just suddenly appears out of nowhere with mass quantities of high grade meth and an appetite for torture. But nothing on him. No photo, no investigation, no file. So I did a check on Bradley. The only weird thing is that his entire military record is classified. You know I have a pretty damn high security clearance, but I couldn't touch it. Access denied. I mean 2001 to 2003 is a black hole. I talked to a contact in DOD, and they said missions are usually classified, but not somebody's entire career. They think that's CIA. Or NSA."

"The guy that interviewed me in the hospital—"

"Could be. Definitely not FBI. I double-checked. So I asked Yazzie what he knew about Bradley's military record. He says nothing. Bradley never talks about it. But he's supposedly highly decorated. Got the Chief of Police job unusually fast."

"Yeah, I asked him about that."

"Well, get this. Yazzie remembers that Bradley's got a photo on the wall of his office with his Army Ranger company. This morning Yazzie gets to work real early and sneaks into Bradley's office and makes a copy of the picture and faxes it to me. With serious enhancement you can read the names off their dog tags or their nicknames off their jackets or helmets."

"You mean the intern could."

"No, I went to my DOD contact."

"Who is that, by the way?"

"Stop it. The important thing is I got these guys' names, and guess what, they are all dead, KIA circa 2003. All except one guy. A Corporal Hargrove. And you are going to love this."

"What?"

"He lives in Delta, Colorado."

"No shit, that's like an hour from here. I love you, Aimee."

"I know."

He hung up the phone and cautiously pushed open the folding door to the booth. He looked both ways and shuffled across the street with the tiny deliberate steps of an invalid. He went back to the tavern and ordered a beer. It had filled up with a happy hour crowd, most of the tables and bar stools were occupied, loud with the sound of conversation and a jam band playing on the jukebox. As Jake took the first sip of his beer a black Suburban braked hard and parked at an angle in the street in front of the phone booth. G-ride for sure. Two suits got out and circled the booth. Agent Colton emerged from the backseat. Black suit, earpiece, dark sunglasses, shoulder holster. The suits looked up and down the street in equal parts aggression, purpose and panic. They fanned out up and down the block.

Jake slipped from his bar stool, turned the collar up on his duster, and side-stepped around people to the back of the bar. He thought about the men's room but knew that wouldn't work. That was the first place he always looked when he was hunting someone. He pushed open the swinging door to the kitchen. A dishwasher with long grey hair pulled back in a pony tail under a hair net looked at him blankly.

"Uh, can I help you?"

Jake dug in his pocket for his bottle of oxycontin.

"Looking for a place to do a line. You want in?"

"Sure, man."

The dishwasher grinned at him, brown teeth, missing a canine, and let the coiled spray hose for pots and pans dangle in the sink. He grabbed a black leather jacket off of a coat rack in the kitchen corner. The jacket had insignia from a biker gang that Jake recognized from a newsletter that used to be emailed to him weekly by the High Intensity Drug Trafficking Areas Program—a federal, state, and local partnership that congress began funding at the height of the drug war in the eighties. These days most of the newsletter was filled with Narco messages with pictures of beheaded or mutilated corpses hanging in dusty town squares and off of freeway overpasses in Mexico by the Zetas or some other cartel, but good old fashioned motorcycle gangs still piqued law enforcement's interest. The jacket was worn thin by age and use, and oddly soft and conforming, whatever protective stiffness, useful for preventing road rash, long beaten away. He slung the jacket over narrow shoulders and led Jake into the walk-in cooler and brushed off two pickle buckets to sit on. Jake cleared a space on one of the metal shelves and crushed a pill into powder with a ketchup bottle. He used a credit card to push the powder into lines. Jake rolled up a dollar bill and they each snorted a fat line. Jake rocked back on the heavy plastic bucket and pinched his nose. He exhaled deeply and rested his back on tubes of vacuum packed deli meats. He felt instantly content. Time slowed. The world dimmed, blinked once, and faded away.

"I'm gonna do another rail if that's cool."

"Help yourself."

The dishwasher closed a nostril and sniffed up two lines. He handed the rolled up bill back to Jake. Jake took his time. He was in no hurry now. He inhaled a line, leaned on a frozen ham, and grunted. A hum rippled through is body. The pain was gone. He dug into his jeans pocket for his Winston Lights. He picked one out and felt around for his lighter.

"He man, that's not cool. Cigarette smoke will fuck up the food."

Jake paused, nodded at the dishwasher, and put the cigarette back in the pack. The metal shelves receded. He saw his breath but didn't feel the cold. There was a light bulb with a pull string above the door. The heat from it caused condensation to bead on the ceiling and run in streaks down the walls that froze and turned into in crystals half way down.

"So, were you a biker?"

"Was. Am. You don't never really leave a club like that."

"Maybe they leave you."

The dishwasher laughed. His eyes were close set over a long narrow nose. His cheeks were pockmarked and covered by a white scraggly beard, thicker where there'd once been a goatee. There was something rodent about his face, but there was a kindness there too.

"You know, you just wake up one day and you're someone else completely."

"Don't I know it." Jake tried to laugh but ended up wheezing, spittle dangling from his lower lip. His face felt numb.

"They say people don't really change, but your motivations sure do. I used to be motivated by anger. Fear. Freedom. Can't really say why I did what I did. Now I'm just happy to have a job. Dishwashing. Move up to line cook soon. Used to be scared shitless of having job. Spent almost half my life doing anything to not have a job. Ran dope. Did some time. Thought that boredom was death. Having a boss was being a slave. Now, I like the repetition, like knowing what each day will be like. Good thing about working 40 hours is I know my time, is my time. But hell, I don't know, could be I got used to the yoke. Maybe I'm just a dog done been beat too much."

"No. You're just a man that knows what he wants."

"Or maybe I'm a man that just don't want nothin no more."

Jake was having trouble with his eyelids. He finally shut one eye and looked at the dishwasher with the other. The man's ponytail was more white than grey. He couldn't have weighed more than one hundred and twenty pounds. The light bulb flickered once and dimmed a shade. The metal walls were sweating.

When Jake refocused the dishwasher was gone and he was

alone in the walk-in. He was cold. The oxy was gone, not a trace of white powder on the shelf. He found the rolled up dollar bill tucked into his jacket pocket. He pushed open the door to the walk-in. The kitchen was empty, and the bar was dark, save for auxiliary lights over the exit signs. He paused at the back door, and opened it a crack, listening for a piercing alarm that didn't come, and surveilled the alley. It was black outside. He gently shut the door behind him. He walked east down the alley to the street. There were distant voices, laughter, low talk. A few cars were on the street. It couldn't have been that long after the bars let out. Maybe 2:30, Jake guessed. When the coast was clear he hustled across the street and continued down the alley east, to the far end of Main Street. At the end of the block the Marriott was in sight. He hugged a wall in the alley and waited. When five minutes passed without any sign of traffic, he walked calmly to the garage. The Sentra was still there. He got down on the ground and checked the undercarriage for GPS. He couldn't be sure, but it looked clean. He executed an eight point turn to unwedge the Sentra from a row of tightly packed cars and crept it up the ramp and out of the garage. He drove the speed limit back to Ignacio. He couldn't believe he'd lost them, but then again, he could. The world is a big place.

The parking lot of little roadside motel outside of Ignacio was empty. He parked the Sentra behind the propane tank and stamped out a cigarette. He fumbled with the key to his room. No cars passed. It was quiet except for early morning birdsong. He pushed his way in and fell back heavy against the door. He locked it, took a swig off the handle of whiskey, and lowered himself carefully, and painfully, onto the bed.

SIXTY-EIGHT

There is a certain clarity that comes with age and loss. The Shaman was not old. By American standards he was in the prime of middle age. But he had plenty of loss. His wife and children were killed before the CIA could get them out of Iraq, if they had ever tried. He didn't know. It no longer mattered. Life was reduced to its simplest form. He saw his existence in binary terms. Decisions were not really decisions at all. There was action, and there was inaction. And he would not live out the remainder of his days on Earth in inaction. He had achieved a sublime clarity.

He walks through the doublewide trailer barefoot. It is a dangerous thing to do. The carpet is threadbare with patches of plywood showing through, and littered with used needles, cigarette butts, and empty bottles and cans. But he has perspective on danger. Danger is relative.

There are a dozen of his army strewn about the compound, maybe two dozen. He doesn't know. They are hard to keep track of. They are wild. Unkempt. Most haven't slept in weeks. They are losing it, he smiles to himself. They see Shadow People everywhere. They are afraid of open spaces, but terrified of their own shadows on walls. They prefer to huddle in corners and dark rooms. For their next mission he'll have to get them higher. He will blow their minds.

He opens the front door and stands on the narrow porch. He looks out at the desert. It is a beautiful desert. So different from the one he left on the other side of the world. Compared to home, this desert is teaming with life. There are birds. Hummingbirds poking into the budding cactus flowers. Quail, dove, crow and hawk. Animals abound in all shapes and sizes. From deer and elk and the wild pigs they call javelinas, to the littlest chipmunks, mice, and lizards. Dozens of tree species, hundreds more grasses and flowers. Even the rocks come in a splendor of diversity. Black and red volcanic rocks, like the skin of meteors. Sandstone, granite, quartz, coal, uranium. Endless varieties. There is no plan. Whatever is there, is there. Whatever lives, lives. The rest dies.

His head begins to sweat. He rubs it with a handkerchief and then ties it around his neck. He watches a trail of dust approach. A fast moving pickup truck. The bloom of dust in the truck's wake rises like a mushroom cloud in front of Shiprock. It is a terrifying and beautiful sight. The two thousand foot monolith is the perfect backdrop for the apocalypse.

The pickup pulls up to the front door. To the Shaman. Two 55 gallon drums of gasoline are lashed to the bed. There is a ruckus behind him and the army unpacks from the house and fans into the sunlight. They smile. They hug. They begin to chant. To scream.

Fresh ammunition for the coming war.

SIXTY-NINE

Yeah, that was a fucked up deal."

William Hargrove had the look of someone who fell down hard but had gotten back up. Eyes crystal blue, whites clear, close cropped haircut that hid his prematurely thinning hair, and a chestnut beard covering up pockmark scars. Now thirty-two years old, off everything except the beer, not steady work but enough to pay the bills. Work that kept him outside, in the cold, crisp mountain air. He stood in waders, the suspenders over long sleeve thermals and under a top of the line Mountain Hardware jacket, balancing on an outcropping of flat rocks in the Animas river, a fly reel in his hand. Hargrove worked as a fly fishing guide for a company out of Telluride. Jake had hired him.

"You ex-military?" Hargrove looked back toward the river bank. Jake sat on a downed log with a fishing pole wedged in the crook of his elbow. Cottonwoods provided cover from a gentle snowfall.

"Yup," Jake said, lighting a cigarette. He shivered and pulled the collar up on the duster.

"Thought so. That or CIA. As soon as you showed up this morning. Hell, as soon as I got the call last night. Full day out of nowhere, asking for me, paid in cash, and then you show up all battle scarred. Where did you serve, Iraq or Afghanistan?"

Jake thought for a moment.

"Both."

"Where'd you get wounded?"

"I got shot in Gallup, New Mexico."

"No shit?"

"Got out of the shit without a scratch. But New Mexico might just kill me yet."

Hargrove flicked his wrist and cast upriver, a hand-tied fly landing just beyond the ice that crept out from the river bank. He watched the fly bob on the current downriver.

"Funny you should say CIA," Jake said. "Saw a lot of black Suburbans in Durango. Why did you think I might be CIA?"

"They're who got him out. Bradley. You come all the way out here to ask about Bradley, right?"

"So why'd you take me out here if you made me from the get go this morning?"

Hargrove yanked the fly out of the water just before it drifted under an eddy covered by a sheet of ice, and reeled in the line.

"Sir, I'm not going to turn down two hundred dollars for a day of fly fishing. It is my favorite thing to do. What I'm best at, these days."

"You weren't worried I was here to kill you?"

Hargrove lowered his shoulders and looked at Jake. His hand drifted toward the hunting knife sheathed on his belt.

"Naw. You looked too sick."

"Lucky for me."

"Yeah, you look lucky."

Jake dragged his cigarette through the snow next to the river to put it out, and flicked off the remaining wet tobacco, and put the used filter back in the pack, so as not to leave nonbiodegradable litter on the pristine river bank.

"So what happened?"

"Like I said. Fucked up deal."

"So Bradley comes out of the bunker with an Iraqi, presumably some scientist or technician."

"Yeah, in a blood splattered lab coat. And a minute later three Blackhawks are landing and we get the fuck out of there."

"What about the other guys in the squad? This Emiliano Hernandez, your squad leader, what happened to him? Uh... Denton, Zapata, Miller."

"Careful now. You're talking about some very good, very dead friends of mine."

"KIA?"

"That's right. The desert took Denton. Hernandez, Miller and Zapata died in the firefight."

"Why was Bradley the only one to make it out—what—with this Iraqi?"

"I don't know. Like I said. The CIA guys came in and we got the fuck out of there. I never saw the inside of that bunker."

The wind picked up and set the Cottonwoods swaying, the wood popping and cracking with the movement. The branches overhead shook, dislodging several inches of snow that had settled in the tree tops. A clump floated down and landed on Jake's shoulders and inside the duster's collar. The snow stung the bare skin on the back of his neck. As it melted, his cotton sweatshirt grew wet, heavy, and cold.

"But what was so special about this Iraqi. Everyone dead and he gets this guy out?"

"Guy said he knew where the WMD was."

"That why the CIA was there?"

"Well, they sure as shit weren't there for me."

"But they never found any weapons of mass destruction in Iraq."

"Who knows. And you know what? I don't give a shit anymore. I used to think it was a big deal. But hell, the Russians had ten thousand nukes trained on us for decades and life went on. Let em have their WMDs. Everyone knows we'll nuke anyone who uses 'em on us. We'd do it too. They all know we're crazy. Crazy is our best defense."

"So you don't think it was worth it?"

"Not for the shit I've seen. Not for all the tea in China. People getting blown up in markets everyday. Beheaded. Tortured with power tools. Car bomb kills thirty people in Bagdad, even now, and nobody bats an eye. Doesn't even make the news. You were there. What do you think?"

Jake tried to dry the back of his neck with his sleeve.

"Not for all the poppies in Kabul."

SEVENTY

On the morning of the first day of the Pow Wow, Jake awoke in the motel room outside of Ignacio. It had snowed during the night and pale blue light leaked through the curtains. The room smelled fetid, old bandages and iodine swabbed gauze piled up in the wastebaskets. The sheets had not been laundered during his stay. He was fine with it. He felt safe in the room. Off the grid. They hadn't found him yet. Car hid. Fake name in the motel's office register. The world was a big and random place. He didn't want to leave the room. It was cold outside. Hell, it was cold inside. He turned on the TV and ate Apple Jacks out of the box. The beef jerky, Pop Tarts, and Goldfish were all gone. There was an inch left at the bottom of the handle of bourbon. His wounds still oozed, but he could move better each day. What he needed to do was think. He was working on it, laying off the oxy the best he could.

So Bradley rescued this Iraqi scientist. Could he be the Shaman? They both showed up on the reservation around the same time. Bradley returned from war and then the Shaman first appeared. But why were the two of them such fast friends? What happened in the bunker? And why was Bradley working with the Shaman now, after all these years, assuming that he was? Turning to crime was completely out of character for

Bradley. So the war jaded Bradley and he grew fat and lazy. But in cahoots with a meth dealer? Why?

He got out of bed and lit a cigarette. The wind moaned outside. He walked to the window and cautiously parted the curtain an inch. No new vehicles. Snow blew across the parking lot and swept onto the empty highway. He exhaled and smoke settled just below the ceiling. He realized it didn't matter why. What mattered right now was saving his ass. And Aimee. And maybe Cally, Mary, Yazzie, anyone else he's gotten to know over the last year. Maybe the whole damn reservation.

Jake inserted the SIM card into his phone and tried calling Yazzie. He knew he was traceable again. The phone's screen showed only one bar of connectivity, but after a long pause, the phone rang on the other end.

"Is this who I think it is? Or is this someone who just killed whoever I think it is?"

"It's me."

"It does sound a little like you."

"It's me. I ain't dead yet."

"Okay, it sounds like you, but more redneck."

"Listen, where's Aimee?"

"She's going to the Pow Wow. Everyone is."

"She's not safe. He knows about her. The Shaman. And so does Bradley. They're working together. I just don't know why."

"The Contest Pow Wow starts today. It is her niece's first dance with the Tiny Tots. My son is dancing in the Young Warrior Division. I will keep an eye on her."

"So will I."

SEVENTY-ONE

Agent Aimee Begay's alarm went off at 5:30 a.m., as it did every morning, regardless of time zone. She was staying at the Gallup Hampton Inn. She could have stayed with family but she preferred the Hampton Inn. The room was familiar, identical to many she'd stayed in, in the dozens of cities and towns across America that her job took her to. The room was clean, sterile even. She wasn't traveling on official government business so she had to pay for the room herself, but she had enough Hilton Honors points to stay there free for a month, if she wanted to.

She put on her favorite yoga pants, black, Lululemon, one hundred and eight dollars online, and a black lycra sports bra under a frayed white tank top. She tied her hair back in a ponytail and took the elevator down a floor to the exercise room. It was empty, as was the lobby and the reception desk. She plugged earbuds into her iPhone and watched CNN on mute as she did an hour on the treadmill.

Pleasantly drenched in sweat, she returned to her room. She set the in-room coffee maker on brew, and took a long shower and washed her hair. When she was done, and the bathroom was so completely fogged she couldn't see the mirror, she wrapped a towel on her head, applied ample moisturizers, and began her day.

She grabbed a complimentary orange from a tray in the

lobby and drove her little white rental car to the FBI's Gallup Field Office. She was surprised that the door was unlocked, and even more surprised that Mary was at her desk in front of her computer. Mary's eyes lit up when she saw Aimee. Perhaps not her favorite niece, but certainly her most interesting and mysterious. She adored little girl Aimee, the one who learned the hoop dance by age five, who insisted that mangy cahouly dog sleep in bed with her each night until the thing got kicked by a horse and died. This Aimee she loved, but worried about. They both worked for the Bureau, so if anyone understood Aimee, it would be her. And she did not understand Aimee. The two women hugged.

"I don't know why, but didn't think you'd be at work. I thought they hadn't staffed an agent to replace Jake," Aimee said, examining the small office.

"They haven't yet."

"So you're just collecting a paycheck?"

"And why wouldn't I?"

"I mean, what do you do all day?"

"There's filing to catch up on. Jeez, it's not my fault they haven't staffed an agent here."

"Do they know you don't have anything to do?"

"No, and I'm not going to tell them."

The two women looked at each other for a long minute. Finally Aimee broke the impasse.

"So, I was going to take a look at Jake's office."

"You haven't been in there yet?"

"No, why?"

"Someone's been in there. Thought it was you. I mean, who else would it be?"

"I don't know."

They both went up the stairs to Jake's office. The door was locked. Mary removed her federal credentials that hung on a lanyard around her neck. A key was inside the plastic sleeve that held her PIV identification card. She unlocked the door and propped it open. The room was a mess.

"Jake was always unorganized, but someone's been in. Whoever it was tried to put stuff back where they found it but with an office this disorganized, that makes it tough. I can tell stuff was moved. I think they were into my desk too."

"Did you tell anybody?"

"Who would I tell?"

"The ASAC, for starters."

"Don't trust that guy. He fired Jake."

"Maybe Jake deserved it."

"Jake is a good guy."

"There are a lot of good guys out there."

SEVENTY-TWO

Jake took the SIM card out of his phone. He put on his boots, covered the Mossberg with the duster, and walked out the door. The ground was icy. The snow over the motel's dirt parking lot was hardened by the wind. Jake walked in short steps, each slight slip sending warning shocks through his healing body. He had to wedge open the door to the Sentra, the joints frozen stuck. It was just as cold inside the car. His breath fogged the windshield. He said a prayer before he tried starting the car. He should have started the car first, before making the call to Yazzie. He was a sitting duck here. Stupid mistake, the kind that get you killed. He turned the key and dashboard lights came on but the engine didn't turn over. He pumped the gas to prime the starter and tried again but still nothing. He jiggled the key in the ignition. It was stuck on the wrong position, sending juice to the electrical but not to the starter. He forced it one click over and the little engine started and then coughed on the grinding ignition. He cranked the heat and turned down the stereo. He couldn't see anything. The windshield was covered by three inches of snow and ice. He cursed himself for not having an ice scraper in the car. Then he remembered it was Cally's car, and cursed her. The call to Yazzie had put him back on the grid. They knew where he was. The internal clock clicked away in his head. Every second counted. He needed something heavy. He leaned his shoulder into the door and got out and used the butt of the Mossberg to clear the snow and dislodge the ice from the windshield. He did a half-assed job and got back inside the car and directed all the heat to the front defroster. He reversed back from the propane tank and then put it in drive and bounced over the hard packed ruts in the snow to the highway and drove south. He knew they could be minutes away, whoever they were. Whether they were CIA or NSA or some covert arm of the FBI didn't really matter, only that they wanted him stopped, probably killed. It had taken them less than an hour to track down where he'd made the call from in Durango, and since then they must have left someone stationed in the area. He figured they didn't have a tracking device on him or the car or they would have already found him. With any luck they didn't know what he was driving. But his best defense was taking as many roads as possible, each turn was a fifty-fifty decision whomever was hunting him would have to make.

His first opportunity to get off the highway was La Plata County Road 318 which doubled as Indian Route 110, and he took it west, deeper into the woods. A grater had passed recently piling snow on either side of the road. It was probably a dirt road, he couldn't see the surface under the snow, hard packed in washboard ruts. But the front wheel drive Sentra was surprisingly good in the snow. The engine was small but placed in the front end so the weight was over the wheels, and the car was light, so he could take the mountain road at forty miles per hour, feathering the brakes on the turns, keeping the car out of a slide. After twenty minutes the defroster melted the last of the ice on the windshield and he could see clearly.

He rolled down the window and lit a cigarette. There was no one behind him. He hadn't seen a soul since he left the motel.

The driving grew trickier as the road jackknifed into Little Cow Canyon, crossing the Florida river at the bottom before straightening. He reached the junction with Highway 550 and relaxed some. His neck ached from being hunched over the steering wheel, trying to feel the tires on the icy road.

Highway 550 was well plowed and sanded. There was a steady flow of traffic. Safety in numbers. The Sentra was coated in frozen mud and road grime. Ice dyed the color of dirt hid the original paint and obscured the license plate. He hoped the car was inconspicuous, maybe even unrecognizable.

At Farmington he took State Route 371 south, rather than continuing on the busier U.S. 64 to Shiprock. The road descended and the land opened up. At the lower elevations the snow stopped, just a white dusting over the empty expanse. The land turned familiar. He knew he was back on the Navajo Nation by that sense of isolation, raw nature. Dry mountains and barren valleys. No manmade structures for as far as the eye could see. Peace. He took solace in the distinct colors of the reservation, unique in the world. The faint wintergreen of high desert sage in the washed out sun under thin silver wisps of the trailing edge of snow. Mountains striated with perfect rings of pink, yellow, and peach, with a layer of white at the base. He felt nostalgic. Like coming home.

Near Crownpoint he turned west on Little Boy Road which turned into Navajo Route 9 and ran to Highway 491, a road he knew well. He turned south into a migration of traffic, all traveling east on Navajo 264 to Window Rock, to the Pow Wow. Three miles from the fairgrounds Jake turned onto a BIA service road that ran behind the iconic arch rock formation that gave Window Rock its name. The dirt road circled the town and ended at a sand and gravel pit that the BIA leased from the tribe for its road crews. Jake turned the Sentra around so it was parked facing out toward Navajo 264, grabbed his gear, and started hiking. One slow step at a time, he walked up the hills to a rocky perch overlooking the fairgrounds. He laid down with a grunt and rolled to a tolerable position on his side. He took the field binoculars out of the inside pocket of the duster and scanned the vast crowds below.

SEVENTY-THREE

Aimee sat on the first row of bleachers at the fairgrounds arena next to Mary, surrounded by aunts, uncles, cousins and her last surviving grandparent, her grandmother Dolee. The Tiny Tots kicked off the Contest Pow Wow, performing first because the youngest children represented life and the future. Aimee's four year-old niece Anhinga was dressed in a bright orange shawl, delicate face paint and tight braids harnessed by a beaded headband. The drums began beating and the children began moving, cautiously at first, some watching each other, some watching the sidelines for encouragement, and some watching their footwork on the ground. The girls wore knee high moccasins, ornate long-sleeve blouses, sides open, with flowing bright colored fringe, tied with a concho or sash belt. Anhinga spun a circle and then began moving her shawl in the air like a butterfly. Each child's dance was slightly different based on family tradition. Twenty-five years earlier Aimee had done the same dance in front of a much smaller crowd. A little girl mimicking a butterfly in flight.

Aimee was amazed by the size of the gathering. She had not been back to the Pow Wow for several years. Cases did not accommodate young agents' vacation schedules. And the passage of time was different in Washington D.C. The Pow

Wow had grown considerably in her absence. In recent years the Contest Pow Wow was combined with the Navajo Nation Fair so now there was a full Indian rodeo and livestock show, an arts and crafts expo, and a hundred and fifty thousand dollars in prize money for dancers, singers, and drummers in dozens of contest divisions. There was a midnight showing of Star Wars dubbed over in Navajo. Fireworks every night. Rascal Flats was headlining the last night of concerts.

When the drums stopped for the Tiny Tots the families spilled out from the bleachers and hugged their little ones and held them up and spun them around, no longer worried about ruffling their beautiful ceremonial dance clothes. Anhinga was swept up into her family's arms and carried to her great grandmother Dolee, who looked into Anhinga's sparkling bright brown eyes and caressed the sides of her face, delighting in the flawless baby soft cheeks. She leaned her face in and touched noses with the child.

A man across the arena stared at them. He was a redhead with red skin to match, deep freckles from too much sun, white man, Aimee guessed, but there are gingers in all races, and it was impossible to be sure. Thin, tight fitting leather jacket, and jeans that looked two sizes too small, unexpectedly shrunk in the laundry. Pocket chain. He made no attempt to be inconspicuous, shifting from foot to foot, holding a thermos like it was a live grenade, he looked straight at them, straight at her, Aimee realized.

The family drifted toward the concession stands for grilled corn on the cob, churros and cokes, Anhinga holding hands with two of her aunts while the cousins held Grandma Dolee's elbows, escorting her across the dirt fairgrounds. Aimee brought up the rear, looking back at the strange man who made no attempt to look away. He didn't follow them. He just idled in place, his feet doing an odd involuntary shuffle.

They took their time perusing the various food carts and stalls, loading up cardboard trays with snacks. Aimee bought a diet coke for herself and a cotton candy for Anhinga, for which she received several disapproving looks, as the child had already consumed a week's worth of sugar. As they made their way back to the bleachers Aimee noticed someone else staring at her, a teenage Indian girl with limp, greasy hair, and scabs on her face. She wore just a long sleeve T-shirt with thumbholes in the cuffs, inappropriate for the weather, muddy sweatpants, and sneakers with no laces and holes in them. She also held a thermos. Aimee continued walking as she watched the teenage girl. The girl locked eyes with her, half dead eyes. Aimee scowled. The girl smiled. A hint of recognition. Her mouth was a black hole. Aimee shuddered. The girl had no teeth.

SEVENTY-FOUR

The ground was cold. Jake lay on his belly, looking through his field binoculars, conscious that every passing minute his body heat leached into the earth in a desperate and futile attempt to warm the ground to his own, ever declining, body temperature. Most of his recon work had been in warm temperatures, exceedingly warm temperatures, although there was cold work—Helmand Province, North Waziristan, Tora Bora.

He focused his binoculars on the fairgrounds arena where the Contest Pow Wow was beginning. Children in bright colored ceremonial dress danced to drummers. From this distance their movements looked minute, but in their brilliant shawls and serapes, they were like gemstones sparkling in the sun. He could barely make out Aimee. The binoculars were a far cry from the precision scope on his old sniper riffle.

He saw some characters he didn't like. Tweakers, plenty sketchy. He counted four of them within a hundred yards of Aimee. They didn't seem to be doing anything, keeping tabs on her, perhaps. They all carried thermoses. There could have been more. There was distance and thousands of people to account for. Two drunks started to fight on a set of bleachers across from Aimee. A barefoot old man wandered on the outskirts of the arena with a blanket wrapped around his shoulders and wild matted hair. But the tweakers stood out precisely because they weren't fighting, or talking to anybody, or watching the dancers, or the rodeo. They weren't doing anything. Except watching his soon to be ex-wife.

Jake put the SIM card into his phone and called Yazzie. He had one bar on the phone. He got nothing. He cursed and dialed the number and then held the phone high over his head. He put it back to his ear and heard the crackly sound of a ringtone. After an eternity, Yazzie answered.

"Do you see her?"

"She's in the bleachers. Mmmm, the children were wonderful. Everybody loves to watch the Tiny Tots dance. It is a great day."

"She's being followed. I have eyes on her now, but I won't if she moves."

"I will call you if she goes anywhere. My son's division is about to be called. I am helping him get ready. Can you see from where you are? Will you watch him dance?"

"Yes, I'm on high ground."

"Good."

"Okay."

Jake felt like there was more he needed to say, but Yazzie was watching her like he said he would do, which was a lot to ask on such an important day for him. He hung up the phone and took out the SIM card. When they traced the call they would find him along with two hundred thousand other people.

Jake re-situated himself atop the hillside and focused the binoculars on the arena just as the Southern Young Warrior Division was beginning. The dancers were in full regalia, moving forward or side to side, never backward. Backward represented cowardice. Jake easily spotted Yazzie's boy. He wore a brilliant green ribbon shirt with horsehair fringe and eagle feather bustles on his waist and shoulders, a bone breastplate, bandoliers, and a breechcloth over buckskin leggings. Barely fifteen, he looked like a man. His face was fierce, painted with crisp lines, jaw set, eyes sharp and clear. Jake could see the whites of his eyes flash even from where he lay in the yellowed grass.

He focused the binoculars on Aimee, and then swept for the four tweakers he was keeping under surveillance. One of them was moving. Jake popped in the SIM card and texted Yazzie:

Someone's moving.

A skinny man in a leather jacket and jeans with either red or bleached hair was jogging into the arena. His face was red, his eyelashes looked blonde, like they'd been burnt. He had no eyebrows. Jake tried to text Aimee but he knew there would be no time. He looked up from his phone long enough to track the man's trajectory. He wasn't headed toward Aimee. He was running toward the dancers.

The man ran along the first row of dancers. The dancers spun in semi-circles, never completing a full circle—symbolizing that no man is perfect—but rather rotating back and forth to keep balance in the world, moving with the drums, feathers and fringe fluttering up and down. The man stopped in front of a dancer in green, Yazzie's son. He held up a thermos. He stopped and stared at the boy and then braced the thermos against a bone thin leg and unscrewed the cap. The boy looked at him, seeing the man for the first time, and scowled. The boy held his head up and stuck out his jaw. Defiance to whatever insult this deranged man intended. The man twisted the cap to the thermos loose, stood up, and threw a clear liquid onto the boy. The boy stopped dancing and his hands flew to his face.

He collapsed into a crouch. The liquid was in his eyes, and it burned. Gasoline. It mixed with his face paint and ran into his eyes and mouth. The man fell to one knee and took out a Zippo lighter. He flicked it against his thigh and got it lit on the first try. He cupped his hand, nurturing the flame. Jake recoiled in horror, screaming from atop the mountain. No one could hear him. The man stood up and took the time to dust off his knees and straighten his tight leather jacket. He watched the boy squirm on the ground. And then he tossed the lighter at him.

Yazzie was there, charging like a bull. The burning Zippo lighter bounced off Yazzie's broad chest and landed on the dirt arena floor. Yazzie slammed into the thin man with his head and shoulder. All the air left the man's body. Yazzie launched his weight into the man, driving him into the ground as hard has he could. He heard the splintering of bones and the man gasping fruitlessly for air. Yazzie brought a ham fist into the side of the man's head and propped himself up enough to see the man's T-shirt under his jacket begin to turn red from where broken ribs had punctured through skin.

SEVENTY-FIVE

Aimee had Anhinga on her lap in the bleachers. The child felt warm in her arms. It wasn't an especially cold day, but when the wind blew she was happy to have the little thirty-five pound space heater in her lap. She was happy to have her in her lap no matter what the temperature was. She was surprised that the child's body heat seemed to sink into her chest, into her core, warming her from the inside. She could feel the child breathing, the little contractions an affirmation of life itself. For the first time in her life she thought she saw why people had these little creatures. She looked down the row of bleachers and saw Dolee smiling at her. Aimee shook her head.

And then her attention was drawn to a commotion on the arena floor. She did a double take. Yazzie was on top of the skinny ginger she'd seen staring inappropriately at her earlier. Yazzie thundered away at the man's face, his fists were covered in blood and every upswing and backstroke sent blood splatter through the air and spraying across the dirt.

Aimee handed Anhinga to Mary. She scanned the area but didn't see anyone casing her. She gathered her purse and coat. She didn't know what was going on but she had the feeling that she was putting her family in danger by being with them. She had to get to the office. She needed help from D.C. She should have been pushing harder for more intervention from Washington. Pushing to be officially assigned the case. Something seriously fucked up was happening on the reservation. She knew on some level that she was protecting Jake by not involving the FBI more, not pressuring her superiors for manpower and resources. But shit was getting out of hand. She could feel it in the air.

She made her way out of the arena. There was a buzz in the crowd, a tension. The crowd swells were becoming erratic. People moving one way and then the other. The patterns of order dissolving. She fought against the tide of arriving spectators, craning their necks, agitated, so different from the usual sloven rhythm of slow time. She sensed the people's curiosity. And their fear.

She crossed a vast parking lot. The wind blew wild in the open, buffered only by rows of parked RVs that rocked on their suspensions. Her long hair whipped violently at her face. Her rental car looked like many others, and she endured several false positives before finding the little white car, parked close to a long line of motorcycles, veterans taking part in the honor guard. She shielded her eyes with her hand and pressed her forehead against the rear window of her car, checking to make sure no one was hiding in the backseat. When she was satisfied that the car was empty, she got behind the wheel. It was immediately warmer and quieter with the door shut, out of the wind.

She inched the car against the flow of traffic, waiting a long while for a gap in the stream of vehicles entering the parking lot long enough to shoot out to Highway 264. She headed east slowly on the two lane blacktop to avoid the masses of people walking along the shoulder. All vehicle traffic headed west. After a few miles the foot traffic eased, but there was still an unbroken line of cars in the westbound lane traveling in the direction of the fairgrounds.

She pushed it up to forty miles an hour as the road cleared. The heater was blasting at full now. She absently drummed her thumbs on the steering wheel to an Albuquerque Top 40 station relayed out of Gallup. She let her eyes scan the wide open high desert running to the horizon. Then she saw red and blue flashing lights in the rear view mirror.

"Oh, you've got to be shitting me."

She was getting pulled over. When she first slowed down and crept toward the shoulder she was sure the cop would speed past her to some real emergency. But no, she was really being pulled over. A police cruiser with full siren lights blazing in the grill and on the roof rode her bumper all the way onto the shoulder until her little white car was half off the pavement and half on the long dry buffalo grass that sloped down off the road.

She twisted the key in the ignition and turned off the engine. The radiator ticked intermittently and then was quiet. Passing traffic rocked the car back and forth. She watched the grass wave in the wind. She waited. What the fuck is he doing? she thought. She unbuckled her seatbelt and grabbed her credentials and looped her front two fingers around the door handle to get out and ask what was going on, when she glanced in the side mirror and stopped cold. It was Bradley.

Something told her to stay in the car. Bradley stepped out of the cruiser and cinched up his belt. He straightened his hat and then walked slowly toward her car. His right hand was on his holster. She took her phone out of her purse and scrolled through her contacts to Jake's number.

Pulled over by Bra—she typed, but before she could finish, there was a loud knock on the driver's side window next to her ear. She rolled down the window with the hand crank. Cheap fucking rental.

"Chief?"

The window was taken up by his enormous gut. She was speaking to a wall of fat.

"Hello? You want to explain this?"

The mountain of man shifted, lowered, and she found herself looking square into mirrored sunglasses. She read nothing. She saw nothing there.

"Get out."

"Excuse me?"

"Agent Begay. I know you. I know your family. You should not have come back to the reservation. You were told not to."

She pressed send on the text message waiting on her phone. He snatched the phone out of her hand. Reflexes too quick for a man of his size. He looked at the phone and read the screen, expressionless, and then threw the phone into a rocky ravine at the bottom of the grassy slope. Her eyes involuntarily followed the arc of the throw. The silver glint of phone broke into several pieces and clattered into the crags and seams of the rock strewn earth.

"What the fuck?"

Bradley punched her in the face and she flopped onto the passenger seat. He opened the car door and wrapped his hand around her neck. He lifted her out of the car by her throat and dragged her that way to the police cruiser. She gasped for air. Her legs kicked helplessly. Her heels barely scuffed the dirt.

SEVENTY-SIX

Jake looked down from his perch above the arena, a sick feeling growing in his gut. A familiar feeling. At first, no one reacted too much to Yazzie beating his son's attacker, a drunken fight, unfortunate perhaps, but not unheard of at a pow wow. And then the boy continued to claw at his eyes, on his knees, and the other dancers must have smelled the gasoline. Someone wrapped the boy in a blanket and looked around for a medic, calling frantically for an ambulance. And Yazzie kept beating on the man until the dancers pulled him off, frothing at the mouth, Yazzie so unlike anyone knew him to be, and a circle gathered as other dancers, who had smelled the gasoline, wanted to join in and begin the beating anew. Someone held Yazzie back until he spun away and pointed out into the crowd, shouting orders, warnings. Jake figured he was imploring people to look for the others. Anyone with a thermós similar to the one the red haired man had used as a weapon. The undulations of the crowd changed. Jake could see the wave and crest of the crowd spiral around a new axis. And then a blaze caught his eye, someone was on fire. Jake focused his binoculars on a figure running in between vender stalls, possibly a girl. Formerly a girl. The figure collapsed on its knees. Some people ran toward her, some ran away. Flames engulfed the girl. She crawled feebly for a few more feet and then rolled onto her back, charred arms frozen in front of her. Then all hell broke loose. Like ants scurrying after someone kicked the top off the ant hill.

Jake scanned the bleachers but saw no sign of Aimee. Her family was still there, huddling together, trying to understand what was going on, but Aimee was gone. Jake struggled to his feet and hurried down the mountain. The descent seemed steeper coming down than going up. He scampered from rock to rock to brace himself and slow his descent, but his speed quickly got out of control and he slid on a patch of loose dry dirt and his legs went out from under him. He landed on his back and slid on his legs, opening up the scabs from the buckshot. He couldn't breathe. He clutched his chest, sure he'd broken his patched up sternum, held together by screws and a metal plate, but he'd only knocked the wind out of himself. After a minute of sheer pain, he could breathe again.

He found the Sentra at the bottom of the mountain. He started it and put the SIM card back into his phone. He was about to call Yazzie when the phone buzzed. An incoming text message: *Pulled over by Bra*—appeared on the screen.

"Shit." He looked back at the mountain and squinted. He called and texted her but nothing went through. He held his stomach.

"Fuck." He called Yazzie. It rang for a long time before he answered, out of breath, not sounding like himself.

"Did you see what happened?" Yazzie said, speaking faster and higher in pitch than normal.

"Yes, is your boy okay?"

Breathing on the other end of the line.

"Yes, I think so. It's just—"

"I know, it could have been bad."

"Yes."

"Listen, they got Aimee."

"No. How? Did you see it? She was just here. Before—"

"Bradley's got her."

"Did you see it?"

"No. She texted me. Bradley pulled her over. And now her phone doesn't work."

"Cell reception's bad on the rez."

"He took her."

"Arrested her? I'll meet you at Tribal Police Headquarters." Yazzie paused and let a minute pass, thinking, while Jake was quiet on the other end, unable to find the words.

"No. That's not where he's taking her. I know where they're going."

SEVENTY-SEVEN

The Navajo woman is on her knees in the dirt at the base of a red cliff face scorched black. Her wrists are handcuffed behind her back. The handcuffs are hers. They were taken from her purse along with her wallet and her FBI credentials, which have already been burned in a giant bonfire to resounding applause. She is drenched in gasoline. Her long black hair is soaked with it. A crowd around her jeers. Someone throws a half-full beer can at her. It glances off her cheek, angering an already swollen knot under her eye where she took a punch from a policeman who outweighed her by a hundred and fifty pounds. She did not get abducted without a fight. Her lip is bleeding. Her sweater is ripped exposing a bra strap. Her left shoulder is dislocated. With her arms cuffed behind her back, the pain is excruciating. But she hardly feels it. She only thinks about fire. Fire is a terrible thing for a beautiful person. It is a terrible thing for anyone, does terrible things to anyone. But she wants to be remembered as beautiful. She does not want to live. She does not want to be left alive.

The gasoline runs into her eyes. It is difficult to keep them open. But she wants to see what is coming. See when it happens. The people dancing around her are hardly people. No longer people. They are skinwalkers. They are witches. Their skin sloughs off of their frames. They are covered in scabs. They smell of rot. Their eyes are red, dark circles underneath. They are thin and twitchy. They move like stick figures. Their limbs jerk. Marionettes made from sticks. Warped tattoos. Their clothes are rank, decaying. What they wore when they were human, before they reemerged from their graves. Before they were reborn.

A man is speaking. His voice is not loud, but he is heard by all. His head is bald and tan. His skin a rich shade of brown. His eyes exude warmth. They are seductive eyes, iridescent red in the darkness. He is speaking gibberish. He speaks of Shadow People, of a spiritual battle between good and evil, between the powerful and the weak, between worlds. It is all cyclical. A mad circle. The woman tries to follow what he is saying, but it is nonsense. The policeman stands next to the bald man with the copper skin. He wears mirrored sunglasses. His arms are crossed. He holds a torch. She snorts in disgust. Gasoline blows off her lips and sprays onto the ground in front of her knees. The driblets make some kind of pattern on the dusty ground, but it's meaningless to her.

SEVENTY-EIGHT

Jake drove straight to the doublewide trailer in the shadow of the Shiprock monolith. He floored the Sentra, but it topped out at a dutiful seventy miles per hour. His heart seemed to be arhythmic, but it could have just been the metal in his chest. Finally, he reached the turn off from Highway 491 to the dirt road running west to the ominous rock formation. His pale sweat dried and his breathing calmed. Feeling faded away. His focus narrowed. He had a job to do. Again the familiar feeling hit, right before going out on patrol. Before a mission. The smell of sand and dirt. The feel of it beneath tires, the sound of it at high speed, a cadence of anticipated horror.

He turned onto the jeep trail. It was dusk. He could see fire and smoke in the distance. There were a dozen cars and trucks parked in disarray beside the doublewide. Flames from a giant bonfire licked the night high above the backyard fence. He could hear garbled voices, staticy music, and one voice slipping though it all, rising above. The Shaman.

He parked the Sentra close to the front door and backed it up so that it was facing out toward the jeep trail. He grabbed the Mossberg and buttoned up the duster so that he was cloaked in black leather. He walked toward the house. His boots clomped loudly up two bent and sagging steps to the wooden porch. The front door was unlocked. He quietly turned the door knob and nudged the door open with the barrel of the shotgun. The living room was empty. Everyone was outside, in the backyard. He walked past the couch where he'd found the high school girl, Cally's friend, blowing the tweaker, methed out of her mind. He remembered the feel of his fists hitting the man's face, and the give of teeth yielding from gums. Jake swiveled the Mossberg to cover the hallway and the kitchen, but they were empty. Same with the interior doorways and the corners. Whatever was happening, was happening outside.

Jake slid back the glass door to the backyard. There were at least thirty people in a rough semicircle. Their backs were toward him. Aimee was in the center, on her knees, with her arms bound behind her back. She held her head high, chin out, long slender neck. She was wet from head to toe. The air was rank with the smell of gasoline. Her eyes were nearly swollen shut. Gasoline dripped off the ends of her hair, shiny black in the night.

The Shaman was speaking. Jake walked into the circle, barrel of the shotgun pointed straight ahead, brushing past a line of tweakers fixated on the suffering woman, and the dancing flames from the bonfire, whipping around at the mercy of the winds, lashing out toward the woman like a serpent's tongue, threatening to ignite her at any moment.

Aimee became still, her burning eyes trying to reconcile what she was seeing, who she was seeing. Jake locked eyes with the Shaman. He smiled. Bradley stood next to the Shaman. A pair of mirrored lenses trained on Jake. The tweakers began to notice the man with the shotgun. In the duster, Jake was covered in black from head to toe. The tweakers nearest to him did double takes, and backed away, startled, trying to figure out if he was real. Someone screamed. He looked exactly like one of the Shadow People, especially to those who had never seen one before.

Jake raised the shotgun and shot Bradley in the face. Aimee pitched onto her side and rolled away from the bonfire. Bradley's neck opened up and his head flopped back on a thread of exposed spinal cord. The big man stumbled back, feet working on muscle memory, and ran into the cliff face and collapsed in a pile and bled out from the neck hole. The Shaman looked genuinely surprised.

Jake wheeled the shotgun onto the crowd. He backed toward Aimee, guarding her flank as she struggled to her feet. A girl with one side of her head shaved, the other side, a ratty side-mane, raised a torch and cocked her arm to throw it, and Jake shot her in the chest. He could have sworn he saw her breasts blown clean off. The tweakers scattered but had nowhere to go. Aimee began running with her hands still cuffed behind her back. Jake followed her, training the shotgun on whoever was closest to them. He heard gunfire and saw a muzzle flash out of the corner of his eye. He felt the rush of wind from a bullet missing him by inches. He spun and faced the shooter, the man whose teeth Jake had smashed rescuing Cally's friend. Face lopsided, one eye still black and half shut, he fired a 9mm as he walked directly at Jake. The bullets peppered the dirt around Jake and ricocheted off the sandstone behind him sending sparks into the night. Jake pulled the trigger and the Mossberg cut the man in half.

Jake caught up to Aimee but there was nowhere to run. They hit the fence line and followed it to the back corner, but there was no gate. The tweakers scattered. Some ran into the house, fighting to get through the back door. Others drew weapons and rallied. They formed a pack. Jake shielded Aimee with his body and fired the shotgun at the fence. The wood exploded. He dropped the shotgun and picked up Aimee and shoved her through the hole in the fence. She landed on her face. Still half blind from the gasoline, she rolled onto the flats of her feet and thrust herself up into a dead run.

Jake searched the ground for the shotgun but only saw dirt. He dropped to his hands and knees and waved his arms across sand, rocks, and cactus, until he felt the metal barrel. He heard a boom and a round of buckshot tore the ground away in front of him pelting his face with dirt, pebbles, and shards of rock.

Suddenly, a collective wail echoed off the canyon wall. People poured into the yard. The tweakers who had ran into the house were spilling back outside screaming and shrieking in panic. Jake found the Mossberg and fired at the pack running in his direction, blowing a man's legs off. The torso went face first into the ground and bounced past him.

The pack running toward Jake splintered. Some turned back toward the house. The yard erupted in gunfire and smoke. Jake felt himself gagging, choking. The air filled with a poisonous haze. Teargas. Three men were cut down in front of him. Jake dropped his gun and threw his hands up. Floodlights lit up the yard, illuminating a melee, tweakers in a frenzy, running into each other, and a phalanx of tribal police in full riot gear beating them with billy clubs and squaring off with anyone who wouldn't drop their weapons and lie on the ground. Yazzie came through the back door, sighting an assault rifle. Jake searched for the Shaman. But he was gone.

SEVENTY-NINE

A week later Aimee drove to the Albuquerque International Sunport. Her left arm was in a sling. The dislocated shoulder made driving painful, but at least the doctors were optimistic that she wouldn't need surgery. She'd had several offers for rides to the airport, including one from Jake, but she wanted to keep things simple. She drove herself from Albuquerque, she would drive herself back. And, someone had to return the little white rental car.

The flight time to Washington, D.C. was only three and half hours. After takeoff, she watched the land pass below. The yellow, orange and brown gave way to various shades of green as the miles scrolled by. Night fell and the veins of electricity spread out in the darkness underneath, outlining towns and sometimes the highways that connected them.

After three hours she felt the throb of the jet engines change in ferocity and the plane drop slightly in altitude, and she steadied herself for a bumpy but familiar descent into D.C. The approach into Reagan National Airport was always choppy, the flight path following the Potomac, the clouds and fog reaching almost to the ground, engulfing the tops of the buildings in Rosslyn and Crystal City, the Washington Monument seemingly scrapping the tip of the plane's wing. Water ran horizontal along her window. It was raining hard.

She was relieved when the plane touched down and deployed its flaps, braked hard, and slowed down enough so that even if there was an accident, at that point, she would probably survive. It was childish, she knew. But she felt that way on every landing. Every time.

She traveled with only a carry-on roller bag and she was quickly outside in the humid east coast air. She smelled water, ozone, rain on pavement. She walked briskly to the taxi stand and waited in the cab line. Relaxed. A familiar ritual. She watched some confused and bumbling tourists, and pitied them. She felt at home.

The city was beautiful, especially at night. The monuments all illuminated still moved her, still gave her a sense of wonder that she actually lived and worked here, in the nation's capital. When the taxi crossed Pennsylvania Avenue she caught her favorite view, the Capital building lit up at night, rotund and majestic, anchoring the end of the street, looking exactly as it did in every painting or photograph she ever saw of it.

She lived in Dupont Circle in a new apartment building, or at least one that had been newly renovated. She had signed the lease only two months ago and she loved it. She would never say it out loud, but she felt like the building matched her style—sleek, pretty, upwardly mobile.

She paid the cab driver and went inside. Her heels clicked across the polished marble floor. The front desk was empty, which was unusual. Concierge service was included in the rent. She took the elevator up to her fifth floor corner unit. She turned on the lights and let the roller bag stand up, wobble, and tip over. She hung up her coat and eased off her shoes with audible gratitude. She massaged the deep lines on her feet where the shoes had pinched and cut her circulation. She pulled open the curtains and admired the view of the rain over Massachusetts Avenue. A nimbus of mist hung in the trees and around the street lights.

It was a one bedroom apartment, but that bedroom was spacious. She changed into sweatpants and a long sleeve Georgetown Hoyas T-shirt. She set her watch and turquoise earrings into a dresser drawer where she kept her passport and metro pass and a few knickknacks. She noticed a necklace Jake had given her once upon a time. It was a silver sun on a thin chain from Tiffany's. Her first real jewelry, or at least the first time anyone had given her anything from someplace as fancy as Tiffany's. She still had the pretty blue box. Jake had given it to her when they were living in Adams Morgan, in a basement studio apartment smaller than the bedroom she was in now. She put on the necklace. It was very light, delicate, but the feeling was unmistakable. After all, she'd worn the necklace almost every day for a year. It made the nape of her neck tingle.

She put on her slippers and padded out to the kitchen. She opened a bottle Pinot Grigio and took a wine glass out of the rack mounted under a cabinet, and poured herself a glass. It was smooth and sweet. She approved.

She walked to the living room and dropped the glass. It shattered at her feet. She was too shocked to scream. Agent Colton sat on her couch. He held a pistol with a very long barrel. He uncrossed his legs and stood up. She realized the barrel wasn't that long, but it was made long by a silencer at the end. It was her last thought. Agent Colton raised the gun and shot her in the head.

EIGHTY

The Shaman paces back and forth across the length of the six thousand square foot house in North Scottsdale. His feet are bare. His hands are behind his back. His head is slightly bowed. He is deep in thought.

The house is a one level territorial. The walls look like they are made from adobe, but they are not. The wood beams, columns, and inlays are polished and lacquered; sealed and preserved against the dry air and the near constant sun. The wood shines and is perfectly smooth to the touch. His bare feet pad on travertine. The countertops are all cut from twenty thousand dollar slabs of granite. He does not particularly care for such things. But one must put their money somewhere. And real estate in Arizona is cheap. Everything in this country is cheap. It is a great country. The land of plenty.

There are others in the house. But no one from the double-wide trailer outside of Shiprock, on the rez. He does not allow them in the house. Those that are left. He does not mind those people, his followers. But, they smell bad. And, it is a fine house. The house reminds him of home. It is a house that belongs in the desert.

The doors to the outside are all redwood with Spanish mission style iron crosses. The door to the back opens soundlessly, effortlessly, as if aided somehow, defying its weight. The Shaman walks outside. It is hot, well over one hundred degrees. He feels the heat penetrate his body, his bones. It feels wonderful. He walks up a staircase to a roof deck. He takes a piece of rolling paper out of the pocket of his robe and layers in Turkish tobacco and hashish. He is thinking about Bradley. He thinks often about Bradley. This surprises him. The night Bradley died—while others were scrambling about, the air full of smoke and dust, cars and trucks spinning their wheels in the dirt, running into each other, cornered, nowhere to go—the Shaman slipped behind the fence to a notch in the cliff, a dry wash that rarely ran, and followed it up and up, to the top of the mesa. He looked down from his perch on top of the mesa as his followers were captured or killed. Looked down as he now looks down from his roof deck. He was not much interested in the mayhem below, except for Bradley. He could not take his eyes off of Bradley, near headless, only a lump of flesh now. He sat cross-legged on top of the mesa and cried. He didn't know why he cried. Why he cried for Bradley. Although bound to him, he had never understood Bradley. This man who had protected him to hide the secret that he had murdered his own comrades. Murdered them so that he, the Shaman, could live. He had never questioned Bradley. Why he did what he did. But that night he cried as if his whole soul was pouring out of him. He realized he cried because Bradley was his only friend. And his only friend was dead.

The Shaman licks the paper and pinches it shut. He lights the cigarette and rests his hands on the iron railing. Beneath him is a swimming pool with several fountains. There are young people at the wet bar in a red-tiled casita. A girl is stretched out in a lounge chair. She is exactly six foot, one inch tall. He knows because he measured her once with a tape measure, looping the metal end to her big toe and rolling out the tape along her slender body to the top of her head. He would not have believed it if he had not measured her himself. He inhales the sweet, pungent smoke.

Yes, this is truly the land of opportunity.

ACKNOWLEDGEMENTS

Many thanks to Kjetil Hestvedt and the hard working crew at 280 Steps. Thanks to Jon Bassoff for giving me my start, and to Matthew McBride for showing us all how it should be done.

Special thanks to Mike Walsh, Eric T. Knight, Mark Bailen, Adam Bernard, Mary Pender-Coplan, Vikram Bellapravalu, and Noah Edelstein.

Thank you to my family and friends for your support and enthusiasm. And, as always, all my love to Oli and Raja, and to Mon, my best friend and consummate editor.

ABOUT THE AUTHOR

C.J. Howell spent many years bartending and writing in mountain towns before getting a master's degree in creative writing from the University of Colorado, Boulder. He has published short stories in various literary magazines and his first novel, *The Last of the Smoking Bartenders*, received a starred review and was named a best crime fiction debut of 2014 in Booklist Magazine. He lives in Scottsdale, Arizona with his wife and two beautiful children.

CPSIA information can be obtained at www.ICGtesting.com
Printed in the USA
BVOW03s0847250316

441453BV00002BA/15/P